PERSONA NON GRATA
TIMOTHY WILLIAMS

Published by
Soho Press, Inc.
853 Broadway
New York, NY 10003

Library of Congress Cataloging-in-Publication Data

Williams, Timothy.
Persona non grata / Timothy Williams.

ISBN 978-1-61695-464-2
eISBN 978-1-61695-465-9

1. Police—Italy—Fiction. I. Title.
PR6073.I43295P4 2014
823'.914—dc23   2014027604

Interior Design by Janine Agro, Soho Press, Inc.

Printed in the United States of America

10 9 8 7 6 5 4 3 2 1

a Maria
C'eravamo tanto amati.

Glossary

ARMA: Arma dei Carabinieri, a military corps with police duties

AUTOSTRADA: highway

BUONA SERA: good evening

BUONGIORNO: hello, good morning

CAPITANO: captain

CASERMA CAIROLI: the Cairoli barracks

COMMISSARIO: commissioner

DOTTOR: doctor (mas.)

DOTTORESSA: doctor (fem.)

ESPORTAZIONE: an Italian cigarette brand

FINANZA: autonomous police force concerned with customs and excise

GRAPPA: a dry, clear brandy distilled from fermented grapes

I PANINARI: a youth group centered around a consumeristic, globalized way of life

ISPETTORE: inspector

MARESCIALLO: warrant officer, senior NCO

MATURITÀ TECNICA: high school technical exam, akin to British A Levels

OSTETRICA: maternity ward, obstetrician

PALAZZO: building, palace

PAZIENZA: patience

PIAZZA: plaza

PIEMONTESI: people from Piemonte

POLICLINICO: hospital

POLIZIA STRADALE: highway patrol

PRONTO SOCCORSO: first aid

PROVINCIA (PADANA): an Italian newspaper

PUBBLICA SICUREZZA: Italian police force

PUBBLICO MINISTERO: public prosecutor

QUESTURA: police headquarters

QUESTORE: chief inspector

REPUBBLICHINI: Republicans

SCIENTIFICA: forensics

SCUOLA MEDIA: middle school

SIGNORA: madam, lady

SIGNORINA: miss, young lady

SQUADRA MOBILE: first response team

TENENTE: lieutenant

VIA: road

ZIO: uncle

1: Body

THERE WAS THE smell of coffee on his breath and, as he spoke, small clouds of moisture escaped from his mouth into the chill air. "I am too old."

Pisanelli smiled but said nothing. He bumped the car up onto the pavement. The two men got out of the Lancia.

The first light of the new day rose above the colorless buildings. No wind, no traffic and, apart from the changing lights at the crossroads, the city at four o'clock in the morning was dead. Dead except for the distant whine of a siren.

Accompanied by the echo of their footfalls they crossed Piazza Castello.

On the far side of the square, a police motorcycle stood at the entrance to an apartment building. There was another vehicle, with the blue lamp revolving unheeded in the silent, first dawn.

They went through the open doors.

A non-commissioned officer saluted and accompanied Trotti and Pisanelli up the stairs. A building that was neither rich nor poor, it had been built at the time of Fascism and was still hanging on to its fading respectability. The walls had once been painted but were now grubby; no graffiti, just the marks of rubbing shoulders and the contact of dirty hands and greasy clothes.

The air carried no smell other than that of the chill September morning and the policeman's cigarette. Pisanelli took the stairs two at a time; Trotti followed him.

Families, dressed for the night, but with faces already accustomed to the new day, had come out on to the landings. They watched interested and unblinking at the passage of the three men. Trotti was out of breath by the time they reached the third floor. The doorway on the left side was wide open and yellow light flooded out.

Bloodstains.

Thin traces of splashed blood across the stone floor and the sound of somebody crying.

Trotti bit his lip.

The NCO placed his hand on the door handle and Maresciallo Santostefano stepped forward. He was wearing boots and had not removed his motorcycle helmet; the chin-strap hung at the side of his round, unimaginative face.

"The girl has been taken to the hospital—she's just left."

"What girl?"

"The girl, Laura, she's . . ."

Trotti interrupted, "What happened?"

"I was called at half past three. Why me, I don't know; I don't work for Pronto Soccorso." He made a movement of irritation, then Santostefano gestured through the open door to the far side of the landing. "The neighbor's got a phone. He phoned one-one-three."

"What happened?"

Santostefano hesitated, taken aback by the brusqueness of the question. "Somebody tried to kill the girl." Santostefano turned to look at the other people in the small room: a room that looked lived in, with a heavy sideboard, a wooden table and a divan that had been pulled down to form a bed. Dark smears on the white bedsheet. "Signor Vardin was next door sleeping and he was woken by the screaming of his daughter." The policeman nodded uncomfortably towards the narrow-shouldered man dressed in a pajama bottom and a singlet.

Trotti turned and looked at the man. The face was creased and the eyes appeared as if they were accustomed to suffering. Vardin had placed his arm around the shoulders of the weeping woman.

"Signor Vardin jumped out of bed and came in here. He

had just enough time to turn the light on and see somebody darting out of the door—out of the door and down the stairs." Santostefano added, "Signor Vardin says that he tried to follow the aggressor . . ."

Vardin removed his arm from the woman's shoulder. "Of course I would have followed him and I would have killed him." The voice was a hoarse whisper devoid of menace. "I would have followed him but I saw Laura and I saw that she was covered in blood and she was moaning and calling out, 'Papa, Papa.'"

"What did you do, Signor Vardin?"

There was dry saliva at the corner of his lips. "Laura is twelve years old—a little girl. My daughter is a little girl."

Santostefano said, "The work of a maniac." He crossed his arms against his leather jacket and, for an instant, a grim smile lingered on the full lips. "At least ten stab wounds, Commissario—not deep, I think, but blood all over the body. The ambulance was quick, and she was breathing normally when they took her away."

The southern accent grated on Trotti's nerves.

"I couldn't tell if there was internal hemorrhaging, but there was no blood in the mouth."

The woman had been crying in silence, a knuckle pushed hard against her lips; she now started to slump forward. "My baby is going to die." She would have fallen to the cold floor but her husband held her. "To die."

"Commissario." Santostefano took Trotti by the arm—a strange act of intimacy for a member of Polizia Stradale—and led him towards a corner of the room. Trotti noticed the bronze tower of Pisa on a shelf and the unframed picture of the Pope. "She wanted to accompany the child in the ambulance but I told Vardin that she would have to stay here until you came." He shook his head. "I think she's going to need treatment. Something to calm her. Before you came she was screaming hysterically."

Trotti turned and looked at the woman and, beyond her, at the paling morning sky over the city.

2: Papa

THE CUP OF coffee was half-empty and fast growing cold. The smell coming from the hall had destroyed Trotti's desire to drink.

"Time?" The eyes were pale grey and they looked at Trotti cautiously.

"What time did you get back with your family from Piazza Vittoria?"

The man fumbled with the packet of cigarettes that Trotti had given him; the green packet of Esportazione appeared strangely small and crumpled in the large, work-worn hands. "Time?" he repeated in his hoarse whisper.

"You went with your family to the piazza, didn't you?"

The man was silent.

"Signor Vardin, you went with your family to the piazza last night."

He looked up. "I'm sorry, but I haven't slept." He ran a hand across his forehead. "I can still see that screen dancing in front of my eyes." He rubbed at the side of his nose while screwing up his eyelids. "I was sitting too close to it and the man in the white coat . . ."

"Signor Maserati?"

Vardin nodded. He spoke with difficulty and Trotti wondered whether the man's lungs or larynx had been damaged. "I was trying to help him. The man in the white coat, I think he was getting impatient with me. But I only saw him—the man who attacked my daughter—I only saw him for a second—for a fraction of a second."

"However, you have managed to give Maserati a description, haven't you?"

"On the machine. What do you call it? On the computer." The face brightened for an instant. "He got me to help him draw the face—but I can't be sure. The attacker—I scarcely saw him."

"You say he was a young man?"

"He looked young to me—I saw him as he ran down the stairs. I saw that he was wearing a jacket and that he had long hair."

"You had never seen him before?"

"No." The reply was prompt.

Trotti smiled. "It is very good of you to help."

"I just want to help my daughter."

"You can help her by trying to answer the questions, Signor Vardin. I realize how you must be feeling but please—please try to cooperate as much as you can. You want us to find the man who did these terrible things to Laura." Trotti took out his pen and started drawing lines on the yellow stationery. "Can you remember at what time you got back from Piazza Vittoria last night?"

A hesitant nod. "It must have been after twelve."

"Not very late, then?"

"School starts next week. I don't want my girls to be tired." He paused, added, "A good education is the most important thing."

"Of course," Trotti said. "What school does Laura go to?"

"She is an intelligent girl—like her mother." The hint of pride while the eyes remained on the packet of cigarettes. "And she is going to do well for herself. Not a job in a factory for Laura—she is going to go to university to become a teacher."

"What school did you say, Signor Vardin?"

"She is at the Scuola Media in via Amfiteatro—and one day she is going to be a teacher. A math teacher." For a moment he looked up and the dusty, grey eyes met Trotti's.

Trotti said nothing.

"If she lives," the man added in his whisper.

Trotti spoke briskly. "There was a public dance in the square and the girls were treated to a pizza that you bought for them at the Pizzeria Bella Napoli?"

Signor Vardin said, "My two daughters and Bettina."

"Signora Vardin?"

"Bettina is my niece. You saw her. She and Netta, my other daughter, are good friends—they always have been, ever since they were little; and now with Bettina's parents in Piemonte for the funeral of Zio Moisè, she is staying with us until the end of the week."

"Until Sunday?"

"She is a friend of Netta's."

"And your niece is staying until next Sunday?"

He nodded. "She's a sweet girl."

"How old is your daughter Netta?"

"Netta—and Bettina—are seventeen. There's two months' difference between them."

Trotti opened the drawer and slid his hand inside. "So there were five of you—your wife, you and the three girls?" His hand found old wrappers but no sweets.

Signor Vardin's glance remained on the cigarettes. "It is nice to get out once in a while. And the mayor organizes the dances at this time of year. A chance to get out and meet old friends. Friends from the factory. The evenings are still quite warm and it is good to talk."

"You work at the sewing-machine factory?"

"I used to work. Until last year." The lips pressed against each other. "For six years. Not a bad job and I couldn't go back to the quarries. Not after I started to lose my voice." He nodded, without looking at Trotti. "The silicon in the air."

"And then later, after the girls had danced and you had danced a couple of waltzes with Signora Vardin, you returned home? At midnight?"

"We went to the gelateria and had an ice. But the air had grown chill and we sat inside." He added, "A mist coming up from the river."

"And when did you get back to Piazza Castello?"

Their eyes met for a fleeting moment. "Just after twelve—the clock at San Teodoro was striking midnight."

Trotti looked at the man and felt sorry for him. He was not very old—perhaps even younger than Trotti—but his pain was like a weight bearing down on the narrow, bony shoulders. He had put on a blue suit, but the collar of his shirt was undone and unshaven whiskers stood out from the skin of his neck. There was a quiet humility about Signor Vardin and the Friuli accent seemed to render him more vulnerable.

"You think she's going to die, Signor Commissario?"

"Of course not."

"She is a lovely child."

"As soon as there is any news, the hospital will ring. Tenente Pisanelli is there with your wife."

"If anything happens to our little girl, it will be the death of my wife. She has a poor heart—ever since she came to this city she has had trouble with her heart and if we didn't need the money she would have given up working years ago. It is all my fault."

"Please take a cigarette, Signor Vardin."

"I never smoke," he said simply and dropped the packet of Esportazione. "Not with my lungs."

"Then perhaps some more coffee?"

"It is all my fault. Normally she sleeps in the big bed. But because of Bettina being there, we told her to sleep on the couch."

Trotti frowned. "Who slept on the couch?"

"And the two big girls slept on the bed."

"I don't understand." Trotti had been about to lift the coffeepot; now his arm was motionless and his eyes—tired and bloodshot—were fixed on Signor Vardin.

"The two big girls—Netta and my niece—slept in the bed."

"Who normally sleeps on the couch?"

"On the couch?"

Trotti did not hide his irritation. "Where does Laura normally sleep?"

"When I was working at the factory . . ."

Trotti cut him short by banging the coffeepot on the table. "Did Laura normally sleep in the bedroom?"

The man looked at him in hurt surprise.

Speaking slowly and carefully as if he were dealing with a child, Trotti asked, "Are you saying that normally Laura slept in the big bed in the bedroom?"

"In the old days I would get up at half past five and have my breakfast." The man nodded his narrow head. He had high cheekbones and sunken cheeks that were already dark although he had shaved. "In the old days, when I was working at the factory. But that's nearly a year ago—a year that I haven't had a job. And the wife doesn't get up until after seven. So there's no harm in letting Netta sleep there. She likes it. Don't know why—it's small for her."

"Netta sleeps in the kitchen?"

He nodded slowly. "I haven't had a proper job now for nearly a year. So rather than sleep with her sister . . ."

"But last night Netta was sleeping with her cousin Bettina? That's right, isn't it?"

"I don't get up early in the mornings."

"And your younger daughter, Laura, was sleeping in Netta's place—on the couch?"

Then Signor Vardin frowned. "There's nothing wrong in that."

"It is possible the r— . . . the man . . . it is possible he knew your house?"

"Why would he know my house?"

"And it's possible he was expecting to find not Laura but her seventeen-year-old sister, warm and tucked up on the kitchen couch?"

"But he attacked Laura—not Netta."

"Does your elder daughter—does Netta have a boyfriend, Signor Vardin?"

Only then did the eyes seem to register what Trotti was saying.

3: Hospital

THE FLOWERS HUNG loosely from Vardin's hand.

They entered the large waiting room and his wife stood up.

"Is there any news?" She did not notice Trotti but moved towards her husband, her eyes searching his face. Even though the air was now warm, she wore a green overcoat with a fur collar. She had been crying but she seemed calmer than before, calmer and slower. In one hand she held a crumpled handkerchief. She repeated, "Is there any news?"

Vardin kissed her and handed her the flowers.

"Tell me."

He shrugged.

Trotti went over to where Brigadiere Ciuffi stood. A brief nod of her small head with its carefully brushed hair. "Any joy, Commissario?"

"Where is Pisanelli?"

"The ostetrica."

"The maternity ward? What on earth for?"

"To have a baby."

"A baby?"

Ciuffi did not smile. "Pisanelli went off about an hour ago. He said he would be back."

"I told him to stay with you."

"He's with Commissario Merenda."

"What does he think he's doing? He works for me, not Merenda."

"Any luck with the father?"

"I need Pisanelli." Trotti turned to look at Ciuffi in puzzlement. "Father?"

Ciuffi nodded towards where Signor Vardin was talking with his wife. There were red rims to Signora Vardin's eyelids and her husband was standing close to her. His hand held hers. The flowers had been placed on the stone bench.

"Maserati's got a computer portrait of the attacker. We've had it distributed over the printer. But Vardin only saw the man for an instant—and I'll be surprised if the identikit brings us anything." Trotti shrugged. "How's the little girl? She's going to be all right, isn't she?"

Ciuffi said, "There's been a nurse—but she doesn't seem to know anything."

Trotti clicked his tongue with impatience. "You've been here for more than three hours."

"I thought the best thing was to stay with Signora Vardin. The nurse gave her a couple of pills."

Trotti pushed past Ciuffi and went through the green door into the hospital corridor. It smelled of floor wax and antiseptic and muted suffering.

There was nobody.

He started walking down the corridor. Flooding morning light came through the windows. At the end of the corridor he found a nurse.

"The little girl with stab wounds?"

She was plump and beneath the gull-wing coiffe of her religious order she looked stocky. The face was pale; a crucifix hung at her neck.

"I'm looking for the girl who was stabbed early this morning."

"Who are you?"

"Pubblica Sicurezza," Trotti said tersely. "Squadra Mobile."

"What little girl?" She softened her Rs with a Piemonte accent. Before Trotti could reply she turned on her heel and said, "You'd better follow me," heading off along the rubber-tile floor.

They went down the corridor, past the busts of earlier benefactors, now sightless in their whitewashed niches.

CHIRURGIA D'URGENZA—Emergency Surgery.

The nun raised her hand and knocked on a door that had been painted mustard yellow. She turned to him. "Sit there." She indicated a short bench. She then went through the door. It hissed shut behind her.

Trotti stared at his hands.

The nurse came back five minutes later.

"Vardin?" she asked. "Laura Vardin?"

Trotti nodded and again the nun went away, this time to return with a young doctor who was in the process of peeling rubber gloves from his long, thin hands.

Trotti stood up and the two men nodded to each other without shaking hands. On one of the gloves there were dark traces.

"She's sleeping." His Italian was good but he spoke with a marked accent.

"Sleeping?"

His name was on his lapel. Dottor James Wafula. An African with large, brown eyes and a flat, intelligent face. His white coat was undone at the neck and there was no shirt beneath but several tight curls of dark chest hair. "You have just operated on her, Dottore?"

"Goodness, no." The doctor noticed Trotti's glance to the bloodstains. "We finished with the child a couple of hours ago."

"Then she's all right?" He was surprised by the excitement in his own voice. "She's going to live?"

The laugh was infectious. "Of course." Dottor Wafula added, "But there may be scars."

"Her life is not in danger?"

"She is going to live to a ripe old age, I am quite sure, with children and grandchildren." The eyes were rapidly squeezed shut with amusement. "She was covered in blood—she had been stabbed ten times." The face immediately grew serious. "There was only one dangerous stab wound—on her shoulder and not really very deep. It was probably what woke her—perhaps saved her life. But I am not sure that her attacker was trying to kill her. If it was a knife he used, it was sharp but not very long. The wounds are not deep. I don't think it was a knife."

"What was it?"

"You see, I didn't give her more than three stitches in all, and apart from the shoulder wound, everything was very superficial."

"What instrument, Dottore?"

The doctor raised his shoulders slightly. "Perhaps they were just playing games."

"They?"

Dottor Wafula looked at Trotti but he said nothing while he rubbed the gloves into a ball and placed them into the pocket of his white coat. He lit an English cigarette. "Stab wounds can leave traces," he said, after exhaling smoke into the air. "I think I have done a useful job." The teeth were not white but yellow; against the black skin, the smile was brilliant. "You white people are lucky."

"Lucky to have you to sew us up?"

"You've never noticed the navel on African children?"

Trotti shook his head.

"Black skin can swell up when it heals. It is a phenomenon that is rare in white-skinned people."

"Why don't you think her attacker was trying to kill her?"

Wafula shook his head as he inhaled the cigarette smoke.

"In your opinion, why was she attacked? The wounds are not deep . . . it doesn't seem to make any sense."

"What did you say the name was, Ispettore?"

"Trotti, Commissario Trotti."

"The girl's name?"

"Vardin—Laura Vardin."

The doctor stood still as he looked down at the ground. The cigarette was in his mouth and the smoke curled upwards into his eyes, causing him to squint. He put his head to one side, as if inspecting his shoe.

(It was in 1945 that Trotti had first seen a black man—an American soldier who had handed him chocolate and who had smiled from ear to ear.)

When the African doctor looked up, the dark eyes were moist. "Not a common name in this part of the world. A name from Friuli—and there can't be many of them in this city, can there?"

"Friuli?" Trotti repeated in surprise but the surgeon hurriedly turned on his heels and disappeared through the mustard-colored doors. The smell of Virginia tobacco lingered in the air.

The nun accompanied Trotti back to Brigadiere Ciuffi.

4: Abandon

"THE WOMAN REFUSES to talk."

"Where the hell have you been, Pisanelli? I thought I told you to stay with Ciuffi and the Vardin woman."

"I've been in Ostetrica."

"I never told you to go to Ostetrica. I told you to do a job—and instead you leave Ciuffi by herself."

"Ciuffi didn't need me."

"It's not for you to make the decisions."

Pisanelli shrugged sheepishly.

"Ostetrica? You're pregnant?"

"Merenda is over there."

Trotti's voice was cold. "You don't work for Commissario Merenda, Pisanelli."

A grin. "He's with this woman . . ."

"You work with me, Pisanelli."

"Of course, Commissario, but, you see, the doctors think she's murdered her baby."

Trotti paused, looking carefully at the younger man. "Who's murdered her baby?"

"This woman. She lives out at Sicamario Po." Pisanelli ran a nervous hand through the long hair at the side of his head. "Nobody can get her to talk."

"You can charm her."

Pisanelli appeared offended. "She's a married woman."

"Married?"

Pisanelli nodded. "With two girls. One five years old, the other three."

"How old is she?"

"Who?"

"How old is this wretched woman?"

"Twenty-three." Pisanelli defensively flicked the long hair away from his ears. On the top of his head, Pisanelli had gone completely bald.

"Why does my colleague Commissario Merenda think she's murdered her baby?"

"All the signs of a recent childbirth. She was brought in the day before yesterday—covered with blood. But, despite all the questions from Merenda's team, she still hasn't admitted to anything."

They were standing outside the hospital, the noise of the controller over the scratching radio. Ciuffi was sitting in the car, waiting.

"And so instead of doing as you're told and staying with Ciuffi, you decide to go off and give Commissario Merenda a hand, Pisanelli?"

"I thought I could be of use."

"You're of most use doing what I tell you. If Commissario Merenda feels that he needs you, he will inform me. It's not for you to decide what you want to do and what you don't want to do." Trotti started to move round the back of the car. "And you're telling me you believe her?"

"Believe her?"

"You don't believe she's had a baby?"

A shaft of sunlight caught the pale eyes, making Pisanelli appear innocent and very young, "I don't know what to believe."

"The doctors should know when a woman has given birth. They know when . . ."

"Placenta in the uterus." Pisanelli shrugged the shoulders of his suede jacket. Trotti wondered whether it was the old jacket that had been cleaned, or whether it was a new and equally scruffy one. "And they've put her on a diet for loss of blood, giving her protein and vitamins. As far as the hospital is concerned there's no question. Loss of blood, dilated vagina." He blushed. "Etcetera, etcetera." He hesitated. "Within the last forty-eight hours."

"You know a lot about these things?"

"I did a couple of years of medicine at university."

"And you can't get her to talk?"

"Nobody seems to be able to."

"What's Merenda doing?"

"Commissario Merenda's been with her now for over thirty-six hours. At her bedside. Trying to get her to say where she's hidden the baby. That's why I went . . . I wanted to help."

"Merenda doesn't need help."

"I want to help the poor child." Pisanelli gestured towards the city, now bright with sparkling roofs beneath the mid-morning light. "Out there somewhere is a baby—and perhaps it's still alive. A baby abandoned by its mother."

"Well?"

"That's what the doctors believe—and it's what Commissario Merenda believes."

Silence as the two men looked at each other.

Trotti released a sigh. "Then you'd better get back to Ostetrica and get the damn woman to talk."

Pisanelli's face broke into a wide grin.

"With your boyish charm, you should be able to get her to tell you everything. Get her to talk, Pisanelli. And show Merenda that old Commissario Trotti has still got a few good men with him."

Pisanelli fumbled as he opened the door for him. Trotti got into the Lancia beside Ciuffi. "Even if you have to seduce the woman, Pisanelli."

5: I Paninari

THREE O'CLOCK IN the afternoon on the third floor of the Questura.

The small office was stuffy. Beige files gathering dust on the floor.

She sat opposite him and the young eyes looked at Trotti without blinking. The girl was pretty: the new generation, the generation for which so many Italian parents had made sacrifices, the generation born during the heady years of the Italian Miracle.

She was wearing jeans and a tennis shirt. Soft down ran along her arms. She had crossed her legs and was sitting back in the grubby canvas armchair.

Trotti noticed the nervous tapping of her foot.

Antonetta Vardin glanced from Trotti to where Brigadiere Ciuffi was sitting.

"Your father says you have a boyfriend, Netta."

She shrugged.

"Well?"

"Riccardo and I are friends."

"You like dancing?"

"It depends who I'm with."

"With your boyfriend."

She smiled tautly. "My father can be old-fashioned." There were freckles on her nose and cheeks.

"But your parents don't mind your having a boyfriend?"

A shrug.

(The smell was coming from the hall.)

"And they let you go out together?"

"I am allowed out on Saturday night—provided I am back before eleven o'clock."

"And where do you go with your boyfriend?"

"Riccardo is a friend—that's all."

"Where do you go together?" Trotti took another sweet from the packet he had bought at the hospital shop. Barley sugar.

She shrugged. "There's the Fast Dog Americano in corso Mazzini—we go there for a hamburger. Or sometimes to the gelateria."

"And when you want to be alone?"

The foot continued to tap silently. "Then we go into the piazza and we sit and chat."

"Not much privacy in Piazza Vittoria."

"I don't know what you mean."

"A boy and a girl together . . . there are things you are tempted to do."

"Don't try to get me to say things that aren't true. Riccardo and I are friends—that's all. We are young, we have interests in common and we enjoy each other's company."

"How old are you, Netta?"

No reply.

Brigadiere Ciuffi repeated the question.

Antonetta stared at the dusty desktop. "Seventeen."

"And did Riccardo accompany you to Piazza Vittoria last night?"

There was a pause before she shook her head. "I went with my sister and Bettina. Riccardo didn't want to come—he has some exams that he is working for."

"You mean he didn't want to be with your father."

The girl turned her head, giving a slight shrug, "My father doesn't like Riccardo very much—Riccardo or any other friend of mine."

"What exams is he working for?"

"He failed his maturità tecnica in June."

Trotti glanced out of the window. The sill was a white patch-work of pigeon droppings. "But he has been to your house?"

"You have a very old-fashioned idea about young people today. You are like my father." She looked up at Trotti and added, "Next January, I shall be able to vote."

"Riccardo has been to your house?"

She nodded. "I presented him to Papa once—but Papa was not very friendly."

"Netta, how long have you known Riccardo?"

"My name is Antonetta."

"How long have you been going out with Riccardo?"

There was a long silence.

Brigadiere Ciuffi said softly, "Please answer the question."

The young girl shrugged.

Brigadiere Ciuffi smiled encouragingly.

"He is in the class above me at the Istituto Tecnico."

"How long have you known him?"

"A year—it will be a year in October."

Trotti asked, "Do you kiss?"

Before the first tint of a blush began to color the pale face, Brigadiere Ciuffi hurriedly interrupted, "What the Commissario wants to know is whether there is something special between Riccardo and you."

"We are friends."

"Just friends?" Trotti asked.

Brigadiere Ciuffi glanced at Trotti and frowned. She moved forward and crouched beside the seated girl. Brigadiere Ciuffi was wearing a uniform dress of dark blue serge. It made her look young. The two women could have been sisters.

"These are embarrassing questions, Antonetta—but you must understand that Commissario Trotti has got to find the man who did those things to Laura. Because if we don't stop him, perhaps he will do the same thing to other innocent girls."

"Laura is all right now."

"She will have to stay in the hospital for a few days. You don't want that happening to other little girls." Ciuffi placed her hand reassuringly on the girl's knee. "Please help us."

A flicker of worry in Antonetta's eyes. "I don't see how I can."

"You must tell the Commissario about Riccardo."

Trotti opened the new file and took out the computer-printed picture. "Does Riccardo have long hair?"

"What?"

He handed her the picture. "Do you know this man?"

She hesitated before shaking her head. "Riccardo has shorter hair than that. And, anyway, his face is quite different. It is thin." She pushed the picture away. "Riccardo is handsome."

"Riccardo has been to your house, hasn't he?"

"I told you—I presented him to Papa."

"Has he been to the house when your parents weren't there?" She said nothing.

"Well?"

Her face now was very pale. The freckles had lost their color.

"When your parents weren't there?"

She nodded reluctantly.

"And you kissed?"

Brigadiere Ciuffi cast Trotti a worried glance.

"You kissed, didn't you?"

Antonetta gave a shrug of admission.

"On the settee. On the same settee where your sister was attacked. That is right, isn't it, Antonetta?"

"We did nothing wrong."

"And Riccardo knows that at night that is where you normally sleep. It wasn't the first time, was it?"

"We did nothing wrong."

Trotti waited. "It wasn't the first time."

Brigadiere Ciuffi looked as tense as the young girl.

"He had been to your house before, hadn't he? Not during the day—but at night, when your parents were asleep. That is why the front door was left on the latch, wasn't it?" Trotti laughed, aware of the unkindness in his voice. "Only last night, it wasn't you who was warm and curled up and waiting for him. It wasn't your body . . ."

"No."

"Not you—but the body of your little sister."

"No."

"I don't believe you, Signorina. You're not quite the innocent little girl you pretend . . ."

"You don't understand, Commissario . . ."

"I think I am going to require a medical examination from you, Signorina Vardin."

Then she broke down.

"No," she shouted, "no, no, no." She started to cry and her crying shook her young body with hysterical sobs that seemed to echo through the Questura.

6: Bianchini

BENEATH THE SILENCE, Trotti could feel Ciuffi's anger.

"You are angry, Brigadiere."

They drove across the Ponte Imperiale.

Ciuffi did not reply.

"It's because of Pisanelli?"

She turned and there was a smoldering light in her eyes. "Pisanelli and everything else."

"Everything else?"

"You told Pisanelli to stay with me—and, when he goes off, you say nothing. Just a silly little mistake, an oversight, but it doesn't matter because you are men, because there is a tacit agreement between you. But when I—the first female police officer in the Questura—when I fail to find out what's happened to the child, you attack me. At the hospital, in front of everybody. Because I'm not a policeman, am I? It's my job to run and get the coffee—or buy you your damn rhubarb sweets."

"I never attacked you, Signorina."

"It's because I'm a woman, isn't it? You think that all women are stupid and that we can't—"

"Signorina Ciuffi, you don't seem to realize—"

"I realize only too well, Signor Commissario. You are insensitive." She snorted. "Like all men."

"Keep your eyes on the road."

"I don't like the way you treated Netta."

"I've got a job to do."

"A seventeen-year-old girl and you treat her like a whore. I thought you were a good man—a kind man. Don't you have a daughter of your own?"

"My daughter is in Bologna."

"You can be very cruel at times," Ciuffi said. "As if it weren't already enough for Netta to know that her sister is lying in bed, her body covered with wounds that were perhaps meant for her."

"So you think that Netta Vardin knew the attacker?" He gave Ciuffi a sideways glance.

A dismissive shrug. "It makes no difference. The fact is a man entered the house during the night and with his knife—"

Trotti corrected her, "With an instrument that was perhaps a knife."

"A man attacked Laura on the dining-room settee. It didn't have to be Laura—it could well have been Netta. She realizes that and she feels guilty. Anybody would feel guilty—it's only normal: her sister taking the suffering that was meant for her. But that doesn't seem to bother you, does it, Commissario? Other people's feelings and . . ."

"I have a city to think about."

"A city is made of people—and people have feelings."

"The only thing I'm interested in is catching the man who did those things to a little girl."

A laugh. "The only thing you're interested in?"

"I have to stop him before he thinks he can do it to any other woman sleeping in her bed." He turned and looked out of the window. The river was now behind them and the buildings grew more scattered as they reached the open countryside. It was hot and a thin haze hung over the fields. The car gathered speed.

Ciuffi fell silent, but Trotti could feel her hostility. She kept her eyes on the road.

A few minutes later Trotti spoke. "You've been in the PS for three years, Brigadiere Ciuffi, and you still think that you can act according to your emotions?" He lightly touched her forearm.

"Emotions are important."

"Not when you have a city to protect."

At Gravellino they turned left and, glancing at his companion, Trotti saw she had pressed her lips together.

The mixture of determination and innocence touched him. "Emotions," Trotti muttered under his breath.

They drove through the village and soon found themselves in the new residential area that had grown up in the last few years: houses for the professional people who had moved out of the city, houses with white walls and sloping roofs of tiles. A couple of villas were of two stories but most were low buildings that imitated the style of the farmhouses they had usurped. Gardens hidden by high privet hedges and cypresses that demarcated well-kept barriers between neighbors.

The air still retained the smell of the countryside—a bittersweet mixture of grass, dung and fertilizer. Above the haze, the afternoon sky was a deep, saturated blue. Swallows wheeled overhead to a secret choreography.

The house was at the end of an unsurfaced road. A German car in the garage. Trotti and Ciuffi got out of the Lancia and the young policewoman rang at the front door.

It was a while before a woman answered.

"Signora Bianchini?"

She was wearing a skirt and a loose white blouse. Her dark hair had a blue glint, as if it had just been dyed and set. The lips of the large mouth were carefully made up. Neatly applied mascara.

"Commissario Trotti, Pubblica Sicurezza." A flat voice.

The woman looked at Trotti for a moment without understanding.

"And this is Brigadiere Ciuffi."

"Police?" The woman stepped back and Trotti could not tell whether the surprise was real or feigned.

"Is your son at home, Signora?"

The woman said, "Has Riccardo done something wrong?"

"I would like to speak to your son."

"He has done something wrong." It was no longer a question.

Trotti gave her a brief smile. "Routine enquiries, Signora Bianchini."

"He has done something stupid again." She did not try to hide the resignation in her voice.

Signora Bianchini was an attractive woman, with fine features and good bone structure. Thirty-eight, thirty-nine, Trotti thought. There was no brassiere beneath the blouse.

"My son is a good boy."

Ciuffi spoke reassuringly. "He may be able to help us—that is all, Signora."

"He has been working for his exam. I thought that perhaps . . ." Signora Bianchini gave a hesitant shrug. "This way, please." She turned and led them into the house.

The living room was dark and smelt of varnish; an antique grandfather clock in one corner and a vase of freshly-cut flowers on the polished table. There was an old painting on the wall: a portrait, perhaps, of a long dead relative.

Expensive furniture, dark antiques that had been carefully restored and polished, a Venetian chest-of-drawers.

She squeezed one small white hand in the other. "Can I offer you a drink?" She tried to smile.

"Not while on duty." They sat down on the high-backed chairs. "Your son will be home soon?"

"Perhaps." An apologetic gesture of the two hands: long, well-kept nails. "You see, Riccardo has a motorbike—and he leads an independent existence. I am afraid he doesn't feel he needs his mother anymore."

Trotti frowned.

"My son is . . . he is like his father, a headstrong person. It is not always easy to argue with Riccardo." A smile that reminded Trotti of another woman. "There are times when Riccardo doesn't sleep at home."

"Where was your son last night?"

The dark eyes blinked.

Trotti waited.

"He was here," she said. "With me."

Trotti looked at her in silence. "And your husband . . . ?"

"Commissario, it is a long time since I last saw my husband."

"He's dead?"

"A dead man who pays the bills." She smiled, more for herself than for Trotti. "As far as I'm concerned, my husband died ten years ago."

"Where does he live?"

"Riccardo?"

"Your husband, Signora Bianchini. Where is he?"

"On Lake Como."

"And you live here alone with your son?"

"It is not always easy to bring up a son single-handed." She looked at Trotti as if seeking sympathy in his face. "Riccardo has always been an affectionate boy. But headstrong."

Trotti glanced at his watch.

"Are you quite sure that I can't offer you something to drink?"

It was not yet five o'clock yet already he felt tired. "A cup of coffee, perhaps, signora."

"A glass of wine—and some truffles from the hills?" The nature of the smile suddenly seemed to have changed. "I think I can recognize that accent. Surely you won't say no to a glass of real wine? Wine from the OltrePò." The woman stood up. Her body was trim and the well-cut skirt showed the flatness of her belly.

"Just a cup of coffee." The muscles in his face had relaxed.

Ciuffi pursed her lips and crossed her arms against her chest. Her dark eyes were puzzled. "One other thing, Signora Bianchini . . ."

Signora Bianchini looked at Ciuffi, "Yes, signorina?"

"We shall need a photograph of your son."

7: Discovery

EVENING HAD BEGUN to fall.

"You think it is a good idea to eat truffles and drink wine in the middle of the afternoon?"

As they approached the river, more and more insects were battered against the windscreen. Cellophane wings and viscous body fluids that gave the world beyond the car a brown and dirty cast.

An uninterrupted flow of traffic in the opposite direction coming from the city and the emptying offices.

"You can get more information from people when they're relaxed—and when they think you're relaxed."

"Commissario, I thought you didn't approve of drinking while on duty."

"I am nearly fifty-eight years old. An old man, and the only thing I'm interested in is getting results. How they're got doesn't bother me." Trotti paused. "What is more, the wine was good. And Signora Bianchini is a charming person."

"Very charming."

He turned to look at Ciuffi. "I think I am old enough to decide when and where I can take my pleasures."

For a few minutes there was silence while the car ran along the smooth road. Ciuffi was a good driver.

"I'm no longer a young man, signorina."

"You're not an old man."

"Of course I am."

"I don't think of you as being old." Ciuffi smiled then, and the smile—a mixture of concern and an unavowed fondness—reminded Trotti of his daughter.

"But you are right," he said, folding his arms and leaning back in the seat with a slight sigh. "I shouldn't drink."

A girlish laugh that took him by surprise. "And the photo, Commissario?"

"Photo?"

"Compared with Vardin's description of the attacker?"

"The photo and the identikit certainly look alike. The hair is just a bit longer in the identikit." Trotti shrugged. "But the photo was taken some time ago."

"You believe that the man with the knife was Riccardo?"

"Netta lied to me. I showed her the identikit and she said it was nothing like Riccardo." Trotti paused. "I don't know what to think. Being young and being in love . . ." He raised his shoulders. "All that happened to me a long time ago. Long before you were born, Brigadiere. And a time when everything was a lot simpler."

Ciuffi gave him a questioning glance.

"Things that people seem to take for granted these days—pornography and homosexuality and sadism . . ." His voice trailed away.

"Well?"

"It must have existed, but I was never aware of it. I think that, when we were young, we were too busy wondering where the next meal would come from to be bothered with all those . . . all those strange pleasures."

"You think that Riccardo is a sadist?"

The city was up ahead, the dome of the Cathedral catching the last light of the failing evening; to the east there was a thickening band of darkness. To the west, the sky was red.

"Unruly and spoiled. His mother is a divorcee and Riccardo is probably given too much money by a father he hardly ever sees. I can easily imagine him fixing up a rendezvous with the girl."

"Which girl?"

"The older sister." He shook his head slowly. "But a knife . . . I can't understand the knife."

"An insurance."

"What?"

"Perhaps Netta sometimes left the door on the latch. But that doesn't necessarily mean they slept together, Netta and Riccardo. The knife—it could have been a way of threatening her. The way a man has of forcing a woman to give her body to him."

"Laura was on the settee—not Netta." Trotti clicked his tongue. "Why was the door left on the latch? Why wasn't it bolted?"

"Commissario," she said, mockingly.

Trotti looked at Ciuffi. "You are a very cynical young woman."

She took her foot off the accelerator. A traffic cop stood by the roadside and with his stick he was flagging the traffic to slow down. Ciuffi brought the car to a stop a few hundred meters before the Ponte Imperiale; fifty meters ahead, a policeman in leather boots and a helmet was holding up the flow of traffic with one hand while with the other he beckoned on a white ambulance coming from the city. It turned, crossing the road and taking the unsurfaced track that ran down to the plane trees and the River Po.

"Wait for me here."

Trotti got out of the car and hurried down the sloping path. The air was losing its warmth.

He recognized the strong smell of the river. The Po was turning a bloodshot red in the evening light. The flowing water was low in the riverbed after the long, dry summer.

He pushed his way through a narrow fence of bushes and came onto the short expanse of grass. There was an Alfa Romeo and one or two men in uniform on the far side of the field. He broke into a run, aware of his weight, aware that he had not done enough exercise, aware that lately he had been drinking too many coffees and eating too many sweets. The taste of the wine washed at the back of his throat.

He also recognized the silhouette: Pisanelli's stooping shoulders. Insects flew into his eyes and into his nostrils.

Pisanelli was taking off his jacket.

Five or six men from the Questura Trotti recognized: Merenda, Schipisi, Mangiavacca, standing on the far edge of the field. Near the clump of stunted bushes. Out of sight from the road.

Something on the ground; something dark, like a packet. A bomb, Trotti thought, as he approached them, running with difficulty and a sense of foreboding in his belly.

Commissario Merenda was giving orders and now Pisanelli was crouching. The ambulance had taken the side road and it began to bump over the grass, coming to a halt on the footpath. A couple of men jumped out. The siren lost its force and whined into a dying silence.

"Dead—it's dead."

"How do you know?"

Trotti reached Pisanelli, placed a hand on his sleeve, knelt down, out of breath and sweating beneath his arms. "Who found it?" He looked down.

Commissario Merenda took a couple of steps back.

It was hard to distinguish the face in the dusk. A small, ugly face that was brown from exposure to a relentless sun. Eyes wrinkled shut, glued together by dried mucus. Stains in meandering diagonals across the minute cheeks. Small dark shapes that moved, oval shapes.

Maggots that were crawling across the dirty flesh.

A naked body, smeared and dark.

The long severed umbilical cord snaked from the belly on to the grass.

A minute, motionless body.

Pisanelli took his jacket and now carefully wrapped it round the small baby. It appeared lifeless.

The two ambulance men came running from the footpath.

Trotti stretched out his hand.

"It moved!"

Movement and then something fell from the nose. A worm—a maggot that vanished in the grass and dry leaves.

Trotti touched the skin. Chill and the softness made coarse with dirt and dried blood.

One of the ambulance men picked up the child.

Trotti watched in silence, unthinking and numb.

Merenda gave a couple of orders. The two men hurried back to the waiting vehicle. With a squeal of tires on the track, the ambulance drove away beneath its reawakened siren.

"My God," Pisanelli said.

The ambulance disappeared, hidden by the cloud of rising dust.

8: Home

"BRING THE BIANCHINI boy in tomorrow. I want to talk to him."

Trotti got out of the car opposite the bicycle shop. He felt drained of emotion.

Ciuffi nodded, smiled and said, "Buona sera, Signor Commissario." The Lancia did a sharp U-turn and disappeared along via Milano, heading back towards the Questura.

Trotti walked slowly home. Beneath the bright lamps, the street was empty. The air was still warm, but not as warm as it had been the previous weeks. The first hint of autumn.

Trotti pushed open the garden gate and went up the steps. Lost in thought, he glanced absentmindedly at the potted plants that needed watering. Eight o'clock in the evening and, as he turned the key in the lock, he closed his eyes and made a silent prayer. He felt the temptation to return to the hospital. By being there, perhaps he could help.

Trotti let himself into the house and immediately recognized the reassuring, familiar smell. A smell of floor polish and emptiness. He pulled the door shut behind him.

Pioppi's bear was there, sitting on the wardrobe and staring down at him with its dusty glass eyes.

He went into the kitchen and opened the refrigerator. Cheese from the hills, milk. There was lasagne the housekeeper had made him and which he had not touched. Trotti was not hungry.

The wine and truffles still lay heavy on his stomach. He poured himself half a glass of chilled mineral water and turned on the television. Cold bubbles jumped from the glass onto his hand.

When he closed his eyes, he saw again the small, sunburnt face.

He tried to concentrate on the television program. Maggots and dried blood.

Half an hour later the front door bell rang.

"Do you still go to church, Piero?"

Trotti said nothing, but held out his hand. "Come in." He smiled and led the man into the kitchen.

"More than forty years ago, Piero. You had a lovely voice."

"Have you eaten, Fra Gianni?"

"Turn the television off," Fra Gianni said peremptorily and sat down. "And give me a glass of wine." He nodded to the bottle of wine that stood beneath the sink. "You always said, Piero Trotti, that you were going to become a priest."

Trotti switched the television off. "And instead I became a policeman, for my sins."

"You have done well." Fra Gianni took the glass and raised it to his mouth. "You still go to church?"

"My wife has left me, you know."

The dark eyes stared at the younger man and there was a smile at the corner of his lips.

"She wants a divorce."

"What do you want, Piero?"

"Agnese was never very happy with me."

"Other things to marriage than happiness—I don't have to tell you that, Piero. There is a home, there are the children."

"I have scarcely seen my daughter in eighteen months." Trotti shrugged. "Pioppi's gone to Bologna to study—and she only writes when she needs money."

"Like you, Piero, Pioppi is stubborn. But at least she is eating now. If you hadn't sent her to that place near Ravenna, she'd have died of anorexia."

"I miss her company."

Between the old, gnarled hands and the long fingers, Fra

Gianni held his glass of wine. He was leaning forward on the kitchen chair, his elbows on his thighs. The gentle features were friendly but he had aged and the skin appeared parched. Behind the tired face, Trotti could recognize the young country priest that Giovanni Batelli had once been.

"Now that Pioppi can look after herself, her mother has decided to live her own life. Without me and without her daughter. She phoned the other day to tell me that she's living with an American . . . a rich American." Trotti smiled. "But it wasn't to hear my life story that you have driven down to the city, Father. I am boring you."

He produced a cigarette from his pocket. "You will give her a divorce?"

"I know how the Church feels about divorce." Trotti raised his shoulders. "But if Agnese wants her freedom, why should I stop her? She was never happy with me. The least I can do is give her the chance of finding happiness with somebody else."

"The Church and divorce." Fra Gianni's smile was apologetic. "We really are too old-fashioned. Time for a change . . . I am not alone in thinking that there are more important problems facing the Church than sexual behavior and birth control." The smile broadened. "When I see a beautiful woman I can't help feeling that the Kingdom of Heaven is here on Earth." He paused. "I am sorry to hear about Agnese. She is a very beautiful woman." He held out the packet of filterless cigarettes. "You smoke?"

"I gave up more than twelve years ago—and since then I have been addicted to cheap boiled sweets." Trotti shrugged. "One of the things about me Agnese couldn't stand."

Fra Gianni lit the cigarette, inhaled and then held it between his finger and his thumb. It was a habit that Trotti had forgotten about. He looked at the old priest and felt a flood of affection for him.

"I still think you should have stayed with the church, Piero."

"And then I wouldn't even have a daughter. No, no . . ." Trotti laughed. "I have been happy with my wife and daughter—and like all good things . . ."

"You also had a brother."

"Italo?"

The name hung in the warm air of the kitchen. Outside in the street, someone was whistling.

"A long time ago," Trotti said.

The priest took another long drag on the cigarette. He was wearing an old jacket. The dark trousers were frayed at the cuffs.

Trotti said, "I saw him when he came out of the hospital. Mother and I went to fetch him at the station in Voghera. Italo was already dead."

"You saw him at Voghera?"

"Italo had been my hero. In his uniform he was handsome and I looked up to him." Trotti paused. "I was young and I believed in it all. Everybody in Santa Maria did—we believed in Fascism and we believed in Mussolini. And then Italo went off to fight. To Africa and then to Spain. We never saw him. For seven years we never saw him. Just the letters that he would write. And then he wrote to Mother telling her he was being sent to Russia. You hadn't come to the village yet—this was before September 1943. I think Mother must have prayed every day. And in the end her prayers were answered."

The old priest had closed his eyes.

"We went to the station at Voghera, Mother and I. We knew he had been wounded—but he was Italo, he was my brother. I never . . . Italo—the brother I had loved and admired for all those years . . . He could scarcely speak. His mind had gone. It had started to wander." Trotti bit nervously at his lip. "Sometimes I think the Fascists were doing him a favor when they put the gun to the back of his head."

Fra Gianni shook his head. His hair—in 1944, when he was chaplain to the partisans, he had the long black hair of a matinée idol and more than one girl had fallen in love with him—was now white and thin. He looked long and emaciated as he leaned back in the chair, with his hands holding the half-empty glass and loosely folded over the slight paunch.

The clock ticked on the refrigerator.

(Mother had always spoken well of Fra Gianni.)

The smell of war came back: the smell and the taste of the

coarse maize bread that had been Trotti's staple diet through the long winter.

"I think your mother knew, Piero."

"Knew what?"

"Italo was badly injured. But he could have been called up by the Fascists. By the puppet government at Salò. They were desperate times and there were spies everywhere. Perhaps he shouldn't have lied to you—but I still believe it was a good thing. You were sixteen. A life in the hills, fighting for a just cause . . . the sort of thing that would set a boy's romantic mind ablaze. Your mother didn't want that for you, Piero—and neither did Italo." Fra Gianni raised the glass and held it against his chest. "His mind was as lucid as ever it had been. He was not sick in his head—but he was sick of war, and he did not want to go back, return to fight for a lost cause and empty words. Russia had cured him of all that."

Forty years.

"Russia."

The telephone rang and the sudden sound caught both men by surprise.

Trotti went into the hall.

The priest finished the glass of wine and stared at the blank screen of the television. When Trotti returned he was smiling.

"Good news, Piero?"

"A call from the hospital. Somebody—a friend—I thought he was going to die . . ."

"A friend?"

"A little boy—and nothing wrong with him." Trotti took the wine bottle and filled the two glasses before sitting down. "I feel like celebrating."

"Then let's celebrate." Gianni held out his glass.

The two men smiled at each other and drank.

"We were talking about your brother."

The lingering smile disappeared. "Fra Gianni—what difference does it all make? Italo's been dead for a long time—and Mother died last spring."

"Italo lived with the Garibaldi Brigade. He never fought, he never carried a gun—but he helped with the cooking and did chores. He had seen too much fighting and he had seen too much blood spilled."

Trotti had begun to shake his head. "I don't want to know, Fra Gianni. I don't want to know."

"You loved your brother, Piero."

"I still put flowers on the grave."

"But he was murdered, Piero."

"The Fascists, the Repubblichini killed him. They admitted to it; all that came out at the end of the war, during the trials. They murdered him when the Germans regained control of Santa Maria."

The priest said simply, "They are still murdering in Santa Maria."

9: Bear

"A FRIEND OF yours?"

Pisanelli wore a flower in his buttonhole. He held the door open.

Trotti did not reply. He got into the car and placed the bear on the back seat.

"You look tired, Commissario—both of you."

"I was up late talking to an old friend." He gestured towards the back seat. "As for the bear, he's not tired, just astigmatic. Been astigmatic for the last twenty years."

"You'd better have a look at the *Provincia*. They're having a field day with it." Pisanelli had not turned off the ignition and now he pulled the black Mirafiore out into the traffic. "Where to?"

"Field day with what, Pisanelli?"

"A rapist at large, a monster. Trying to frighten the readers. Trying to create hysteria in the city."

"That's what makes papers sell."

"Where do you want me to take you?"

"The hospital." Trotti glanced at him. "And thanks for coming to fetch me, Pisanelli."

"On the phone you told me to be here."

"I didn't tell you to be half an hour late."

The familiar, sheepish grin. "A bit of a celebration last night. The doctors were amazed—they couldn't believe it. For nearly forty-eight hours the woman refused to talk—forty-eight hours while Ivan . . ."

"Ivan?"

"That's what the nurses in Ostetrica have christened the little boy. Ivan the Terrible. A nice crowd of girls, very friendly . . ."

"I don't wish to know that."

Pisanelli repressed a smile. "The baby was exposed, quite naked and unprotected. Two days and two nights out in the open. At San Matteo they cleaned him up—he was crawling with lice—and they put him in the incubator. And the only thing wrong with him is mild pneumonia."

"So he's going to survive?"

Pisanelli nodded like a pleased child.

"Does that mean that you won't be going on any wild chases today, Pisanelli? Does it mean that Commissario Merenda won't be needing your services? And does it mean that perhaps I can ask you to carry out one or two little chores for me?"

Pisanelli's smile vanished.

"Perhaps even ask you to help Brigadiere Ciuffi? If you don't mind, of course."

Pisanelli frowned, concentrating on driving.

"A few little chores concerned with the Vardin enquiry—but of course, nothing too strenuous." He tapped Pisanelli's lapel. "After all, you are celebrating. Celebrating with Commissario Merenda and his men. And the nice nurses in Ostetrica."

Pisanelli leaned forward in his seat.

"I'm sure that Brigadiere Ciuffi would appreciate some logistic support. Or at least your presence."

Pisanelli spoke in a flat voice. "Brigadiere Ciuffi manages to get by without needing anybody's help."

"Don't you believe it."

"The trouble with Brigadiere Ciuffi—"

"You said something about the paper, Pisanelli?"

"Brigadiere Ciuffi would get a lot more cooperation if she—"

"Where is the article, Pisanelli?"

"The front page."

The air was already tinted with the exhaust of the commuter

traffic. The pavements along the outer boulevards of the city were filling up with erratically parked cars.

They reached the traffic lights in via Milano, went over the canal and took the direction of the autostrada. Pisanelli drove awkwardly, putting his foot on the brake and then accelerating aggressively from the lights.

Trotti tried to read the article. There was a picture of Piazza Castello and another of the Vardin's living room. The print of the photograph was coarse and the details were unclear. A MONSTER, ran the headline, ATTACKS SLEEPING SCHOOLGIRL. In smaller letters: CAN THE POLICE PROTECT US? ARE THE WOMEN OF OUR CITY SAFE?

"Well?" Trotti said.

"And that?" Without taking his eyes off the road—they were approaching the railway bridge—Pisanelli tapped the bottom part of the page. "A secretary attacked," Trotti read. "Another victim of the same monster?" He held the paper up but the movement of the car caused the printed lines to dance in front of his eyes. "What does it say?"

"Read the article, Commissario."

"How can I read it when you're driving this car over cobbles?"

"There are no cobbles."

"Drive a bit more smoothly."

"A woman has been attacked."

"When?"

"At home. In bed. At night, while she was sleeping."

"And she informed the police?"

Pisanelli gave a slight shake of his head.

"How did the *Provincia* know about her?"

Pisanelli stamped on the brake.

Trotti was tugged forward. His forehead would have hit the windshield had he not been held back by the belt.

"For God's sake, Pisanelli."

"Commissario?"

Trotti straightened his tie. "And her address?"

"Who?"

"This woman who was attacked."

"Somewhere near Ciel d'Oro."

"I want to get out of this car. Drop me off at the hospital."

Pisanelli said, "Can I go over to Ostetrica?"

"Follow it up, would you, Pisanelli? Find this woman who says she's been raped and—"

"I'd like to get over to Ostetrica."

"Get her address. Contact *La Provincia*."

Pisanelli repressed a sigh. "This woman, whoever she is, will be at work on a Monday morning."

"Perhaps you can take Ciuffi—she should know how to ask intelligent questions. Just take notes—and shake your head if you think it's necessary. Get a statement from the woman and see if you can get her to come in for a picture on the computer."

"Shall I see you later, Commissario?"

"I'll make my way back to the Questura from the hospital." Trotti put his hand on the door handle. "You didn't use to drive so aggressively. Not in love again, are you, Pisanelli?"

"I beg your pardon, Commissario."

"You can drop me off here."

The car stopped at the railway bridge and Trotti turned in his seat and picked up the bear. "When you've finished with the raped woman, help Ciuffi find the boy." He opened the door and climbed out of the car.

"The boy?"

"Do you think it's a good idea to wear a carnation, Pisanelli?" Trotti slammed the door shut—a middle-aged man on the city pavement during the Monday morning rush hour, holding a moth-eaten teddy bear under his arm.

Somewhere in the city, beyond the ocher walls and the red tiles of the rooftops, a siren began to wail.

"No call for a flower in your buttonhole. You're not getting married today, Pisanelli." Trotti lowered his head and looked at Pisanelli's disgruntled face. "Or are you?"

"Of course not."

"The Bianchini kid—see if you can find out where he is."

Wearily Pisanelli asked, "Who's he?"

"Ciuffi'll explain everything."

Pisanelli put the car into gear.

"One other thing, Pisanelli."

"Commissario?" Pisanelli did not look at him.

"Ivan's mother—how did you get her to tell you where she had hidden her baby?"

"I did as you told me, Commissario—I threatened to seduce her."

Against his will, Trotti found himself smiling.

10: Ward

"WELL?"

"I would like to see the child."

"What child?"

"The girl that was attacked in her bed."

"It is too early for visiting hours."

"I told you. I am Commissario Trotti of the Pubblica Sicurezza." He was not sure whether it was the same woman he had seen the previous day. If not, the two nuns looked remarkably alike: stocky, the wide coiffe that hid the ungentle face.

"You told me nothing."

"I am telling you now."

"It is too early to see the child."

"Sister . . ."

"This is very irregular." She turned away and said, "You'd better follow me." She took short steps down the empty hospital corridor.

Trotti followed the small woman.

"You don't think she's a bit old for dolls?"

"We all need affection, sister. Some of us find it in marrying Jesus. Don't begrudge children the joy of loving a bit of cloth and stuffing and a couple of glass eyes."

"You laugh at me." She stopped so suddenly that he almost walked in to her. She held out a thick, short finger. She had pale eyes and no eyelashes. "I could have married—I could have had children. Don't laugh at what you can't understand. I didn't have to become a nun." She spoke in a flat monotone. "If loving Jesus means emptying bedpans, I am not ashamed of my love for Him." She turned again. "This way please."

They were new wards, part of the expansion at the beginning of the 1970s when there was money coming from Rome for the university. A room with six beds, at the same time both institutional and yet human. Posters of furry animals and television stars on the wall. Inspector Gadget and Heidi. A lot of flowers and two children in red pajamas running hurriedly towards their cots.

"Children!"

The underlying harshness in her voice reminded Trotti of one of his aunts. Zia Martina lost her husband at Vittorio Veneto and spent the next fifty years wearing shiny black dresses and resenting the happiness of others. She went to Mass every morning and lit a candle to the memory of her husband.

The two barefoot children scrambled into their beds and snatched the blankets towards their small, white chins.

A third bed was occupied and at first Trotti thought that Laura was asleep. On approaching the bed he realized that her eyes were open and staring at the ceiling. Beneath the nightdress he could see that her chest was wrapped in tight bandages.

The nun placed a hand on the little girl's forehead and then going to the foot of the bed, picked up the record sheet attached to the bedstead. "You're doing well, Laura. We're very proud of you."

There was no movement in the girl's eyes.

Trotti spoke softly. "Laura, how do you feel?" A long time since he had last been with children.

The girl said nothing.

Trotti smiled. "I have brought you a present." He raised the large bear and set it beside her on the clean white sheet.

She shook her head.

"You don't want a bear?"

The eyes blinked but they did not look at Trotti.

"I want to help you, Laura. I am your friend—and this bear

belongs to my daughter. She is a big girl now and soon she is going to get married. An old bear—his name is Chinotto and nobody has ever found out why. My daughter has left home and she has forgotten about him. And I am a busy man." He tapped Chinotto's chin. "Bears need people to talk to them."

The nun was looking at him with a frown on her forehead.

"Chinotto," Trotti said and he looked down at his feet. "You would be doing me a favor if you took him. For a day or two—or perhaps a bit longer. Every time I see Chinotto looking at me with his cross-eyes, I am reminded of my daughter—and I haven't seen . . ."

Her nightdress did not have long sleeves and her left arm was a series of small bandages, neat flesh-colored squares anchored with sticking plaster.

"I am not a child," Laura Vardin said tersely and, with a sharp nudge of her elbow, she pushed the bear off the side of the bed. "And you are not a friend of mine. I have never seen you before."

11: Stetho

"MY FAULT," TROTTI said.

Dottor James Wafula smiled. "Oh, I wouldn't worry about the nun, if I were you. They're all like that. They're very good—and, unlike the other nurses, they don't have to be reminded a hundred times. Dedicated, but susceptible. Highly susceptible."

"I'm talking about the girl."

Wafula nodded and put the cup of coffee down.

A small room, both neat and comfortable, with two leather armchairs and a large mahogany desk. A white laboratory coat hung from the stand and the stethoscope had been thrown over the back of a chair. The odor coming from the fresh coffee drowned the smell of antiseptic.

"I am not a psychiatrist," the African doctor said. "Although I did do a course in child psychology in Makerere."

"Macerata?"

"In Uganda. But that was a long time ago."

"Strange behavior for a little girl. Eleven years old—my daughter was never like that."

"Times have changed, Commissario. And an eleven-year-old child today is not like an eleven-year-old of ten years ago. Children are growing up faster—a lot faster."

Trotti found himself resenting the suggestion that he was too old to understand.

"Eleven-year-olds are not interested in dolls—and certainly

not in teddy bears. They're interested in boys." Wafula leaned forward and picked up the cup of coffee. "Laura probably feels that she has been betrayed."

"Why betrayed?"

"A girl likes to think that she is coping, that she is in charge. And at puberty most normal children manage to stay in control, even if it is not easy. But suddenly she is attacked—attacked in a way that was probably sexual." Wafula's Italian was perfect; only the slight accent betrayed the fact it was not his mother tongue. "In her mind, she is still just a little girl." He shrugged. "Not the end of the world and certainly not something she'll never get over. She's a tough little thing."

"I hope so."

"We normally manage to forget what we don't want to remember."

"You said you weren't a psychiatrist."

A flash in the doctor's eyes—perhaps even a flash of anger. "We are all psychiatrists to a certain extent. Even policemen." He drank. "The wounds will heal, and so will the wound in her mind. Time cures everything—while gradually leading us onward to the grave." He looked at Trotti. "Death is the cure to everything."

Trotti said nothing.

"I don't think you need worry about Laura. She has had a rather bloody introduction to adulthood. She will recover. And her reaction to you—in the circumstances—seems to me both healthy and normal."

Trotti put his hands on the leather armrests. "Thank you for the coffee . . ."

"But it wasn't about that, Commissario, that I wanted to talk to you. Have another cup of coffee."

"I must be going—I'm driving up into the hills this afternoon."

"The hills? Tarzi? I thought I recognized the accent."

"For a foreigner, Dottor Wafula, you are very good at accents."

"And to think my father ran around in a loin cloth, shaking a spear." A brilliant glimpse of the teeth. "Perhaps you would like to bring me back some wine from the hills—real, full-blooded wine. I'd be—"

"There are a lot of places in this town where you can buy good wine from the hills, Dottor Wafula."

"Good wine, with good anti-freeze."

"I see you have already developed your prejudices about the Italian people."

"We are all prejudiced at some time or another."

Trotti stood up. "I must be going."

"We are not getting on very well." A very wide grin. "Be careful, Commissario Trotti. My Ugandan predecessor in this job went back to Africa and became Minister of the Interior. In six months he managed to murder one hundred thousand of my compatriots." An unassuming shrug. And then, with deadly irony, "We Africans are not always very bright—what can you expect from people who have just climbed out of the trees?—but we can be dangerous."

"I don't doubt it."

"Do please have another cup of . . . Ugandan coffee."

Trotti sat down again.

"I said I wanted to talk to you about the girl."

"We have already discussed her, Dottor Wafula."

"But we haven't discussed her father."

Trotti frowned. The doctor shrugged. "I don't know why I want to tell you all this—I am sure you have got computers. And I know that you have better things to do than waste your time with a stupid black man." A mischievous smile. "But it is not every day that I have the opportunity of chatting with a policeman—a real policeman."

"An ageing policeman, who has been in the PS for too long. A policeman who has got another four years to get through before a well-earned retirement. A policeman who asks for nothing more than to leave this city and to go and live in the hills and make his own wine—wine without anti-freeze."

"Commissario—we all have our bad days." The smile was sympathetic. "Vardin," the surgeon said, "you know who he is?"

Trotti shrugged.

"You haven't always lived in this city, Commissario?"

"I was in Bologna—and in Bari. I came back in seventy-seven."

"Then you do like the city?"

"It was my wife who wanted to return." A dismissive movement of his hand. "Why do you ask about Vardin?"

"You have interviewed him, I suppose, and he has told you where he works?"

"He is unemployed."

Wafula nodded. "And before he was unemployed he worked at the sewing-machine factory."

"Well?"

"And before that he worked for AVIS."

"So what?"

"AVIS, Commissario. The voluntary blood bank. I knew I recognized his name. He was the porter—and it was he who gave evidence about the comings and goings at the dispensary. About Galandra."

"The AVIS dispensary?"

"You have records in the Questura, Commissario—and I can't remember very much. But I remember the name—because I remember thinking that he was courageous. From Udine or Trieste, isn't he? A man with guts."

Trotti had picked up his cup although it was empty.

"It must have been in seventy-five or seventy-six. No, seventy-six, because that was the year I arrived in this city and I was working for Professor Adunata. That's right, seventy-six."

"What happened in seventy-six?"

"The AVIS trial."

"And Vardin was involved?"

"Vardin—I am quite sure. Either him or a relative—or else a coincidence. It's not a common name and I have got a good memory. The people at the blood bank—they were getting all the blood from the donors and then selling it to the hospital watered down. They were selling plasma and pocketing the money. And in the end it was Vardin's testimony that sent them to jail. The man—the ringleader—he was sent away for seven years."

Trotti listened in silence.

"Ten years ago—it took over three years for the thing to get to court. So by my calculations, he should be coming out of prison any moment now. With a grudge against Vardin."

"A grudge?"

The wide grin. "More coffee, Commissario?"

12: Principessa

INSTINCTIVELY HE PUT his hand to his mouth.

Over the last couple of months it had been getting stronger, more assertive, making life on the third floor of the Questura more unpleasant.

Today the smell was overpowering; it worked its way down the back of Trotti's throat.

As Trotti stepped out of the lift, Gino looked up and smiled wanly.

"Any news?" Trotti asked, lowering his hand.

Under the table, Principessa was motionless, curled up and her paws outstretched. Hardly a hint of movement although the dog's eyes were open, pink and looking at Trotti without interest. Gino and Principessa had been together for more than fourteen years.

"A woman waiting for you, Commissario. Signora Bianchini—with her son."

Trotti placed his hand briefly on the blind man's shoulder then went down the corridor into his office.

She was sitting in the canvas armchair. She wore the same skirt and her slim legs were crossed. She turned her head very slightly as Trotti entered his office.

"Buongiorno, Signora Bianchini."

A small smile. "My son has decided that he would like to see you." She gestured to where Riccardo Bianchini stood by the window, staring out at Strada Nuova.

"It is very kind of you to cooperate."

The smell had worked itself into the dingy office. It was coming through the wooden hatch in the wall.

"Riccardo is willing to answer any questions you may have."

Trotti opened the window, took a deep breath and then sat down behind the desk. He moved a pile of dossiers on to the floor.

"I don't want you to think that my son has anything to hide."

Trotti looked towards the boy. Riccardo continued to stare at the street below; the oblique light fell on a sallow, thin face.

"You want to help the Commissario, don't you, Riccardo?"

The boy turned and glanced coldly at his mother. Riccardo had put on a white shirt, a tie and a sports jacket. Trotti noticed the dirty fingernails and the grime embedded in his fingers. The boy—eighteen years old, tall and slim—looked ill at ease in his clothes. The shoes were new and uncreased.

Signora Bianchini placed her hands on the armrests. "If you wish to speak to Riccardo alone . . ."

Trotti gestured her back into the low chair and smiled at her.

She returned the smile. There was something of Agnese about her—the fine bone structure and the way the almond eyes held his glance. But there was a softness to Signora Bianchini—a softness that Trotti's wife had long abandoned in her dealings with her husband.

A breeze came through the window and it partially carried away the sickly smell. The smell of death.

Trotti's mouth was dry. "Something to drink?" He ran his tongue along his lips.

"I beg your pardon."

"Something to drink?" He smiled.

Signora Bianchini shook her head. Her French perfume competed valiantly with the smell of the dying dog.

"You won't say no to a cup of coffee?" He turned in his seat and banged on the hatch. "Gino, get somebody to bring me a pot of coffee from downstairs." Then he looked carefully at the boy.

Riccardo Bianchini fidgeted uncomfortably.

"Riccardo, you know what has happened?"

The boy nodded.

"You know that Laura is in the hospital?"

Another nod.

"You know that she was attacked by a man with a knife."

"Yes." His face was partially hidden by the bright light of the sky behind him.

"And you are Netta's boyfriend?"

"Netta and I are friends."

"More than just friends, I believe."

Trotti saw the slow blush as it moved across Riccardo's face. He stood with his hands loosely clasped. His hair was unruly and, although he had brushed it, it showed a lack of attention. It needed cutting.

"Netta and I are friends—that is all. There was a time . . ." He hesitated. "There was a time when we were a lot closer. Now we are just friends."

"Can you tell me where you spent Saturday night, Riccardo?"

"I was with a friend."

"A friend?"

"From the Istituto Tecnico." He nodded earnestly, stepping forward towards Trotti's desk. "We went to the cinema and then, as it was late, I stayed at his place."

"Who is this friend—and where does he live?"

"Raffaele Arzanti, via Emilia, thirteen, in the Borgo Genovese." The boy spoke fast as if he had been preparing his answers.

"And Raffaele—can he corroborate what you say?"

"Of course."

Trotti opened the left-hand drawer and took out the dossier. He looked at Riccardo carefully before asking, "And does this mean anything to you?" He handed over the identikit pictures, two side views and one frontal.

The boy took the sheet, his hand was shaking very slightly. Then with his eyes on the sheet of paper, he lowered himself on to the armrest of his mother's chair. The light from the window softened the long nose and high cheekbones.

Signora Bianchini looked up at her son; she placed her hand on his arm.

"Well?"

In thought, Riccardo massaged his jaw with his hand, as if he were trying to alter his own features. His face had paled, the blush had disappeared.

"Well?"

Signora Bianchini took the sheet from her son's hand.

"A resemblance?" Trotti asked in a flat voice.

"It's the old man, isn't it?"

Now the eyes were steady. Riccardo looked uncomfortable, but the eyes remained on Trotti. The same almond eyes as his mother. "Signor Vardin—the old bastard. He gave you the identikit." Riccardo Bianchini spoke calmly. "It was Vardin, wasn't it? He's always hated me . . . And now he wants to get me into trouble with the police." A dry laugh. "The cunning old bastard."

13 Sunglasses

A MISTAKE. A pleasant mistake.

The Audi moved effortlessly out of the city and Trotti sat back, enjoying the sensation—the sunlight beyond the tinted windows, the comfortable upholstery of the car and gentle, insinuating perfume that hung in the air.

For twenty minutes he sat in silence looking through the window at the tinted September countryside. A country at work, a people at peace. Italia felix. Trotti smiled to himself. The muscles beneath his eyes seemed to ache.

Signora Bianchini turned her head, raising an eyebrow. "Commissario?"

He looked at the woman, at her regular features, her wide, almond eyes. "Not every day that I have such a charming chauffeur."

"And it is not every day that my son is accused of attacking an innocent child."

"Nobody is accusing him, signora."

The voice was cold. "But you don't believe him."

"I don't believe anybody."

"You believe that my son would take a knife to a little girl?"

"Your son has nothing to be afraid of . . . if he has a corroborated alibi. We will check with Raffaele." Trotti folded his arms. "Understand, signora, that I must look into every possibility, no matter how disagreeable."

"You really think Riccardo is a child molester?"

"I believe nothing without proof, signora."

The woman pursed her lips. "You're a strange man, Commissario Trotti."

"I am interested in facts—not in beliefs."

"A strange man—and harsh."

"An old man—and only a few years away from a well-deserved retirement."

"Old?" She smiled. "You are fishing for compliments."

He put his head back on the rest and closed his eyelids.

"A man in the prime of life, Commissario."

The strange aching of the muscles beneath his eyes.

"A man of probity. A man who has the courage of his convictions." There was a hint of bitterness in her voice. "A man who is not afraid of being unpopular."

"It's not my job to be popular."

"How much do you earn, Commissario? A civil servant, a flatfoot at the end of his career—and just enough to get by on. Off-the-peg Lebole suits and cheap shoes. A nylon tie from Standa. And no doubt a dutiful wife at home, sweating over the kitchen, with her hair falling into her eyes."

"My wife is in New York."

"You're not rich—perhaps not even particularly intelligent."

Trotti shrugged.

"But honest."

"You flatter me."

"An honest policeman."

"Let's just say stupid."

"An honest man—the sort of man that I should have married."

Trotti laughed. "With my salary, signora?"

"Instead I was looking for something else. Honesty, integrity—I thought they didn't exist."

"Perhaps they don't."

"Now you're laughing at me, Commissario."

"An unintelligent flatfoot, Signora Bianchini?"

"Don't laugh at me."

Their eyes met.

"My family was not rich, Commissario. I grew up in Caserta. Not starving, not desperately poor—but poor enough to be determined that my children would have the best. There's nothing romantic about being poor, about being hungry. There is no dignity in poverty—just fear. Fear that you have eaten your last meal. That's why I married my husband." She shrugged; then she tapped Trotti's knee. "There's a pair of sunglasses in the glove box."

He found the glasses—German, with a neat, golden logo on one of the arms—and handed them to her. "You don't need glasses with the tinted window, signora."

She put on the glasses.

"And you have beautiful eyes."

They had reached the foothills; the vineyards ran down the slopes and the afternoon air was hazy with the late summer mist. A castle in the distance stood out from the soft skyline. No smells from the countryside penetrated the cool interior of the Audi. Several road signs indicated the possibility of landslides. "You really don't have to take me all the way to Santa Maria, Signora Bianchini."

"What else have I got to do with my time?" She slowed down before overtaking a tractor. The driver—a wizened peasant beneath a battered felt hat—gave a little wave and then frowned his wrinkled eyes at the silent, powerful car. "It is a pleasure to talk to a man like you, Commissario."

"A man who is not rich? Nor particularly intelligent? With a wife sweating over the cooker?"

"You know, when my husband decided to leave me, it was a relief. He loved me no more than I loved him—he'd married me for my looks and I'd married him for the money. Once I'd got tired of the nice clothes and the nice cars that money could bring, there was nothing left. Nothing except my son." She shrugged. "And about the same time, he realized that I was no longer an eighteen-year-old virgin but a middle-aged woman and mother. With wrinkles and a flabby belly."

Trotti felt uncomfortable. At the same time, it was not unpleasant to be beside this woman, to breathe in her perfume, share her secrets.

"Now it's you who are fishing for compliments, signora."

"Why New York, Commissario?"

"I beg your pardon?"

"What is your wife doing in New York?"

"It's not always easy living with an unintelligent, underpaid policeman."

"And you have children?"

"I have a daughter."

"Then you know how a parent feels." She shrugged. "I never thought I would have children—I was the eldest of seven and I didn't want that. It was so—so animal, so degrading, seeing Mama with her swollen belly and her tired face and her hands roughened by all the hard work. I didn't want that—and instead I made the mistake of having only one child. One child, Commissario, and you are a prisoner. Even when you are angry with him, you dote on him. You dote on him because there is nobody else—there is no one else to share your affection."

Trotti turned away. Seen through the tinted glass, the outside world was unreal, like a moving film.

"And in the end, by loving him too much, by worrying for him, you teach him to resent you."

"My daughter is in Bologna."

"To resent you. And then to hate you." A sigh. "Riccardo is a man. In these last two years, he has grown up a lot—he has changed. And now he no longer has time for me. I am a fool, an old woman. I think he despises me."

"For many years, my daughter admired me, she looked up to me, I was the only man in her life. Now I scarcely ever see her."

"Riccardo thinks that I am mercenary, that all I am interested in is money and the good things. But it was for him that I wanted the best. You can understand that, can't you, Commissario? The good life—it wasn't for me, but for him. So that he wouldn't suffer. That's why I came north, that's why I did what I did . . ."

"What you did?"

The eyes move behind the dark lenses. "I am not a saint, Commissario. And when I came north, it wasn't easy to find a job."

Trotti waited.

"I went to Turin."

An awkward silence.

"I could no longer stay in Caserta. Eighteen years ago I was a pretty girl. From Turin, I sent a lot of the money back to mother—so that my sisters could go to school. And then I met my husband."

"You fell in love?"

"I have never loved any man, Commissario. Not even my father."

"But you love Riccardo?"

"Riccardo is part of me." She took her hand from the steering wheel and brushed lightly at her cheek. "And now he no longer needs me."

"Why not?"

"About a year and a half ago something happened to him. Riccardo went to stay with his father. On Lake Como. And when he came back, he was strange—he had changed."

"In what way?"

"Riccardo has always been very good—very affectionate. And as soon as he came back, I could sense the hostility. He was no longer the affectionate son that he used to be. He resents me. And it was after coming back from Lake Como that he started staying away. He has the motor bike that his father bought for him at Mandello del Lario."

"And when did he start seeing the Vardin girl?"

"Riccardo never told me about her at first." Signora Bianchini opened her mouth to say something else, but instead she fell silent.

"When did they meet?"

"Riccardo deserves better than that girl." The corner of her lip turned down. "She is insignificant."

"Perhaps he is in love with Netta."

"Of course he isn't."

"She is very fond of your son."

"That girl means nothing to him. When she comes to the house she has hardly got a word to say for herself."

"That's not the impression that I—"

"Riccardo may have been infatuated, but he doesn't like her anymore—and, anyway, I haven't sacrificed eighteen years of my life just to see Riccardo go off with the first stupid little girl that comes along. A poor little peasant child—and a father who hasn't got two hundred lire to rub together."

They turned off the main Tarzi road and followed the signposts. Santa Maria, eight kilometers. Trotti's ears began to sense the change in the atmosphere.

"He is a good boy. You must help him, Commissario." She sighed. "Oh my God."

Trotti looked at her again.

"He would never hurt anyone."

A beautiful woman.

"Riccardo is all I have got. You will help me, won't you, Commissario?"

14: Rooftops

FRA GIANNI TURNED and called out, "Too many boiled sweets, Piero, and not enough exercise."

"I am an old man."

"You're fifteen years younger than me—and I am a young and athletic priest." He laughed as he leaned on his stout walking stick.

Out of breath, Trotti caught up with his friend. He wiped his forehead with a handkerchief then let himself sink down on to the soft grass. They had come to a clearing and, through the trees below them, Trotti could see the village of Santa Maria.

Trotti was born in Aquanera but he had gone to school in Santa Maria. Once he had seen the American bombers on their way back from Milan.

Strange that the village should have changed so much. There were villas and apartment buildings where Trotti could remember only fields. A place that had grown richer—a lot richer since the days when Trotti had lived there with his aunt and his cousin, Sandro. And yet, each time he returned, it somehow seemed smaller. Streets that had appeared broad to him as a child, he now saw as little more than alleys.

Fra Gianni said, "I'm so glad you decided to come with me, Piero."

(In 1977, Sandro had phoned from his clinic in Brescia, offering to share the old house with him. It had fallen into disrepair and needed a lot of work. Pioppi was still at school and for a few days, Trotti had been tempted to retire. To move out of the city, to move back to the hills. In the end, he had somewhat reluctantly turned down his cousin's suggestion. Anyway, Agnese would never have followed him into the country.)

Santa Maria.

So many faces—and not even young faces—that he had never seen before; and boutiques where he could remember only shops selling the bare necessities of life. The Santa Maria he remembered belonged to the past.

Fra Gianni handed him the water flask. "Who was that woman in the car?"

"A friend."

"A very attractive friend."

Far below in the valley, the church spire rose grey and austere against the terracotta rooftops.

Trotti drank. "I came, Fra Gianni, because you asked me to." His throat was dry and he did not want to speak. "The woman you ask about kindly offered me a lift."

Fra Gianni took the flask, drank, then banged the cork cap into the metal neck.

"I still don't have a car." Trotti clambered to his feet.

They started walking, following the path that was scarcely visible. A smell of pines and burnt wood hung in the air; a smell that reminded him of his childhood. "You let more than forty years go past—and then all of a sudden you drive down to the city because you have to see me. That is why I came, Fra Gianni."

"Your mother is dead, Piero. It would have done no good for her to know. It was better that she should die thinking her son was killed by the enemy."

Trotti stopped. "Who murdered my brother?"

The priest stopped, too. He shaded his eyes with his hand. "It wasn't the Fascists who killed him."

"Answer my question, Gianni."

"The partisans killed him."

"The partisans? What makes you say that?" A perplexed laugh. "Italo was a partisan."

"He was a witness."

"Witness to what?"

"You don't remember Saltieri?"

"A Carabiniere."

Fra Gianni nodded.

"He collaborated with the Fascists."

The priest shook his head. "Saltieri was not a collaborator—nor had he ever been. Just a policeman—a humble policeman from Ancona province—who tried to do his job at a difficult time." He shrugged and started walking again. "They murdered him and they made him appear as a Fascist—so killing two birds with one stone."

"Them?"

"An unwanted intruder—and, by accusing him of collaboration with the enemy, they passed themselves off as partisans."

Trotti's legs felt heavy and he was sweating; his shirt stuck to his back. "Who are you talking about?"

"Piero—I knew the partisans—and there were many of them that I loved like my own brother. Loyal men and honorable—even in a dirty war. A dirty, civil war. But they were not all innocent choirboys. We had a job to do and that job was to chase the enemy from Italy. The men that lived in these hills—there were Italians. But there were also Poles and South Africans and the English and the Americans. Not to mention the deserters from the Italian army; and even some Germans. Good Germans, Piero. They were wild men and they needed disciplining."

"Who murdered Italo?"

"Do you remember Primula Rosa?"

"Tell me about Italo, for heaven's sake."

Fra Gianni held up his hand. "You remember Primula Rosa?"

Trotti shrugged. "I saw him at the end of the war."

"A good and honorable soldier who looked after his men." The priest was now walking more slowly so that Trotti could keep pace with him. "I think we all loved Primula Rosa."

"Who murdered Italo, Fra Gianni?"

"You saw Primula Rosa?"

"Once—at a victory parade, at the end of the war." Trotti

ran a hand along his damp forehead. "I can recall thinking that he was only a few years older than me. He had lost an arm."

Fra Gianni smiled.

"Primula Rosa murdered my brother Italo?"

"No." Fra Gianni clicked his tongue. "Of course not."

"Then who killed Italo?"

"Come, Piero, another few hundred meters and we are at the spot." Turning forward, the priest marched briskly up the incline.

Trotti sighed, pulled back his shoulders and followed.

It was several years since Trotti had been back.

He felt hot. He was sticky with sweat and out of breath. But then, when he came to the small graveside, Trotti knelt down and lowered his head. He tried to remember an almost forgotten prayer as he stared at the engraved headstone.

ITALO TROTTI, 1921—1945

Then Piero Trotti closed his eyes and prayed, asking for eternal peace and divine love for his dead brother.

15: Cool

"WHY CAN'T YOU tell me the truth?"

He laughed. "You think that I'm not telling you the truth?"

"You talk like a Jesuit, Fra Gianni."

"Is that an insult?"

"What do you want me to do?"

The Fiat 500 went into a slight skid on the unsurfaced road. "Careful." Trotti could feel the back of the car sliding forward. "You are a priest—not a Formula One driver."

The older man gently touched the medallion of Saint Christopher on the dashboard. "Perhaps I should never have been a priest—and perhaps you should never have become a policeman."

"I don't think I would have been a good priest, if that's what you mean."

Fra Gianni was hunched over the steering wheel but he turned to look at Trotti. "You have the dedication, Piero. You have a kind of moral single-mindedness."

"And that's why you asked me to come here?"

"Your mother is dead, Piero. She cannot be hurt."

"There was no need to tell me about Italo. Dead—Italo is dead."

The rubble surface was bright in the sunlight. "Too many people have died."

Trotti frowned.

"You knew la Nini—she sometimes used to help your mother with the animals after the war."

"La Nini?"

"Her real name was Giulia Spallanera."

Trotti nodded. "Well?"

"Two weeks ago she was murdered."

They went through a small copse and the pine trees partially cut out the sunlight. The shadows of the trees danced hurriedly across the windscreen and the air was filled with particles of white dust rising from the road.

"A bit eccentric, a bit old-fashioned. La Nini spent her time living in the past—during the war, she used to carry messages from one partisan group to another. She knew the hills like her own apron. She must have been thirty years old at the time—but in those days she could run faster than most men. Old stock, Piero—hard-working and loyal."

"And?"

"They found her at the back of her house." He raised his right hand and gestured towards the valley. "Since her husband died some twenty years ago, she'd been living by herself. A bit strange in the head—but harmless."

"How did she die?"

"She fell into the stream and cracked her skull. That's what the Carabinieri think." He shrugged.

"You don't believe that?"

"La Nini was murdered."

There was an awkward silence.

"In cold blood, Piero."

"What do you expect me to do?"

Fra Gianni glanced at Trotti. "The sixth person to have died in strange circumstances."

"Six people?"

"Six people in the last twenty-five years. And all of them were directly or indirectly connected with the partisans."

"If one day I get run over in the street in Milan, is that because my brother was a partisan?"

"You don't understand, Piero."

"Fra Gianni, the war ended forty years ago. That's a long time. And it's more than long enough for anybody to carry out their plans of revenge."

"Here in the hills, memories can be very long."

Trotti placed his hand on the priest's arm.

"I am afraid, Piero."

"Afraid?"

"Not for myself—but for other people in the village."

"Afraid of what, Fra Gianni?"

"Revenge."

"Revenge for something which happened in 1944 or 1945?" Trotti tapped his temple. "I think you've been overworking your head."

"Six people, Piero."

Trotti laughed, but without conviction. "Suppose you are right—suppose six people have been murdered. What for? People don't get murdered just like that. They get murdered because they know something or because they are dangerous. What on earth can an old cleric . . . a young and athletic cleric know that would put his life in danger?"

"I never said that my life was in danger."

"Then what are you worrying about?"

"You're forgetting about the others."

"You're reading Agatha Christie when you should be reading your missal."

"The others, Piero."

"There are no others, Fra Gianni. Not after forty years."

"But the money is still there."

"Money?"

"That's why they killed your brother. He had witnessed Saltieri's death—and he knew about the money."

"Italo had no money. He was poor. We were all poor."

"The gold bullion that the partisans stole from the Germans." Fra Gianni shrugged. "Why else did they murder the Carabiniere? Why did they murder your brother? The gold bullion, Piero—somebody must have it."

The sky was a cloudless blue as they came to a bend. The

village opened up before them, like a photograph in a geography textbook.

"Why else have they been killing off these old people—people with an old secret?"

16: Afternoon Tea

FRA GIANNI WAITED until the housekeeper had closed the door before speaking. He sat forward. "It was probably a good thing you left Santa Maria, Piero . . . They used to say, 'Five days in the hands of the partisans, two days in the hands of the Fascists.'"

"A joke."

"A joke that wasn't too far from the truth. There was a lot of fighting in the last months of the war and Santa Maria changed hands frequently. We would chase the Fascists and a few days later they would come back supported by the Germans and take over the town again. Then we would have to run away up into the hills and hide until the Germans had gone off. Gone off with their heavy artillery and their tanks." Fra Gianni laughed as he began to pour tea into the three cups. "Your mother sent you to the city because she thought you'd be safer there than staying in Santa Maria. Or in the hills."

"The city got bombed."

"But by the allies—and they weren't trying to kill. Up here it was the Fascists—Mussolini's Fascists and they were worse than the Germans."

The Baronessa held up her hand—a fragile hand, of an almost translucent white. "You mustn't be so harsh on the Germans, Gianni. There were good Germans, too."

The priest looked at the woman and nodded. "At least when the Germans took a partisan, they shot him quickly."

"And sometimes they released him."

"You are not completely objective, Baronessa."

"I married a German, I lived in Germany. I think I know better than you what the Germans are really like."

Fra Gianni spoke hesitantly. "I can forgive the Germans. But the Italian Fascists were different. I can find no forgiveness in my heart. How can I forgive them for what they did to their fellow Italians? They tortured their compatriots." He stretched forward, handing a cup of tea to Trotti. "Cruel men for cruel times. Your mother did the right thing, Piero. She did not want to lose another son."

Trotti looked out of the window of the presbytery.

The Baronessa said calmly, "That's why your partisans tortured Saltieri."

Trotti turned. "Why?"

"The partisans were no gentler than the Fascists. They had the same methods, the same ruthlessness. And the same mindless spilling of blood. They were no better. Don't listen to this foolish old priest. The partisans were traitors."

Fra Gianni looked at her. "You must not say that, Baronessa."

"Communists."

"We weren't all communists."

"And common law criminals."

"There are times when the Baronessa von Neumann prefers to ignore the truth."

"Traitors."

"The partisans were patriots, fighting to free Italy."

"We had started the war alongside our German allies—and the partisans were traitors."

Fra Gianni asked, "Then in your mind, Baronessa, I, too, am a traitor?"

In offended silence the priest waited for an answer. The wrinkled, kind face looked aggrieved.

"Drink your tea, Gianni—and tell your friend about the partisans. And how they courageously slaughtered young boys."

The tea was bitter and seemed to rasp against the side of Trotti's tongue. He took more sugar from the silver bowl;

granules dropped from the spoon onto the highly polished wood.

The room was almost bare. The walls had been painted a long time ago; there was a painting of Saint Theresa in a dusty gilt frame. A single vase of cut flowers in the middle of the table.

Fra Gianni raised his shoulders in reluctant concession. "The partisans were not all saints." The old priest looked at the woman—they must have been of the same age. But while Baronessa von Neumann looked frail, there was a liveliness about the priest, a warm, human robustness.

"But Primula Rosa was no murderer."

"Then he was a fool."

"A fool?"

"To live among murderers and criminals." The Baronessa snorted. "And traitors."

Trotti asked, "What happened?"

"Happened?"

"To the young boys the Baronessa mentioned."

Gianni hesitated. "I had to give them the last rites. And then they were blindfolded and shot."

The afternoon air was losing its warmth. Trotti put down his cup on the table and stood up; he went to the window that looked out on to the garden and beyond it, at the peaceful panorama of the village.

"I didn't want them to be shot—and neither did Primula Rosa."

"But they were shot, weren't they?" A triumphant smile on the old woman's thin lips. "They refused to come over to us. And if we had let them go, they would've gone straight back to the Fascists and told them where we were hiding."

Trotti continued looking out of the window. "Tell me about Saltieri."

Fra Gianni poured another cup of tea before answering. "A good man—but not wise."

The presbytery was beside the church. The roofs of Santa Maria were spread out beneath the window. The leaves of the chestnut trees were showing their first tint of brown. A bus moved silently along the road from Tarzi. Trotti heard the shrieks of children playing somewhere.

He turned his back on the window and took a packet of sweets from his pocket.

"What Gianni means is that his friends the partisans hated Saltieri because Saltieri was a Carabiniere who tried to do his duty."

"He wasn't a bad man—but most people hated him." Fra Gianni nodded. "There was a black market. From the first day of the war in 1940. Everybody knew that—and I don't think many people really disapproved. Not even you, Baronessa—for in those days, you were no richer than the rest of the villagers."

"Black market?"

"With Genoa and Milan easily accessible, there was money to be made. And the people up here deserved a bit of wealth. It may not be the Mezzogiorno here—but the hills have always been poor. When I first came to Santa Maria in November 1943, I was shocked. Poor and very closely-knit. Just like the south—like Calabria. With the same ancient rivalries between families. And the same tradition of poverty. In a way, the war was a blessing. The war created the market for the people here and it was no secret that some villagers got rich by selling meat on the black market in Genoa. There was a big demand for fresh meat in the towns—and Santa Maria could supply meat. Good, fresh meat. That was Saltieri's mistake."

The woman said, "He did his duty."

A mischievous smile. "Something of a Prussian about the Baronessa von Neumann."

"Saltieri did his duty."

"He should have minded his own business."

Trotti asked, "What did he do, Saltieri?"

"You know what southerners can be like, Piero—one of those southern policemen who are as innocent as some of their colleagues are corrupt. There was a black market—and Saltieri tried to stamp it out. With any sense, he would have collaborated."

The Baronessa said, "He was not a southerner. He was from Ancona."

"He arrested half a dozen of the black marketeers."

"When?"

"It must have been as early as 1942 that there was the first trial. In Chiavari. I wasn't here at the time—but I know a lot of people resented Saltieri. At least two villagers went to jail."

"You met Saltieri?"

"Once or twice." The priest set down his cup and now stretched back in his chair. The Baronessa watched him with a look of friendly disapproval. "By the time I came to Santa Maria there was more for him to worry about than a black market in meat. The whole zone from here to the Po going north and over to Genoa going south—the whole area was like the Wild West. A long, guerrilla war; and nobody knowing who was fighting who, and who was in charge. I was living here"—he tapped the well-worn wood of his chair to indicate the presbytery—"taking mass every day in church. But a lot of people knew that I was chaplain to the partisans."

"Saltieri knew?"

"I could trust him. There was nothing dishonest about him."

"Saltieri was honest, Gianni."

"But unimaginative, Baronessa. He had that slow, unimaginative dullness that you find in some southerners. One day I met him in the street and he asked me if I was a partisan. I told him I was and he just nodded slowly."

"Well?" the Baronessa said sharply.

They were like an old couple, Trotti thought. Fond of each other, yet continually bickering.

"Devoid of guile." Fra Gianni shrugged. "And I realized that sooner or later they were going to kill him."

17: Pauli

"YOU BELIEVE MY brother was murdered?"

The street was empty and Trotti was reminded of the days of curfew. Deserted and silent, except for the creaking of the street lamps hanging above the road; shadows that danced jerkily.

They reached the edge of Santa Maria. The cafe by the bridge was still open and a solitary old man sat outside, caught in the yellow light of the doorway, like a gnarled tree that had taken root.

Overhead, the sky was without a cloud and the stars had formed a dome of twinkling lights. There was no moon yet. Beyond the river, Trotti sensed the hills looming on the far side of the village. For a brief instant, nostalgia pinched at his heart. Nostalgia for Santa Maria as it used to be, nostalgia for the young man he had once been.

Trotti accompanied the Baronessa across the bridge. A wind was coming down from the hills, a sharp wind that announced the approach of autumn. It ruffled Trotti's hair.

"The last months of the war I spent in Germany." The Baronessa was out of breath from the exertion of walking.

"But your husband was here. He told you what happened."

"You mean the bullion?"

"Was there a connection between the gold and my brother's death?" Trotti took her by the arm and helped her down from the pavement. She had difficulty in walking. She took small, careful steps. Together they crossed the road.

(Trotti remembered the road. It had once been made up of cobbles worn to a roundness in the river bed. Then the Americans had come with their tanks and all the stones had been cracked or destroyed. Now the road was surfaced with tarmac.)

"The war was almost over and the partisans were getting bolder. It was very difficult for Pauli. Everybody knows that my husband was a good man—everybody. But for them I was a traitor—even though Pauli and I were married at a time when Italo-German relations were still good." She stopped and it was almost bodily that Trotti lifted her and placed her on the far pavement.

The sound of the river joined that of the wind. The cold smell of the hills.

"You are very kind, Commissario Trotti."

He gave her his arm.

She patted his hand. "I like to tease Gianni—you do understand?"

"Of course."

"Gianni is a fine man—but like so many Italians, he doesn't like to face up to the truth." She had raised her voice against the wind. "Or rather, he prefers to create his own truth. And so he has got it into his head that all the partisans were good and everybody else was wicked. But you know, Commissario, before the war, before everything started going wrong, we all loved the Duce. We were all proud of him, proud for what he was doing to make our country a better place. We were all Fascists then—and the tragedy of Italy is that we didn't all change sides at the same time."

"Baronessa, you talk like a German."

"I spent over twenty happy years in Germany."

"You came back in 1965?"

"Pauli and I were living in Hamburg. He died in 1963 and I returned to Santa Maria in 1965—after my boy got married."

"You knew Italo?"

"Italo?" Her eyes flickered.

"My brother—did you know him personally?"

The Baronessa seemed to hesitate. "Yes, I knew your brother."

"Was there a connection between the bullion and my brother's death?"

"They killed Italo Trotti because he knew about Saltieri. He had witnessed Saltieri's murder." She tugged at his sleeve. "This is my house."

It stood by the river. It was a villa with closed shutters and a steep sloping roof. There was not enough light to see the color, but Trotti noticed the flowers creeping down the walls, a battered Fiat 600 in the drive, a large front garden and an iron gate that creaked as Trotti pushed it open.

They went slowly up the steps, the woman placing her weight on Trotti's arm. She led him into the house.

"I cannot stay, Baronessa."

They entered the drawing room where several photographs of Pauli von Neumann looked down from the immense piano. Pauli in the uniform of the Wehrmacht, Pauli smoking a pipe and swinging a golf-stick. Pauli—his hair now thinner—and a little boy on a windswept beach of the North Sea.

Velvet curtains and dark red wallpaper.

"A little something to drink." A conspiratorial glance. "That priest doesn't like me drinking alcohol. He would have made an awful husband." From a cabinet she produced a bottle of Latte di Suocera. "Not schnapps, perhaps—but it can warm an old heart."

She laughed to herself and Trotti smiled.

"You want to know about the gold?" She gestured him to one of the deep armchairs.

Trotti sat down. "I want to know if there is any connection between my brother's death and the other murders since the end of the war."

"Pauli was here. Over seven thousand German troops and everybody knew the end was near. They were surrounded." She raised her glass. She did not sip her liquor as she had sipped the tea. She drank in two fast gulps. "Surrounded on all sides by the partisans. Pauli had heard about a special SS convoy that had been heading north—heading to the Austrian frontier. But when they saw that their line of retreat had been cut off, the SS people joined up with the other Germans. It was a long time after the war Pauli discovered that, when he and his men surrendered, it wasn't just the guns and armaments the partisans took. Seven thousand soldiers, Commissario. And each man heavily armed—but tired of war, tired of fighting. The partisans took all their weapons . . . They took everything."

"Including the bullion?"

She nodded. "Booty that the SS were hoping to buy their freedom with."

"And it all fell into the hands of the partisans?"

"In the Valley of Tecosa." She put her head to one side.

"Where does my brother come into this?"

"That was before." A click of irritation. "Saltieri was murdered in April—and at the same time they murdered Italo Trotti, April fourteenth. 1945."

"There's no connection between my brother and the SS gold?"

"Italo Trotti was a witness to the murder of the Carabiniere."

"Fra Gianni seems to think my brother knew about the gold."

"Gianni is an old man." A harsh laugh. "And he is from Piemonte. What do you expect the Piemontesi to understand? He still refuses to believe that most of his partisans were criminals and black marketeers."

"Did Saltieri and my brother know about the gold?"

"They were already dead."

"You heard Fra Gianni talk about the deaths . . . the people who've died since the war. You don't think those people were murdered? You don't think their deaths had something to do with the gold?"

"Of course I do." The eyes grew smaller and darker.

"Then who murdered who? And why?"

"I know very little about what happened here at the end of the war. I was in Germany and what I know is from asking questions. And here, when you ask questions, you make a lot of enemies." She paused, poured herself another generous glass of Latte di Suocera. She had kicked off her shoes. Small misshapen feet in dark stockings. "Since my return to Santa Maria I have seen five people murdered. All of them connected directly or indirectly with the partisans. All of them the same age. Like Draghin—Draghin was in the firing squad that murdered the young Repubblichini." There was no softness in her face. "They found his body in the river about ten years ago. The back of his head had been smashed in."

Trotti could hear the whine of the wind.

"And Dandanin. Not an intelligent man, perhaps, but he had been among the partisans. A loud mouth and a drinker. He beat his wife. Then in 1979 he was attacked in the lane that runs at the back of the house. They found his body the following day." She smiled grimly and finished her drink. "His head had been smashed from behind."

"Was Dandanin in the firing squad?"

"You must ask Gianni."

The sound of the wind and the river outside.

"And why have they all been murdered? Why the deaths since the war?"

"The gold, Piero Trotti."

Trotti frowned. "You knew Italo well?"

"A nice boy, but the retreat from Russia had unbalanced him—made him strange." For a moment, she closed her eyes.

"What happened to the money, Baronessa?"

"Perhaps the partisans shared it among themselves."

"They must have spent it—at least some of it . . . in forty years, some of the money must've surfaced."

She shrugged her narrow shoulders. "No flashy cars or nice houses. Just the same old people, living their quiet lives."

Trotti stood up slowly. "Then there is no money."

"Commissario, the money is there. Pauli told me—and Pauli never lied. Rivalries between families," the Baronessa said. "Smoldering anger that in forty years has killed at least ten men and women."

"Ten, Baronessa?"

"In the last days of fighting, about five villagers were killed. Always the same thing—it was never clear whether they had collaborated with the Fascists or whether they were partisans. After that, for about fifteen years, everything was calm. Then just a year or so before I came back from Germany, the killing started again. Since 1964, at least five people have been murdered . . . and nearly always with a blunt instrument." She paused, a brittle smile on the thin lips. "Hit from behind with a blunt instrument."

"And nobody's gotten rich."

"In a small village, you don't always want to show what you've got. Tongues can wag."

"Or of course it could be the opposite."

"The opposite, Commissario?"

"Perhaps the money is there. Somebody had hidden it."

"Somebody?"

"A secret that must be kept. And the only way of keeping it is by killing those who share the secret."

"It is possible."

Trotti set the glass down. "Aren't you afraid, Baronessa?"

"Afraid of what?"

"Of knowing more than you should, perhaps?"

"Afraid of dying?" She laughed again, a strangely girlish laugh, while her eyes remained on his. "My son lives in Stuttgart now, he is married and his children are grown up. The eldest is at university. My two daughters have their own lives to lead. They write regularly but they don't need me—a silly old woman. And as for Gianni, he has got his memories of the life in the hills, of his partisans and of his beloved Primula Rosa." She turned away to look at the photographs on the piano. "I have lived long enough."

18: Voghera

"I CAN'T HELP you."

"Of course you can, Piero."

Trotti shook his head. "I have no jurisdiction outside the city."

They entered Voghera and the priest took the wide, empty boulevards towards the station. Trotti looked at his watch; the train was due in another twenty minutes.

"You can look for Primula Rosa."

"Santa Maria comes under Carabinieri jurisdiction. You can't expect me to tell the Carabinieri they haven't been doing their job properly. Tell them that my good friend the priest has reason to believe six people have been murdered under their noses—and they haven't noticed a thing."

Fra Gianni braked sharply. His lips were drawn tightly against each other.

They parked outside the station, in the bright light of the street lamps. Several billboards announced films at the local cinemas. Cars stood in the forecourt and there was the bustle of anticipation in the station. Trotti went to the ticket office. He joined a queue of people that included a few young men in army uniform.

The priest placed his hand on Trotti's arm. "I'm not asking you to open new enquiries. Of course not."

Trotti paid for his ticket, for a moment surprised how cheap it was. Then they went to the bar and ordered two coffees.

"Primula Rosa, Piero."

"What about him?"

A couple of soldiers were laughing. They wore ties tucked into their shirts and neat jackets, but the trousers were crumpled and the shoes dusty. They had slid their berets beneath their epaulettes.

"Find out where he is."

"Why?"

"Because I think he knows."

They were standing at a chest-high table. Trotti raised the small cup of coffee.

"He knows about the bullion."

"Perhaps he stole it, Fra Gianni."

It was warm in the bar, even though the glass doors were wide open and gave on to the platform.

On the far tracks, in the penumbra, a local train in dark browns, unlit and unnoticed, waited out the night. "In the Questura, you can locate him. Use your computers—and you have your contacts. Find him—because, if you don't, more people are going to be found with their heads smashed in."

Trotti shook his head.

"You won't do that for me, Piero? For an old friend?"

"A young and athletic friend."

Fra Gianni placed his hand on his shoulder. "I'm counting on you, Piero."

"Primula Rosa?"

"His real name is Mario Vecchioni. After the war he went to Milan and worked at Pirelli. I last saw him in 1967."

"And you didn't ask him about the killings?"

He shrugged. "At the time, I believed they were accidents."

The tin voice of the loudspeaker announced the arrival on time of the InterCity train number 48 for Milano Centrale.

"Is he still with Pirelli?"

"He lost his left hand in the last days of the war—picking up a grenade. He did it to protect his companions. It shouldn't be hard to find him, Piero."

Trotti shrugged.

"You can find him."

A few minutes later, the long train pulled on to the platform, an alligator stenciled on to the side of the high locomotive. There was the dull thud of doors being opened and closed, shouts from the soldiers and laughter as they climbed aboard.

The first-class carriage was in the middle of the train. Fra Gianni pulled open the door and Trotti got on to the tram. The air in the carriage was warm and unpleasant; the door to the lavatory had been left open.

"I can count on you, Piero?"

Trotti smiled, the train whistled and then the stationmaster waved his flag.

"You'll let me know, Piero?" Fra Gianni had to shout above the sound of the jolting wheels.

Trotti said, "I'll see what I can do," and leaning against the open windows, he looked down on the platform. It was now empty except for Fra Gianni standing like an old marooned sailor.

Trotti repeated, "I'll see what I can do." He smiled at Fra Gianni, gave him a little wave.

Trotti turned his head. He saw the bright lights of the bar. And, as the train picked up speed, he had the impression of seeing Signora Bianchini beyond the open doors of the café.

She was sitting at a table, drinking coffee. She was not alone.

19: Protuberant

SHE SAT IN the low canvas chair and looked around her, her neck stretching and the pale eyes protuberant. She looked at the old posters and the map of the province.

"It is very kind of you to come into the Questura so early in the morning."

She turned to face Trotti. "I have no intention of being late for work. I have not been late in twenty years." The eyes seemed to take time to focus. "I am a woman of the twentieth century and I earn my living with dignity."

"What exactly . . . ?"

"I told the woman everything last night."

"Then perhaps, signora, you could repeat everything to me."

"Signorina." She folded her arms. "Signorina Podestà. I am not married."

For a moment they looked at each other.

The woman's nose twitched. "There is an unpleasant smell."

Signorina Podestà was below average height and she sat uncomfortably in the low canvas armchair. She had dark hair that was badly cut and needed combing; an upturned nose that pulled at the pale flesh of her upper lip and which gave to her face a look of permanent surprise and disapproval.

Trotti turned in his seat to see that the partition was firmly closed. "I'm sorry about the . . . the smell. It's the drains." Trotti shrugged apologetically. "You would care for something to drink?"

For a moment, Signorina Podestà did not reply. Then brusquely she shook her head.

"You were raped?"

Another firm shake of the head. "Somebody tried to rape me. Somebody very low and revolting. But I am a woman of the twentieth century and I know how to defend myself."

"How did you defend yourself, signorina?"

"There are evening classes in self-defense at the Istituto Magnoni. I have a quick eye and I learn fast."

"Who tried to rape you?"

She snorted. "If I knew, I wouldn't be wasting my time here. And you wouldn't be dealing with a case of rape but with a case of murder or . . ." A moment's hesitation. The pale face blushed. "Or castration."

"You didn't see your aggressor?"

"I was sleeping. Sleeping in my bed."

Trotti pulled the writing pad towards him and wrote a couple words.

"When was this, signorina?"

"About ten days ago."

"What day?"

She thought for a moment, knitting her forehead. "It was the Saturday night." She held a handbag between her large, pale hands.

Trotti wrote down the word Saturday. "At what time?"

"When you're being raped, you don't look at your watch."

"Make a guess, signorina. Was it after dawn?"

She raised her shoulders. "At about three o'clock perhaps."

"Can you describe what happened?"

"Not very well. I was sleeping."

"At home?"

"I don't sleep in other people's beds."

"Of course not, signorina."

"I'm not sure . . ."

"Signorina Podestà, you live where, exactly?"

"Opposite Ciel d'Oro." She now took her time in replying. "My poor mother passed away a few years ago and since then I have been living by myself. And I keep an eye on my sister who lives in the apartment above me. She is not—my sister is not quite normal. You understand?"

Trotti nodded. "And where do you work?"

"I could have got married . . ." She unfolded her arms and played with the clasp of her handbag. "I prefer to wait. We are in the twentieth century and I don't believe there is any need to rush into these things. And I have little time for children." She frowned. "Drains, you say? It's very strong."

An apologetic move of the hand. "And you work where exactly?"

"I am a medical secretary."

"Who do you work for?"

"For the medical insurance company. IMPS."

Trotti nodded. "You live on the ground floor, signorina?"

"On the second floor. But the main entrance is rarely locked because there is this man who . . . The front entrance is rarely locked and anybody can enter the building."

"But you lock your own front door."

"Of course."

"You didn't report the attack immediately?"

"There are some things . . ."

"That require delicacy."

"Precisely." She nodded.

"But you have waited nearly ten days."

"There was no point in coming to the police. I know the police, I know what you are like."

"Like, signorina?"

"But then I read about the poor little girl. And so I telephoned the newspaper."

Trotti nodded. "And what exactly can you tell me about your attacker?"

"Everything."

"Can you give me a step-by-step account of what happened?"

"I always wear pajamas." She leaned forward, her hands clasping her bag, and her voice a conspiratorial hush. "I used to go to bed naked."

"You surprise me."

"It's a lot healthier." The corners of her mouth twitched. She continued, "But I am not as young as I used to be. And so now I wear pajamas."

"I understand."

A distrusting glare of the colorless eyes.

"And what exactly woke you up?"

"He was on top of me."

"A man woke you up?"

"Of course. He was trying to do horrible things—horrible things that men do."

"What did you notice about him? About the way he looked? The color of his hair?"

"Horrible things that you men do."

"How old was he?"

"It was dark."

"Was he a young man? When you tried to push him away . . ."

"I didn't push him away. I threw him. I threw him from me. That's why I wear pajamas—like judo clothes. They don't impede your movement."

"Well?"

"A woman should never be naked in front of a man. It only encourages him to greater bestiality. I make a point of carefully buttoning my pajama jacket."

"Bestiality?"

"All men are animals."

"Signorina, are you certain you were attacked?"

"He wore a bracelet—or else it was a watch strap—because he bruised my face."

"You are quite sure that you were attacked?"

"Of course I was attacked. But I looked after myself." A brief snort. "God helps those who help themselves, and if I count on the police, I might—"

"You don't have any bruise on your cheek."

"He hurt me—the awful man hurt me."

"There is nothing that you can remember that might be a clue to the person's identity?"

"Fortunately the bruise has gone down."

"You didn't see your attacker, did you?"

"I have already told you it was in the dark."

"But you threw him to the ground?"

"And then he ran off." She nodded forcefully. "Men—they're all cowards."

"Some women . . ." Trotti began, then coughed. "There is a school of thought that believes some very sad and lonely women would like to be raped."

The eyes opened wide, as if trying to leave their sockets. "What do you know about women, Commissario?"

Trotti looked down at the yellow paper. He coughed. "There was nothing about him that you noticed? His size or the smell of his breath or the color of his hair? A beard or a mustache . . . ?"

"Perhaps he was one of those southerners. Southerners go in for bracelets. Particularly soldiers."

"A soldier, Signorina Podestà?"

"Why not? Ciel d'Oro is less than three hundred meters from the barracks."

"And so you think he was a soldier?"

She shrugged. The protuberant eyes looked down.

"You don't have any proof, do you, signorina?"

"A couple of days later—it must've been the Tuesday—I found this. It must have slipped under the bed." She opened the large handbag.

20: Belt

CIUFFI HELD OUT the beige folder. "The Vardin dossier, Commissario."

"Are you free now?"

Brigadiere Ciuffi nodded hesitantly.

"Then perhaps we'd better go to the hospital." He held up his hand. "By the way, when you see Pisanelli, thank him for finding the woman."

"Woman, Commissario?"

"Or rather, if you see Pisanelli."

"What woman are you talking about?"

"The spinster with the protuberant eyes." Trotti played with the buckle. "She gave me this," he said.

Ciuffi sounded hurt. "It was me, Commissario. I got her. The *Provincia* gave me her address." She tucked the beige folder under her arm. "It was me who fixed the interview for this morning. I knew you'd want to see her."

"Standard issue army belt buckle." There were crossed cannons in bas-relief, two standards and a coat of armor. "Says it got pulled from the phantom rapist's belt in the struggle. She probably bought it in a surplus store."

"I haven't seen Pisanelli since yesterday, Commissario. As for the woman, they had her address at the *Provincia*." The young face was taut and disapproving. "I located the woman—and I drew up this dossier on the Vardin affair myself. Without any help from Pisanelli or anybody else."

Trotti handed her the belt buckle. "Says she found it under her bed."

Ciuffi looked at the object on her open hand.

"The spinster seems to think she was raped by one of the soldiers from the nearby barracks—the Cairoli barracks."

"If Signorina Podestà is a spinster, it is no doubt the result of having looked after her mother. It's not her fault if she never had the time to get married. I don't see why you have to use an emotive word like spinster."

Their eyes met. She gave him back the buckle. In a lighter voice, she added, "Doesn't have to be a soldier, Commissario."

They left the office.

Waiting for the lift meant being near the dying dog. Together they walked down the stairs of the Questura. One or two men went past, saluting.

Trotti saw Commissario Merenda and nodded.

Merenda lifted his hand. In it he held the newspaper. "I see our friends at the *Provincia* are enjoying themselves." His voice was deep, virile. The regular features on his young face broke into a smile.

Trotti raised an eyebrow.

"The *Provincia* is making good mileage out of your raped little girl. Headlines about a wild maniac. And a police force that is incapable of protecting our womenfolk as they lie in bed at night." He placed his hand on Trotti's shoulders. "Glad you decided to take this one on, Piero. Better you than me. Good luck to you—you'll be needing it."

"Thanks."

Commissario Merenda went on up the stairs, taking them two at a time.

Trotti turned to Ciuffi who was still watching Merenda. "You think Podestà was raped, Brigadiere?"

She looked at Trotti and her eyes came into focus. "Why not, Commissario? Or perhaps you believe that it is just a frustrated woman's repressed sexual drive. A spinster's wishful thinking? Another silly female with sexual fantasies."

"It's possible."

They walked past the main desk out into Strada Nuova. A woman in black, her stout legs hidden behind several cartons, was arguing with the officer on desk duty.

"You can check where she works—she said the man bruised her. See if you can get any corroboration. Unfortunately, after ten days, there's no way of giving her a medical check. But if she's a virgin . . ."

Ciuffi said, "She's not a virgin."

He laughed, then hid his mouth with his hand. "She gave you her life story?"

They walked down the steps.

It was not yet nine o'clock and the city was coming alive. There hung on the air the smell of methylated spirit. Neatly dressed girls cleaning their shop windows.

A low mist, still chill with the memory of the night, hovered over the city.

"Being raped is not a laughing matter, Commissario. It is debasing. A human being—a woman—is treated like an animal; with less respect than an animal. I think that Signorina Podestà merits the benefit of the doubt." She held her head to one side, frowning and in thought. She took short steps. The leather shoes were silent on the pavement. "It is possible that she's making it all up—it's possible. But when so many women are raped—are being raped every day—and they don't dare come forward . . . And when those women who do have the courage to come forward are dismissed as merely sex-starved spinsters . . ." She shook her head. "That's too easy, Commissario." Another vigorous shake. She was not looking at him but at the ground. "Too easy. And it's not fair."

"Signorina Podestà's not my idea of who I'd like to rape."

"You'd like to rape someone, Commissario?"

"That's not exactly what I meant. But if I was going to exert force for my . . ." He hesitated. "If I wanted to force myself upon a woman, there are a lot of women I'd think of before I'd think of Signorina Podestà."

"You'd rape me, Commissario?"

"Of course not," he answered hurriedly. "And anyway, you're not the sort of woman to allow yourself to be raped."

"Then you think that there are women who like to be raped and others who don't?"

"That's not what I meant. But with your police training, I'm sure you could look after yourself. Of course, you are an attractive young woman . . ."

"You are a gentleman." The young face broke into an unexpected smile. It was like sunshine in a cloudy sky. "But men will rape anybody—anybody or anything that moves. Including ninety-year-old women."

They reached the car and, while Ciuffi unlocked the door, Trotti looked at her. Her job in the Questura was hardening her; three years of dealing with the dregs of society had seriously shaken her faith in human nature. She was learning to conceal innocence beneath a series of masks, masks of hardness which she was assuming to protect her own decency.

She caught his look and gave Trotti a hurried smile.

"What did Podestà tell you about herself, Brigadiere?"

They got into the car.

"She just said that she had never married. She'd looked after her mother. But that she had once lived with a man."

"You pronounce the word man with disapproval."

Ciuffi turned on the engine and they left the parking lot. As they went past the Bar Dante, a couple of officers from the Questura looked out at the car and one of them said something to his companion who laughed.

"A married man—a school teacher. She said that they lived together for five years. On and off. Then she discovered that he had been having an affair with her sister—a mentally retarded woman. In the end he went back to his own wife and family."

"They still meet?"

"She didn't tell me, Commissario."

"And you think she was raped?"

For a moment, Ciuffi did not speak. They took via Aldo Moro—the plaques had been recently embedded into the brick walls outside the Civic Museum—and headed towards the edge of the city.

"You think she was telling the truth? Tell me, Brigadiere. You're a woman. You have your intuition."

"You're laughing at me."

"Not at all. But I want to know whether you think it's worth my following up the whole thing—lose hours over an army buckle that was allegedly left by her phantom rapist. Or whether I could be spending my time—and yours—in other fields of enquiry."

The traffic lights and then the canal. Ciuffi drove well. Trotti noticed several foreign number plates—the tail-end of the tourist season, one or two adventurous travelers who had ventured beyond the Certosa eight kilometers up the road.

Ciuffi spoke slowly. "I don't think she's lying."

Trotti noticed the hesitation in her voice. He waited.

"But yesterday . . ." she started, then stopped.

"Yes?"

A different voice, a different subject. "It's not for me to complain, Commissario, but I would appreciate more support from Pisanelli. You said we should work as a team."

"What happened yesterday, Brigadiere?"

"Pisanelli is supposed to be working for you and not for Commissario Merenda."

"Merenda's a nuisance and I'd be grateful if he used his own men rather than poaching mine."

Her hands were delicate and clean. She moved the steering wheel with short precise movements. A smile at the edge of her lips.

They reached the bridge just as the Genoa train pulled out of the station below them. "A lot of people believe that Commissario Merenda is bringing new life to the Questura. New life and new dynamism."

"Then he doesn't need Pisanelli." Trotti's voice was cold. "What happened yesterday, Ciuffi?"

Another layer of mask.

"Well, Brigadiere?"

"I checked with the registry office."

"And?"

"And nothing." She shrugged. "Just that the records show Signora Vardin is not the first Signora Vardin."

"What?"

"His second wife."

The traffic policeman in the middle of the road beckoned them on. He glanced at their number plate but there was no recognition in his eyes as he watched Trotti and Ciuffi drive past. He did not salute.

Past the enormous billboard advertising the local fur atelier.

"Is that important?"

"It could be." The mask now hid all emotion. "Because it means that little Laura and Antonetta are not sisters."

"Of course they're sisters."

"The same mother, Commissario. But not the same father. They are stepsisters. And from what I can gather, they don't get on very well. Netta seems to think that Laura is too spoiled. They quarrel quite a lot it seems. They even fight."

21: Incubator

THE MASKS HAD been dropped, Trotti noticed as he moved towards the incubator.

"Ivan," the young doctor said softly as she came to Trotti's side. "We've christened him Ivan."

They had placed the baby under the plastic dome and he now lay asleep, naked on the sheet. Tubes ran into his arm and into his nostril. They were anchored with plasters. The face and hands were slightly darker than the rest of the body.

"Another few hours and he would have died."

"Such a little thing," Ciuffi said. It was as if her face had been lit up.

There was a clip on the lower belly and Trotti noticed that the doctors had neatly cut the umbilical cord. A bandage on his forehead. The face was strangely old and the spiky hair gave the impression of a grown child.

Ivan slept with his minute fists clenched.

"He was kept alive by the good weather we have been having—and by the rain at night. The human body can survive without food—but not without water. These last few days, the weather has grown chill."

Trotti turned.

"Another night of exposure could have killed him." An acrylic glass door in the wall of the incubator. The doctor opened it and carefully changed the position of the sleeping baby.

The skin of the groin and at the elbows was wrinkled and reminded Trotti of chicken flesh. He moved away.

The doctor smiled. "I think we were all taken aback. Not every day that you see a newborn child crawling with worms. And a full-length umbilical cord."

"An attempted abortion?"

"Not possible. It was a bit late for that sort of thing. He weighs two kilos, eight hundred grams. You're a big boy, aren't you, precious?" She made gentle sounds and Ciuffi moved to her side, looking down at the minute body. The doctor smiled at Ciuffi and then closed the door. She ran her finger down the scale on the thermostat.

"If the mother didn't want the baby, couldn't she have had an abortion earlier—before it was too late?" Ciuffi asked.

The doctor looked at the young policewoman thoughtfully, then shrugged. She wore a gold crucifix at her neck and the lead of her stethoscope hung from the pocket of her blouse. Not very attractive, but with a kind, intelligent face. Blonde bristles along her upper lip and freckles on the back of her hands. "It's not unheard of for mothers to murder their children." Her lipstick was a bright red and ran over the edge of the lips at the corners of her mouth.

Trotti said, "It's abnormal."

"We are all abnormal at some time or another, signore." She turned to give him a blank stare.

Trotti held out his hand. "Commissario Trotti, Squadra Mobile."

They shook hands; her grasp was firm. "Dottoressa Silvan." She added, "Stefanella Silvan."

"And this is Brigadiere Ciuffi."

The two women exchanged brief—almost conspiratorial—smiles.

"And now?"

"And now, Commissario?"

Trotti asked, "What's going to happen to the child?"

She shrugged. "With a bit of luck he should grow into a healthy young boy. Nothing wrong with him that food and warmth can't solve. And love. Above all, love."

Ciuffi bit her lower lip. "But there will be problems?"

"Not necessarily. There's a risk of pneumonia and we've put him on antibiotics. But he's tough, our Ivan."

"And who's going to look after him?"

"Look after him? You don't think we're doing a good enough job?"

He shook his head. "But once he leaves here. Will he go back to his mother?"

"I shouldn't think so. Very unlikely. Probably he will be sent to the Institute—and then I imagine he will be adopted."

"Adopted," Trotti repeated and he turned back to look at the sleeping baby.

"I am sure there are a lot of loving people who would like to look after Ivan."

Trotti frowned. "How many days did he spend like that?"

"At least a couple." Although her face was prematurely wrinkled she had a nice smile. "Have faith in the human body. It clings to life." Her pale eyes looked at Trotti playfully. "We all cling to life—it's all we have."

"He will be adopted, you say."

"In his way, he has been lucky. If it hadn't been for Commissario Merenda, we would never have found the child. And that other nice policeman."

"Nice policeman?" Trotti looked at her and laughed. "Not a contradiction?"

She raised a hand to the side of her head. "The policeman with hair over his ears—and none on top." She added, "And with a suede jacket. An old suede jacket."

"Pisanelli."

"That's right. He was concerned. He was very good with the mother." She gave Trotti a shrewd glance. "I think Signor Pisanelli understands female psychology." She moved towards the incubator and looked down at the sleeping child. "A lucky boy, aren't you, Ivan?"

"Ivan would have been a lot luckier if his mother hadn't dumped him in the middle of the field."

"Perhaps she had no choice."

"She had the choice long before the child was ever conceived."

"Have you ever carried a child in your belly, Commissario?"

He shrugged. "It'd be a bit difficult."

"Then I don't think you're in a position to judge a woman. Do you?"

Ciuffi was still smiling.

22: Police Woman

THE SUN HAD risen above the veil of mist that hung over the city.

"Are you coming with me to see Signor Vardin?"

"But you haven't looked at the dossier yet, Commissario."

"The dossier?"

The policewoman allowed a brief smile to flicker across her lips. The serge uniform suited her. She wore just a hint of lipstick. "You told me you wanted to know how Vardin was involved with the AVIS transfusion center." She took the folder from under her arm. "I was working on it until late last night. By myself."

"Then why didn't you give it to me?"

The young face hesitated between amusement and irritation. The eyes looked tired, weary. "When I wanted to give it to you in the Questura, you said you were coming to the hospital."

"Poor bastard," Trotti said.

"Pisanelli? There's nothing poor about him—just lazy." She pursed her lips.

"A poor child, Ivan—being left like that by his mother." Trotti took her by the arm. "Come," he said, but she had stopped still. In the hospital, in front of the incubator and the sleeping form of the baby, Ciuffi had been subdued, silenced by the miracle of birth, the miracle of life. Now she was reassuming her own identity, her own slightly querulous assertiveness. She stood with her arms folded, the file held to her chest.

They were beside the entrance to Ostetrica. In the hospital grounds, the leaves on the chestnut trees were already beginning to turn brown. The ground was damp with patches of dew in the shadows. Somewhere somebody was whistling—an old, almost forgotten tune. Trotti tried to remember the name. A song from the past.

"Pisanelli is not being very helpful at the present moment."

Trotti said, "Pisanelli has his own way of doing things." He shrugged. "The lady doctor seemed very impressed."

"You asked me to find out about Vardin—and the AVIS blood bank."

"Well?"

"I don't see why I have got to do everything by myself in archives. I am not a secretary, you know." She pursed her lips again. "I worked as a secretary for three years. And I hated it. That's why I joined the PS."

"Signorina Ciuffi, we must all play our part. We're members of the same team."

"Then why doesn't Pisanelli play his?"

"Pisanelli is a good policeman—it's just that he likes to do things in his own way."

"And in his own time—when all the footwork has already been done for him." Ciuffi pulled her arm from Trotti's hand and turned away. The muscles of her jaw were taut and her nostrils were pinched.

A doctor parked his car—Swiss registration from the Ticino canton—and climbed out. He brushed past Trotti and entered the building, leaving a faint odor of antiseptic and tobacco.

The whistling stopped and then started again. Perhaps a janitor or a cleaning woman in the maternity section. And the repeated melody that Trotti could not put a name to.

There was a packet of Charms in Trotti's pocket. "A sweet, Brigadiere Ciuffi?"

She shook her head.

Trotti put an aniseed-flavored Charm in his mouth. "A bit of sugar in the bloodstream can calm your nerves."

"My nerves don't need calming. I need support. And

help. I don't see why Pisanelli thinks he can go off when he pleases."

"Go off where?"

"To the hospital."

"There's no need. The baby has been found."

"He's getting married." Ciuffi shrugged. "He's getting married to a nurse."

A dry laugh. "Pisanelli has been about to get married for the last three years. Two years ago, it was with a little slip of a girl from the university."

"If we're to work as a team, Pisanelli must help."

"You heard what the lady doctor said. Pisanelli understands women."

"A pig-headed phallocrat, you mean." She spat the words out, "A balding, ineffectual, greasy phallocrat. And stupid. And ugly, too."

"Pisanelli?"

Ciuffi looked at Trotti carefully before answering. The young eyes were tinted with blood. Ciuffi had not been getting enough sleep. "Pisanelli," she said. "And all the other men in the wretched Questura."

"A bit harsh, Brigadiere?"

"It's not always easy for a woman."

"You do very well." He slipped into the familiar "tu" form.

Ciuffi seemed not to notice the change in the form of address; it was as if she were talking to herself. "After all, what are we women but poor, weak, mindless creatures?"

"Single-minded."

"There you are wrong, Commissario." She shook her head. "Competent—just like men. No better, no worse." Ciuffi looked up at Trotti.

"What have you found out for me?"

"On Vardin?"

Trotti nodded.

She folded her arms before answering. "I told you—the two girls, Netta and Laura, are half-sisters. They don't get on very well."

"And Vardin—what do you know about Vardin?"

She took the dossier from under her arm. "At least Maserati and Schipisi were willing to help. Most of the stuff is on the database."

"Database?"

"Maserati has filed everything onto his computer."

Trotti raised an eyebrow. He took Ciuffi gently but firmly by the arm and started walking towards the main entrance of the hospital. "I think we could do with some breakfast."

She looked at her watch. "At half past nine, Signor Commissario?"

Verdi, of course, Trotti told himself, recognizing the whistle as an aria from *Simone Boccanegra*.

One of the porters got up from his broken chair in the entrance hall and saluted as they went past. Trotti led Ciuffi across the road and they entered the Bar Golliardico. The smell of roasted coffee and fresh lemons.

Two girls were playing on the pinball table. One of them wore a loose necklace and a cigarette hung from her lips. They had placed their medical textbooks on the top of the pinball table. Electronic bleeping and the slightly raucous laughter of the girls.

"Something strong perhaps? A grappa? Or brandy? To cheer you up."

"While on duty?" Ciuffi gave him a worried glance. "A cup of coffee will do. I don't need cheering up."

"A young woman like you—you look tired and fed up."

"I need help, Commissario."

"Something to eat?"

"I need cooperation."

Trotti ordered at the bar and then held a chair for her and they sat down at a window-side table. Outside the yellow buses rumbled past the Policlinico.

"Tell me about Signor Vardin."

She had set the file down on the table. "Commissario, I don't like complaining like this."

"I will tell Pisanelli to stop acting like a phallocrat."

Ciuffi leaned forward and placed her elbows on the edge of the table. She propped her clenched fists beneath her chin. A gesture that reminded him of Pioppi when she was little.

The waiter brought two cups of coffee. On a small plate there were a couple of croissants.

Trotti handed her a croissant.

"Thanks." Ciuffi gave him a brief smile and, for an instant, she allowed her fingers to touch the back of Trotti's hand.

23: Plasma

PROVINCIA PADANA, 11TH September 1972:

"As technical director of AVIS, it has never been my intention to harm the organization of which I am proud to be a member. However, my first responsibility is to the people of this city and this province and, in the last resort, it is their welfare that I must protect."

So speaks Giuglielmo Azzali. The professor—born 49 years ago in Livorno—appears troubled, upset that his action has caused so much anger within the city's medical community. But he regrets nothing. "My being dismissed is a political action. It is not by getting rid of me that the problem is going to go away. I have faith in the officers of the Ministry of Justice and I know they will do their utmost to cast light on this affair. I feel no bitterness towards the AVIS administration in Rome. They no doubt believe they are doing the right thing in giving me the sack. However, I can assure them that I am not a troublemaker. My only concern is the good name of AVIS in this city."

The AVIS scandal exploded last week when the Rome paper La Voce del Secolo announced that the Pubblico Ministero was looking into serious allegations of malpractice within the AVIS organization of our city. What were these accusations? Who made them?

Professor Azzali gives a brief smile. "Monday before last,

I found myself in the anteroom to the operating theater at the San Matteo Policlinico. I noticed four phials of blood sent from AVIS. One of the phials seemed strangely clouded. There seemed to be a lack of plasma. I asked the anaesthetist whether he had requested pure blood—plasma and red corpuscles—or merely red corpuscles in a physiological solution. He replied that he had asked for blood. We then analyzed the four phials and observed that the protein content was extremely low, which could only mean one thing—absence of plasma. There was no label on the phials. When I discovered that in all the operating theaters and throughout the hospital this so-called blood was being freely administered, I immediately gave the order to withhold the distribution of the phials."

And the AVISini?

"I am sorry for what has happened. But I am sure the AVISini will understand my action. I have nothing but admiration for the blood donors who over the years have unstintingly given their blood in good faith. It is thanks to the AVISini—and to all the donors throughout Italy—that AVIS has been able to build up such a dynamic network. In this city, we have one of the most advanced transfusion centers. There are about three thousand donors on our lists and we can produce about thirty thousand phials a year. I am proud to be a member of AVIS. I have nothing but respect for the national AVIS organization."

Dottor Azzali wishes to be reasonable, "It is not rare for doctors to ask for low-protein blood; in certain instances, it can be administered safely and effectively. However, the fact remains that, while many of the doctors at San Matteo have been asking for normal blood, they have been receiving watered-down plasma."

Dottor Azzali is too discreet to mention that whereas a phial of blood costs the Policlinico five thousand lire, a phial of non-plasma blood costs only two thousand lire. It follows logically then that if someone at AVIS has been selling non-plasma as blood, he has been making a profit of three thousand lire per phial.

Dottor Azzali is adamant. He knows nothing about any mal-practice. In informing the Public Minister, he says he was merely carrying out his duty as technical director of the local AVIS.

A couple of questions remain unanswered.

How long has this malpractice been going on? Dottor Azzali has been the technical director of this city's blood bank for more than three years. Why is it only now that a suspicion of malpractice has come to the notice of Dottor Azzali?

24: Files

"WELL?"

Ciuffi said, "It's all there."

"If we're going to see Vardin, I haven't got time to read the entire dossier."

She leaned across the table and flicked through the pages. There was a lot of computer typescript as well as the occasional newspaper cutting, one or two smudged photocopies. "I should like to remind you that I put this together all alone, Commissario."

"Well done."

"I was up until two o'clock."

"Where does Vardin come into this AVIS business?"

"Read the file, Commissario."

"I haven't got the time." He clicked his tongue. "Not if we're going to see Vardin now." He glanced at the clock on the wall, advertising a local coffee—Mocka Sir's. "Tell me what happened."

She held her breath as she ran through the pages. With her head held down, her hair fell forward and partially hid her face. She had put the empty cup of coffee to one side and she reminded him of a thoughtful, hardworking pupil, upset at not having met with the teacher's approval.

"Forgive me, Brigadiere." Trotti smiled as she raised her head and he was touched by the youthful innocence of her face. "I am being ungrateful." He squeezed her forearm.

She looked down at her arm. Then she raised one eyebrow.

"You're not meeting enough appreciative men." He gave her arm another squeeze. "I'm afraid we are all phallocrats."

"I don't think you are a phallocrat, Commissario." The eyes had softened. "I think you are a good man—with a good heart."

Surprised, Trotti found himself smiling. "I am an old man—and I am getting too old for this job. Too old and too irritable. It is time I took a well-deserved retirement. It is time I went back to the hills, where I belong."

"By yourself, Commissario?"

"I've had enough of this city."

"You could never go back to the hills. You need people too much."

"People?" A brief laugh and a shrug.

"I think you'd be very lonely. You need people—and you like them."

The image of the small, maltreated form beneath the incubator.

"Who knows? Perhaps I could adopt a child." Trotti finished the cup of cold coffee and brushed at the grains of sugar that had fallen from the croissant on to his jacket. He made an effort to concentrate, and he tapped the dossier. "All I really need to know is how Vardin fits in."

Ciuffi nodded and the softness in her eyes disappeared. She took one of the sheets. "Listen," she said, and she began to read. She spoke in a flat monotone. "'The behavior of the accused is particularly disturbing if we consider the scale of his actions, the period of time, the nature of the fraud and the danger to human life. Patients at San Matteo were receiving little more than fresh water when what they needed was life-giving blood.' This was the summing up of the public prosecutor."

"Against Azzali?"

Ciuffi shook her head. "Against Galandra."

"Who the hell's Galandra?"

"Azzali was the technical director and it was he who brought the affair into the open. And, once he did, there were several arrests, including Conti, the priest, who was the nominal director of AVIS. But in the end, most of the accusations centered on Galandra and his wife."

"What did they do?"

"The problem was finding out who was responsible for what. Watered-down blood was being sent to the hospital. Apparently, in one year, the demand for saline solution at the transfusion center had gone up ten-fold. Although nobody really believed that Azzali was guilty, it was far from clear why he had authorized the delivery of adulterated blood to the hospital."

"And?"

"In the end, Azzali's defense was able to show that he was not responsible for the deliveries. He was merely responsible for the running of the center, the collection of blood. It was Galandra, the accountant, and his wife—she was a secretary—who must have added the saline solution."

"They would have been seen."

Ciuffi nodded. "That's just it. And there's where Vardin came in. He was a witness."

"What to?"

A shriek of laughter and one of the girls at the pinball table said, "Tilt." The other girl glanced briefly at Trotti and Ciuffi before looking through her handbag. She produced a couple of coins and inserted them into the slot of the blinking machine.

Ciuffi frowned disapprovingly. Turning back to the file, she riffled through the pages, her tongue sticking from the corner of her lips in concentration. "Ah," she said, and again she read from the pages like a dutiful schoolgirl. "'The fraud was carried out in the following way. Blood was put through the centrifugal spinner, which separated the plasma from the hematin. Azzali gave permission for the hematin to be diluted with forty-five centiliters of saline solution, on the understanding that this liquid was used within four hours. On each phial, there should have been a label with the following legend: "Hematin for immediate use." Instead of diluting the hematin with forty-five centiliters, Signor Galandra and his collaborators added an equal amount of salt water. The labels were removed from the bottles and as the mixture was not much different in appearance from normal blood, doctors at San Matteo couldn't have been expected to distinguish between the phials of normal blood and those of diluted hematin.'" She smiled with satisfaction.

"And Vardin?"

"Precisely," she replied.

"What do you mean, precisely?"

"The fraud was on a large scale. And spinning the blood and then adding saline solution to the hematin—it was something that took time. And since nobody really questioned Azzali's probity, the unanswered question was when did all this manipulation take place. And that's when Vardin came forward."

"He was the janitor at the transfusion center?"

"Before AVIS moved out to the university campus on via Mantova." She nodded. "The trouble was that Galandra and his wife were blackmailing various people. And throughout the trial they made threats of damning revelations. At one point Galandra accused Azzali of having killed a patient by making a mistake in a blood analysis. Galandra and his wife were unscrupulous—and people were scared of them." She flicked through the pages. "That's why Vardin's testimony came as a surprise."

"What testimony?"

"The presiding judge asked him if he had ever seen Galandra or his wife return to the transfusion center in the evening." She read from the dossier: "'Yes, I saw them repeatedly when they went to the plasma laboratory. They'd come at nine and leave around midnight. It was my job to keep the place clean and I'd always find empty phials everywhere. Phials marked, "Physiological solution."'"

"He should have reported it earlier."

"When the judge asked him why he hadn't reported anything he replied that he took his orders not from Azzali but from

Galandra. He then went on to say that he and his wife had received threats."

"Threats?"

She nodded. "But he said that AVIS had been a good employer. And that he was not afraid of doing his duty. He then added that he was a competent hunter, he knew how to manipulate firearms and, if necessary, he would know how to protect himself."

For a moment they sat in silence. Trotti looked at the young woman and she looked at him. Trotti repeated, "He knew how to protect himself."

"That's what he said—but that was nearly ten years ago."

"And you think that the knifing in Piazza Castello was Galandra's revenge?"

"Why not? He was released from jail three months ago. After serving the full term. In Verona."

"And he had made threats at the time of the trial?"

"Yes." She hesitated; her voice changed. "Commissario Trotti..."

"Well?"

She shook her head.

"What is it, Signorina?"

"No." She was staring down at her hands. "It's got nothing to do with Galandra—or with the case."

He smiled. "Tell me."

"It's about your retirement."

"My retirement?"

"Yes." She raised her eyes. "Are you serious?"

"Serious about retiring? But of course. In just over a couple of years I'll be sixty."

"Serious about adopting a child?" Again she lowered her eyes.

"Why not?"

"Why not?" Ciuffi repeated.

"I would love to adopt." He paused. "But I doubt if it is really possible."

"You'd really adopt a child?"

"I have a grown daughter—but I have always dreamt of having a son. But I don't suppose it's possible. I'm old—and now I live by myself."

"But you are a man," Ciuffi said. Her young face gradually turned a deep scarlet. "You don't need to adopt. Men aren't like women, there's no age limit to parenthood for you. If you really want a child, you can easily have one of your own."

25: Monotony

TROTTI WAS OUT of breath by the time they reached the third floor.

With the morning light coming through the window, the small room was less depressing. A room that looked lived in, with a heavy chest-of-drawers, a wooden table. The bedsheets had been removed and Trotti sat down on the bulky folding settee. Everything was clean and neat.

The thin traces of splashed blood across the stone floor had been scrubbed and now there was just the slightest discoloration. A light, warm breeze came through the window and rustled at Frate Indovino's calendar on the wall.

Ciuffi took a chair and placed her elbows on the table.

Trotti smiled. "Where's your husband, signora?"

"He has gone fishing."

"A strange time to go fishing."

"What else has he got to do? He sits in the house and he gets miserable." She shrugged. "Would you care for a drink?" Signora Vardin used the polite form, addressing Trotti and Ciuffi as "they"—*would they care for a drink?* In her mouth, the expression sounded servile—a lifetime of humility, of limited expectations.

"We have just had a late breakfast." Trotti brushed at imaginary grains of sugar on his lapels. "I would like to talk to your niece, signora."

"To my niece? To Bettina?"

"I think that she might be able to help us."

"You have already talked to her."

Trotti shook his head.

"Not you, Commissario—but the other policeman. The nice young man." She touched her forehead. "He is losing his hair."

"I would like to speak to her personally."

"She's not here."

"Where is she?"

A slight sigh. "She is in Piemonte . . . at Ovada."

"Your husband told me that she was staying with you for a week. That her parents had gone to the funeral of Zio Moisè."

"Bettina said she wanted to go home." A resigned shrug. "And so we took her to the station." A plain, dull face, used to the monotony of hard work. "She is a good girl—but the doctor told me that it would be better for everyone if she went home." She sighed again. "The doctor has given me these pills. For my nerves, you see, because I worry about Laura. Laura is her father's favorite and even though she is going to get better, I can't help worrying." A hand to her forehead. "And I feel so tired. I love Bettina, but it is better for her to be out of the way." She raised a hand. "And the way that the newspaper is talking about us—Bettina said that she had to go home."

Trotti gave her a smile. "I understand."

"You are a good man, Commissario."

Trotti turned his head away, looked at the table. Then he stood up, moved towards the sideboard and picked up a red cardboard box. On the packet, there was the printed sketch of a dog's head; between its jaws, a dead duck. "Your husband has a gun, signora?"

"A gun?" She shook her head. "My husband is a good man, he has never harmed anybody."

"He keeps a gun in the house?" Trotti raised the empty box of cartridges. "A thirty-two caliber."

For a moment the eyes looked at him without understanding. Then she nodded.

"Can you show it to me?"

"Why? There is nothing illegal. He has a permit."

"Of course, signora," Ciuffi said, giving a reassuring smile. "It is only normal that your husband should want to protect his family."

She turned back to face Trotti. "My husband uses his gun for hunting—and now that he is unemployed . . . He hasn't been out with it more than twice in the last two years."

"Then what is this packet doing here?"

She tapped the ample slope of her chest. "With my heart troubles, he can ill afford small pleasures. We are not rich."

"Your husband has received strange letters lately, signora?"

The woman said nothing.

Ciuffi's voice was gentle. "Signor Vardin should have told us if he was receiving threats."

In silence Signora Vardin wrung her large, pale hands.

"It is our job to protect you," Trotti said.

"I know nothing about threats."

"In your opinion, who attacked your daughter, signora?"

"Laura is getting better. Soon she will be out of the hospital." The face tried to smile, while the eyes went from Ciuffi to Trotti, looking for understanding. "And that nice doctor told me that there will be nothing to pay."

"Who attacked her?"

"Laura?"

Trotti nodded and gave a sideways glance at Ciuffi.

"A madman, I suppose." She pronounced her words with difficulty. "A sexual maniac."

"Nobody ever threatened you, signora? You or your husband? Or the girls?"

The eyes were brown—like those of a cow at pasture. Signora Vardin shook her head.

"And the name Galandra means nothing to you?"

"Galandra?" Signora Vardin thought for a moment. She frowned and looked down at her shapeless slippers on the cold, stone floor. Then she nodded slowly. "A long time ago. That was when my husband was working at the AVIS." A pause. "It was a good job at the AVIS—he got it because the priest helped him. And with his lungs he could no longer work in the quarries.

Ciuffi said, "Galandra came out of jail earlier this year."

The light of understanding began to dawn upon her face. "You think my husband has been receiving threats from Galandra?"

"Galandra has spent the last seven years in prison. In Verona. Sent there thanks largely to the testimony of your husband."

"My husband is a very proud man," she said simply.

"Signora Vardin," Trotti said, "I think you'd better show me the gun."

The chair creaked as the woman placed her hands flat on her thighs and wearily stood up. She was wearing a black blouse and beneath it her body was shapeless. She wore ankle socks.

An old body battered by a life of hard work. Difficult to believe that not much more than a decade earlier she had been fertile, that she had given birth to Laura.

Signora Vardin left them and, walking heavily, she went into the bedroom.

The sound of traffic came from Piazza Castello.

Ciuffi said in a quiet voice, "You haven't asked about the girls, Commissario."

Trotti glanced at Ciuffi and grinned. "You believe the older sister took a knife to Laura?"

"Unlikely—particularly since the cousin Bettina was there. But it is just possible that as a stepfather—" She lowered her voice to a hoarse whisper. "Stepfathers aren't always very nice people."

"Vardin seems a kind person." He placed his hand on the table. "These are good people—from the Friuli, country folk, undemanding and honest. And proud. The backbone of Italy—its only true wealth."

Ciuffi raised an eyebrow.

"Don't forget that it was his blood-daughter—not Vardin's stepdaughter—who was attacked."

"Strange how Vardin's identikit of the attacker was so much like Riccardo."

"Perhaps it was Riccardo."

Ciuffi shook her head.

"Or perhaps Vardin chose to make him look like his step-daughter's boyfriend." He frowned. "What makes you think Riccardo couldn't have attacked the little girl?"

The sound of cupboards being opened and closed in the next room.

"Riccardo's not the type."

"We are all the type at some time or other. We are all capable of criminal behavior if the temptation is great enough." Trotti unwrapped a boiled sweet and placed it in his mouth. "It's possible Riccardo attacked her—just as it's possible he attacked Signorina Podestà." He took the belt buckle from his pocket and played with the sliding clasp. "But I'm not sure Riccardo is the type to wear army surplus. Lacoste and Enrico Coveri seem to be more his style."

Ciuffi laughed. "I didn't realize you knew so much about clothes . . ."

Trotti raised his shoulders. "A wife and a daughter—and magazines hanging round the house . . ."

"Now you believe Signorina Podestà was raped, Commissario?"

"A boy whose father has run off. A boy who has been smothered by his mother—and who is perhaps afraid of his own sexuality."

"A sweet boy."

"Don't trust your emotions, signorina."

"Yet you trust Vardin, Commissario—just because he's hard-working and from the Friuli."

"Don't trust your emotions—and don't trust appearances. I was once a sweet boy."

Ciuffi stretched out her hand, and ran the index finger lightly across his knuckles. "Hard to believe." Her eyes—no longer tired—watched his. There was a smile at the corner of her lips.

Signora Vardin appeared in the doorway.

Ciuffi quickly removed her hand.

The plump, white arms hung at her side. "I don't understand," Signora Vardin said. In one hand she held a cheap canvas case—a case for holding a rifle. "He keeps it in this but the gun is not there." The cow-like eyes looked at Trotti and the young police woman. "I didn't see my husband take his gun this morning."

26: Gino

"WE'RE NOT GOING to look for Vardin?"

The lift doors opened before Trotti could answer.

Gino slowly raised his head. "Two love birds," he said and from behind the desk gave his tired smile. "Ciao."

"Ciao, Gino."

The smell of death as they stepped out of the lift. Ciuffi put her hand to her face, her fingers against her nose.

The corridor was empty on the third floor and although the windows gave on to Strada Nuova, the sounds of outside traffic were muted. The blind man gave a little wave of his hand. At his feet Principessa slept her mid-morning siesta.

"Where's Pisanelli?"

Ciuffi began opening several of the windows.

"Only creates a breeze," Gino said irritably. "These women always wanting to organize."

"A woman," Trotti said lowering his voice, "but a good policeman, Gino. Believe me."

"Still a romantic, Commissario?"

"Gino, have you seen Pisanelli?"

"Merenda was looking for him a minute ago."

"Pisanelli works for me, not for Merenda."

"Must've been about ten o'clock." A muffled voice, as if the dentist had anaesthetized his mouth. "Said he was going to see the Vardin man."

"Pisanelli's probably gone off to see one of his girlfriends." Trotti clicked his tongue. "We've just been to the apartment in Piazza Castello."

"Commissario, I am not party to Pisanelli's methods of enquiry. I am just the old man who answers the phone."

Trotti placed a hand on Gino's shoulder. "You know, you're really beginning to sound like an old man."

"Old enough, Piero, to see that you're too hard on your men. That's how you lost Magagna—and, if you're not careful, Pisanelli'll go the same way." He added, "Not all your men can be pretty girls in uniform."

"Trouble with you, Gino, is you're a phallocrat." Trotti took a packet of Charms from his pocket. "You and all the men in this Questura. Here, have a sweet. Fennel flavor—it should sweeten you up. If I didn't know you so well, I would be tempted to think that you are brooding. The male menopause, Gino?"

"Piero, I'm retiring at the end of the year."

"And you should be glad to be getting out of here. A lucky man, Gino."

"I'll miss you all."

Trotti asked, "And Principessa?"

"The vet says . . ." Gino began, then shook his head quickly. The stained teeth worried at the lower lip.

"We'll get you another dog."

"Another dog after fourteen years?" The sightless eyes peered from behind the thick lenses. "A dog isn't like a wife. You can't just change like that when the first one gets to be too old."

Ciuffi had gone into Trotti's office.

"You must cheer up. Retirement—you'll be able to get out, to meet your friends. And you know you'll always be welcome here, among us."

"Pazienza." Gino raised hands in an Italian gesture of resignation.

"You've always been like a father to us, Gino."

"Father? There can't be more than two years' difference between us, Piero Trotti." He laughed. "There was a phone call for you."

"Who from?"

"He said to ring Gianni in Santa Maria."

Trotti sighed. "A priest who has been reading too many detective novels." He gave Gino a friendly slap on the shoulder. "You'd better give me a line," he said.

"I hear the *Provincia* is stirring up trouble."

Trotti left the old man and went into his office.

"You must do something about that wretched dog, Piero."

He looked at Ciuffi as he stepped past the files cluttering the floor. A raised eyebrow. "Christian name, Brigadiere?" He found himself smiling as he picked up the telephone and dialed.

"If you don't want to do anything, I'll kill the dog myself—the smell is unbearable."

"I don't think it's a good idea for you to call me by my Christian name."

"You said we were friends."

Trotti nodded. "Outside the Questura, Brigadiere." He frowned as a voice came on the line. "Fra Gianni?"

"Don't you ever work, Piero?"

"I was at the hospital."

"Have you started checking?"

"Checking for what?"

"The man I told you about."

"Primula Rosa, you mean?"

"Yes."

"I have been busy all morning. I do have a job to do—and a city to worry about."

"You promised me you would start looking for him."

"I told you. Santa Maria is not part of my jurisdiction."

"But you are concerned."

"A trace on somebody—somebody who has no criminal record, who has done nothing wrong—do you realize the effort involved?"

"You have computers."

Trotti laughed. "You don't even know what a computer is."

"You promised, Piero."

"It's not up to me. It's up to the Carabinieri."

"And you know what the Carabinieri are like."

"Fra Gianni, I am not—"

"Piero, you gave me your word."

The pigeons. They were cooing beneath the roof; beyond the window, the terra-cotta tiles of the city, the towers and the dome of the cathedral were bright and clear now that the mist had lifted.

"Piero, you gave me your word."

"And how am I going to find him?"

"Use the computer."

"Primula Rosa is not his real name."

"Don't make excuses. You know his real name."

Trotti waited.

"His name is Vecchioni, Mario Vecchioni. Class of twenty-three."

Trotti was silent.

"Well?"

"What was it you said the other day? That, with my singing voice, I should have gone into the Church."

"Don't change the subject."

"That's what you said, isn't it—I should've gone into the Church?"

"I've always thought that."

"And you, Gianni, you have all the single-mindedness of a policeman."

The priest laughed, said, "God bless you, Piero," and hung up.

27: Spadano

THE TWO MEN shook hands.

"You're not looking any younger, Trotti."

Trotti sat down in the leather armchair.

Spadano returned to his desk and picked up the stub of a Toscano cigar from where he had placed it on the ashtray. A plastic ashtray, chipped and advertising the *Provincia Padana*. "What brings you here?"

"Good to see you, Spadano."

"It's always good to see you, Trotti—when you're not asking for favors."

"I need a favor, Spadano."

"Coffee?"

"I need a favor."

"Then you know the answer."

The office was spacious and well-furnished. For unimaginative southerners, the Carabinieri did well for themselves.

Spadano lit the black end of the cigar with a kitchen match. "Trying to give them up." He looked at Trotti, "One of the remaining vices." He blew out the match.

Later a man in uniform brought in a tray of coffee. Little cups with the insignia of the Carabinieri. There was also a bottle that Spadano took and opened, twisting the cap with a rapid movement.

"Grappa?"

Trotti shook his head. "I'm having lunch soon—with a friend."

"Never known you to refuse, Trotti." Spadano poured grappa into both cups.

They drank—Spadano in one gulp, Trotti slowly.

"Lunch with a lady friend, Trotti?"

Trotti nodded.

"And the family?"

"My wife's in America."

"So I heard." Regular features, tanned skin and hard eyes behind the acrid cloud of cigar smoke. A perfectly ironed khaki shirt. "So I heard."

"Probably better for everybody."

"A very sophisticated woman, Signora Trotti."

"Too sophisticated for me."

"Being a policeman is a full-time job—and it takes the place of wife and family." Spadano leaned forward and placed the cup on its saucer. "You have a wife. And you have your daughter. You must not complain."

"Pioppi is in Bologna."

Spadano tapped his left shoulder. "The pips and the insignia. This is my life. Nearly thirty years in the Carabinieri. They have been good years—and the friends are good friends." He gave a brief shake of his head. "At least those who are still alive. The Years of Lead haven't been kind to any of us."

"The Years of Lead are over, thank God."

"We knew then who the enemy was. Urban terrorism. And in Dalla Chiesa we had a man—a Carabiniere—who knew what he wanted. Terrorism was the enemy—and we defeated it."

"The Carabinieri defeated terrorism?"

"Italy, Trotti. The Italian people—it was they—us—who said we'd had enough of kneecappings and bombings, trains being blown up and policemen murdered. Innocent people being blown apart in Brescia or Florence. Terrorism from the extreme left and the extreme right. Years of Lead—but they were also years of hope."

"And now?"

"They sent Dalla Chiesa to Palermo—this time to combat the Mafia. Within three months he was dead."

"The Mafia killed him."

"Rome killed him—because between an honest Carabiniere and the Mafia, Rome will always prefer the Mafia." For a moment he was silent, his eyes bright and watching Trotti through the rising clouds of smoke. "Rome needs the Mafia because Rome is the Mafia!"

"You are bitter."

Spadano put the cigar back on the ashtray and fumbled in a drawer. He produced a letter that he held out to Trotti.

Trotti did not take the letter. He recognized the heading: Ministry of Defense.

"They are sending me to Sardinia."

Trotti whistled softly.

"Orgosolo in Nuoro Province."

"At least you won't be bothered by the Pubblica Sicurezza coming to ask you for favors."

"I have grown to like this city."

Trotti raised an eyebrow as he set the coffee cup down on its matching saucer.

"A northern city. Hard-working, conservative and quietly xenophobic. But kind. And decent—in its own provincial way."

"Sardinia is the south, Spadano. You're going home."

"Who told you I wanted to go home?"

"We all want to go home. We are getting old—and there is nowhere else."

"I like this city—and they're sending me to Nuoro. Working with helicopters, looking for the shepherd kidnappers and their wealthy victims in the barren mountains of Sardinia."

"Promotion, Spadano."

"All my life I have thought about the Arma—about doing my duty. And about promotion. And the insignia have grown into my flesh, have become part of me. There has never been anything else. And now . . ." He shrugged. "The Ministry is pleased with me." He glanced at the letter and shook his head.

"What more do you want?"

"I want what you have always taken for granted."

Trotti smiled without understanding.

"The best men, the best equipment, helicopters and land vehicles. Night vision equipment and the full support of the Finanza. I will be part of one of the biggest attacks mounted against organized crime in this country's history. A direct line to Rome and the Ministry. British and American advisers—there are even going to be watchers from the UN."

"Isn't that what you've always wanted?"

"When all the time I find myself looking at the kids in the street, Trotti, and wishing that one was mine—wishing that instead of a barracks to come back to, there was a little boy just a little bit like me—perhaps a bit cleverer—who was going to grow up and become like me. Like me, but wiser."

Trotti shrugged.

"I never gave marriage a second thought. Not once in thirty years. But now I am suddenly afraid that all that I have worked for will die with me. You have a daughter, Trotti."

"I scarcely ever see Pioppi."

"But you know that she is there." Spadano sat back. "You know that when your time comes, a part of you will live on."

"I genuinely believe that the Captain of Carabinieri is feeling sorry for himself."

"A life in the hills, chasing bandits . . . How can I ever hope to find a . . . to start a family now if I am away from civilization?" A deprecatory shrug.

Trotti laughed, not unkindly. "We can't all be Dalla Chiesa, Spadano. We can't all be high-ranking generals. We can't all be the man the country turns to in its moment of need. And above all, we can't all hope to find a beautiful young wife to share the evening years of our lives. Dalla Chiesa had money and fame. A wealthy background—Piemonte. And an international reputation. But where are you and I—ageing policemen, Spadano—where are we going to find a young wife half our age?"

"You don't need a wife, Trotti. You have a daughter, you should be happy."

"My wife is in America and I see Pioppi at best a couple of times a year. She has decided that she's happier without her father."

"One thing's certain—I'm not going to find anything in the Sopramonte. Other than sheep, wind and rain. And foul-smelling Sardinian peasants and murderers." He poured himself another cup of coffee from the stainless steel pot. Spadano swallowed in one fast bob of his adam's apple. Then he looked at Trotti, his face set. "Well?"

"I told you—I want a favor."

"I don't owe the Pubblica Sicurezza any favors."

"Spadano—you don't owe me a favor. But I have known you long enough . . . ?"

The short hair was turning white at the temples. "What is it you want? About the little girl who was attacked?"

"You heard about that?"

Spadano said, "I can read, Trotti. I can read the *Provincia*—for the last couple of days, it hasn't mentioned anything else. I can recognize your name. I can see that our local newspaper is intent on creating an atmosphere of hysteria." He paused. "And the Bianchini boy?"

"I beg your pardon."

"The Bianchini boy is innocent."

"What are you talking about, Spadano?"

"I knew the father—a drinker and a womanizer. But he is my friend. And I know the son. Riccardo may be a bit reckless, a bit spoiled by his mother—but he is not a criminal."

Silence.

"We all get telephone calls, Piero—that is what power in Italy is all about. People you've never heard of asking for favors, asking you to forget your responsibilities, your duty to your job and your country. It's something I've never accepted—because my only duty is towards the Arma. So if you think I'm interfering, forgive me. I know the Bianchini family—and I know Riccardo. For your sake, Piero—for your sake and so that you don't waste any time—I can tell you now that Riccardo Bianchini is innocent."

Trotti was silent.

"Angry, Trotti?"

"Surprised, Spadano."

The Carabiniere coughed. "More coffee?"

"No."

The two men looked at each other without speaking. "You wanted to ask me a favor, I believe."

Trotti lowered his voice. It was flat, devoid of emotion. "Access to Carabinieri archives, Spadano. That's what I need."

For a moment Spadano looked at Trotti in silence. "I don't think I can help you."

"You don't think you can help me find out who murdered a Carabiniere in Santa Maria in Collina?"

"Saltieri? That was a very long time ago, Trotti."

Trotti nodded.

"I'd like you to follow it up. Find out as much as you can from archives about Santa Maria."

"You have your own good men in the Pubblica Sicurezza, Trotti."

"Santa Maria is not in my jurisdiction. And I want to know about the murders—the mysterious deaths—that have occurred there since the war. At least six deaths in the last twenty years. And all within a few meters of each other."

"Why?"

Trotti shrugged.

"Why?"

"As a favor to an old friend."

"You mean the crazy old priest?"

Trotti tried to hide his surprise. "What do you know about Santa Maria, Spadano?"

"Slow, unimaginative southerners, Trotti. But careful and painstaking."

"What do you know about Santa Maria? And about Fra Gianni?"

"An old man living in the past. Who hasn't stopped pestering the Carabinieri for the last five years with his theories of mass murder."

"Fra Gianni is a friend. And a friend of my brother."

"You have a brother?"

"Italo Trotti was killed in the hills. At about the same time as Saltieri."

Again the two men looked at each other. Rivalry and the unavowed affection of years spent working for and against each other.

"I've come for a favor. The Arma, Spadano—with its tradition of loyalty? Loyalty to the State—and to the partisans. The insignia tattooed into your flesh? You are a Carabiniere and I want to find out who killed the Carabiniere Saltieri because perhaps the same people killed my brother."

Silence.

"The same people who have been murdering for the last forty years."

"I don't think I can help you."

"You can help me."

Spadano's dark eyes remained on Trotti. "Will you do it, Spadano?"

"Do what?"

"Will you let me have a look at the Santa Maria dossiers?"

Spadano said nothing.

"Not just for me or for the priest. But for Saltieri."

"Saltieri is dead."

"And for the good name of the Arma."

Spadano took a deep breath.

"Well?"

"Have some more coffee, Trotti."

Slowly Trotti's face broke into a smile. "You forget I'm having lunch with a young lady, Spadano."

28: Maserati

"Ah, Commissario."

Trotti turned and squinted against the light.

"I hear you were looking for me," Maserati said and gave a forced smile. It was rare that he was to be seen out of his white lab coat. "Actually, I was about to go to lunch."

"Bit early for lunch, isn't it?"

He wore jeans and a loose jacket; the top three buttons of his shirt were undone. Although casually dressed, Maserati somehow appeared ill at ease away from his machines.

(Cardano in Scientifica maintained that Maserati was intending to get married before the end of the year.)

"I hear that Ciuffi dragged you in early this morning for an identikit. Our Brigadiere Ciuffi can be a very determined police woman."

"But nice." Maserati grinned and perhaps even winked, it was hard to tell in the light. "And very fond of you."

"Did you get anything from her?"

"From Ciuffi?"

"Did you get anything from the raped woman?—Signorina Podestà?"

"Not an ideal witness, I'm afraid. Best to use the kid-glove approach."

"You think she was raped?"

"Ciuffi does."

They were standing at the entrance of the Questura. Outside the sun shone on the city. A couple of students—girls who had primly tucked their skirts under their saddles—cycled slowly along Strada Nuova.

Italia felix.

Maserati touched Trotti's arm and said, "Shouldn't take more than five minutes . . ." For a brief instant their eyes met.

"As much time as you want, Maserati."

They went back into the building and took the new lift. The two men stood in silence without looking at each other. There was the smell of mint on Maserati's breath. Then the sliding doors drew apart and, from the interior of the lift, Maserati unlocked the heavy door.

"I'll also be needing a general search put out."

"Who for?"

"An old partisan . . ." Trotti let the breath escape noisily from his lungs. "Who hasn't even got a record."

They entered the basement and Maserati's antiseptic World of Science.

"What do you want him for?"

"Somebody thinks he might be connected with a series of killings. Killings up in the hills."

"A bit out of our jurisdiction, Commissario?"

Trotti did not reply. In the last year, the basement had been completely reorganized and renovated. The archives had been put on to microfiles and in the place of the old shelves—Trotti could remember them bulging with beige files gathering dust—there were now metallic cupboards, painted a functional, impersonal grey.

They had also installed several fire extinguishers and a telephone on the wall.

Maserati walked across the rubberized floor and sat down on a stool in front of a screen. He turned on a switch and the console bleeped.

He typed out several words on the screen. Trotti recognized the name Vardin.

The air-conditioning was chill.

"Somebody's been lying." A little laugh. "If you want my opinion."

"I would have thought, with all the wonders of technology, it shouldn't be difficult to find out who's lying and who's telling the truth." Trotti pulled up the stool beside Maserati. He noticed that the younger man's clothes had acquired the same antiseptic smell as the basement.

"Lie detectors? You can't really trust them. The Americans went overboard for polygraphs. But of course the polygraph doesn't actually detect lies—it simply detects signs of emotion. You can pick up the same signs in facial expressions, gestures and voice. To be fair, the polygraph can give a better than fifty-fifty chance of determining if somebody is lying. But that means you can be fifty per cent wrong." He shrugged. "After a while the Americans realized they were sending too many innocent people to the electric chair." A series of electronic bleeps, signals that exploded and then vanished from the screen. "Here. This is the picture we got of the attacker."

"Wasn't there talk of your going to America for a course?"

"Who needs America, Commissario? When we Italians put our minds to it, we don't need Americans."

Trotti looked at the green image on the screen. "The attacker of the Vardin girl? You've already given me copies."

Maserati gave an imperceptible nod. His eyes were on the monitor. "Laura's father said he didn't see the attacker properly. But once Cardano and I started asking him questions, he managed to remember well enough. He was a good witness to work with . . ."

"But?"

"I couldn't help wondering if he was making things up. Just to please us." He tapped the screen where a face had already appeared. "If you want, we can move the face around, get a different angle." He pressed one of the keys on the computer.

"Impressive."

"An Italian program. For once it's us who are selling to the Japanese and the Americans. Devised by the criminology department at the University of Pisa." He nodded enthusiastically towards the screen. "You see, if you want, this is a picture of the whole body—it gives an idea of the man's age and build." On the monitor, there appeared the silhouette of the human figure. "And this is the composite picture we've sent out. Over the phone." He got up and went to a filing basket that stood on the tabletop. Maserati had forgotten about his lunchtime appointment. His entire attention was upon the work in hand. He gave Trotti a sheet of paper on which the screen picture had been printed.

"You've already given me copies," Trotti said.

"But this is the other picture." He returned to his seat and the screen went blank. "The identikit from the girl . . . Signorina Podestà." He turned and gave Trotti an unnatural leer. "I felt that Podestà's own face could do with a bit of rearranging." He tapped the computer. "With this program, you've got five degrees of exorbitant eyes." A laugh that Trotti found unpleasant. "Poor thing, I could make her a bit more presentable—with this Pisa program. Straighten out the nose, put the eyes back into her skull. And a completely different figure. Then perhaps she could find a man who'd give her what she needs. And she'd stop bothering us with her sexual fantasies."

The picture had come up on the screen.

He shook his head. "She says she threw the attacker off her and then he got up and escaped." Maserati laughed. "Woman of the twentieth century—that's what she called herself."

Trotti nodded.

"Of course, there was little to go on. Both Cardano and I felt that she was making things up. But not like Vardin—it wasn't that she was trying to please us. It was more . . . I don't know . . . more personal."

Trotti waited.

"Here's the printout."

Trotti took the second sheet of paper that Maserati handed him and compared the two faces.

"You see, Commissario—either one of them is making things up. Or else there are two rapists at large in this city."

29: Caserma Cairoli

THE GATES OPENED and, turning slightly, Trotti glanced at Ciuffi sitting in the car. She gave him a little smile and a wave as he entered the barracks.

A conscript in ill-fitting trousers and heavy boots accompanied him. They crossed a courtyard.

Several vehicles painted in khaki and the letters EI in red on the white number plates. Esercito Italiano—the Italian army. Part of NATO, an integral part of the West's defense.

Trotti looked at the somnolent buildings, at the billowing, grubby curtains, at the chipped ocher paintwork and he smiled to himself. If the Russians were to come now, there would not be much of a fight. They would find the soldiers of the Caserma Cairoli preparing for lunch. The smell of tomatoes and onions hung in the air and from the open windows of the cookhouse came the sound of casseroles being banged together; someone shouting in a dialect that Trotti could not understand; guffaws of laughter.

Trotti followed the soldier up a couple of flights of stairs.

Architecturally, the building was part Habsburg, part Italian Miracle. Along the long corridor, the smell of tomatoes and pasta was less pervasive. The plasterwork had been painted a dark ocher. Several framed photographs on the wall—pictures of soldiers in action or training, stun guns in hand and berets pulled menacingly down to one side—had turned a pale grey with the passage of time.

They came to a door. The conscript raised his hand, grinned at Trotti, knocked deferentially, opened the door, saluted and then disappeared.

Trotti entered the office.

"You phoned, Commissario." The man half-rose from his chair, and then inelegantly dropped back on to it.

Colonello Vincenzo was a large, florid man with fat cheeks and broken blood vessels. The cotton shirt had lost both its gloss and its creases. The collar bit into the bulging flesh of the neck.

They shook hands. "It's very good of you to receive me like this, Signor Colonello."

"Even though the PS is no longer a military force."

Trotti shrugged. "Mere civilians, I'm afraid."

"And perhaps it is better that way," replied the soldier. There were orange hairs on the back of his large hands. "As a civilian force, the Pubblica Sicurezza can better complement the Carabinieri, who remain part of the army."

"It is not always easy for the two police forces to collaborate. On both sides, there is a feeling that we have a different job to do, a different way of doing it."

"Of course." Colonello Vincenzo glanced at his gold Rolex watch. "How can I be of use to you?"

Trotti could almost hear the man's belly rumbling.

He took the identikit from his pocket. "A rapist who has already attacked a middle-aged woman. This is a graphic transcription of her identification. As you can see, the man would appear to be fairly young."

"Ah, I think I read something in the paper." He took the identikit and frowned at it. "Please sit down, Commissario."

Trotti lowered himself on to a wooden chair. The leather upholstery was worn and had lost its color.

"You think that one of my men . . ." He frowned as he studied the rumpled identikit. "You think that one of my men is involved? Is that it?"

"Three nights ago, a little girl was attacked in her bed. Attacked with a knife." He nodded towards the piece of paper. "The identikit would give the rapist the age of twenty-one or -two."

"I am not an unreasonable man, Commissario. I am willing to admit that soldiers can get a bit, well, sex-starved. Except for a few officers and NCOS, I've got nothing but conscripts under my command. Good boys—but lonely away from home, away from the people they love. More than fifty per cent of the men are from the south—south of Rome. Away from home and lonely at an age when sexually . . ." A cough, he put his hand to his mouth. "But I don't see why you come here. Do you think that one of my men is this . . . is this rapist?"

"We cannot afford to leave any stone unturned."

The head to one side in a gesture of acquiescence, the thick hands fanning out on the desk. "But I fail to understand . . ."

"You say you've been reading the paper."

"I am a busy man."

"The *Provincia* has been putting the story on the front page—talking of a monster, of a mad sex maniac at large."

The Colonello gave an indulgent smile.

"The last thing I want in this city is mass hysteria."

"You can always tell the *Provincia* to lay off, Commissario."

"I want to get the whole thing sorted out as fast as possible. That's why I need your cooperation, Signor Colonello."

"See the *Provincia*."

"One of the basic tenets of democracy is the freedom of the press."

Again the indulgent smile. "A strange idea of democracy."

"We have to live with the press."

The man was about to say something. Trotti noticed the hesitation.

"A drink, Commissario?"

"I beg your pardon?"

"Would you care for a drink?"

Trotti smiled and shook his head. "I'll be going for lunch in a minute."

"You can have lunch here in the officers' mess."

"You are very kind."

There was an old Savoy flag on the wall; it had been flattened and placed in a glass frame. The edge of the flag was badly frayed.

"I want to help you of course, Commissario."

Trotti took the buckle from his pocket and placed it on the edge of the desk. "A woman who claims she was raped says she found this under the bed. She claims that it was left by her attacker."

"A belt?" The large face cracked into a smile.

"She lives about two hundred yards from here."

"A standard army buckle—of the type that anybody can buy in any surplus store from Palermo to Padua—and you believe that the rapist is one of my men." Colonello Vincenzo placed both hands on to the desk.

The ginger hairs on the back of the hands had been shaved and formed a thick stubble.

"Commissario. Please—let us be serious."

"You recognize it as standard army issue?"

"This is how you undertake an investigation?"

"What do you know about police investigative methods?"

The red face hardened, the lips pursed. "I have a minimum of common sense."

"So do I, Signor Colonello. But I also have a city to protect. You do understand. Somewhere in the city is a rapist—and the identikit and this buckle are the only clues I have to go on. It is not much and please smile if you choose. By all means laugh if you think that the PS is no more than a bunch of stupid civilians—I won't stop you. But I ask you for just one thing. Not for me, not for the PS, but for the city—for the women of this city. Signor Colonello, I ask for your help. For your cooperation."

30: Pizza

"I DON'T UNDERSTAND why you don't want to look for Vardin."

"There's no hurry."

"But he took his gun. Without telling his wife."

Trotti played with the starched napkin. "There are a lot of things a man doesn't tell his wife."

"You think Vardin has been receiving threats."

"Perhaps."

"I don't understand you, Commissario."

"A minute ago you were calling me Piero. I was beginning to get used to it."

"At last we've got a motive for the attack on the little girl. But all of a sudden, you seem to lose interest." She shook her head, as if she failed to understand Trotti's obduracy. "Galandra comes out of jail after a seven-year sentence. Seven years is time enough to work out a way of getting revenge. Revenge on the man who put him there in the first place." She stopped, ripped the end off the packet of grissini and started nibbling nervously at the long stick of bread. "You're not listening, are you?"

"I beg your pardon."

"You're thinking about something else."

"I don't think I really like pizza." He shrugged.

She sat back and folded her arms. Her chest rose and fell. "I've been working for you for nine months."

They were sitting on the terrace, beneath the awning.

Trotti turned and looked towards the interior of the pizzeria. A cook in a singlet and a paper hat on his head stood in front of the open oven. From time to time he slid his flat spade under the embers and removed a pizza that he placed, perfectly round and steaming, on to a marble tabletop. Nimble-footed waiters—short-sleeved white shirts and thin bow ties—ferried the pizzas to the diners waiting in the red-tinted shade of the stretched canvas outside.

"Nine months, Commissario. Why this sudden interest in me?"

Trotti turned to face her.

"I know it's not for professional reasons—because you don't listen to a word I say."

"This sounds to me like a quarrel."

"You think I'm a silly little girl."

"You are a very good policeman."

"Then today both breakfast and a pizza lunch. I'm being spoiled, Piero. Why?"

Trotti looked at her and there was surprise in his eyes. For a moment he was silent. "Drink up, Brigadiere." He poured mineral water into the two glasses. "We've got a lot to do this afternoon."

A lopsided smile, but she did as she was told.

They sat in the shade. Just past one o'clock and it was nearly as hot as the month of August. The sun was overhead and battered down on to the empty piazza and on to the deep-red awning of the Pizzeria Bella Napoli. A feeble breeze rustled the potted plants.

"Why are you spoiling me like this, Piero Trotti?"

"You are hungry, Brigadiere?"

"Why don't you answer my question?"

"Are you hungry?"

She shrugged. "I don't get much time to eat."

"Let me take you somewhere proper one evening."

Her laugh was cheerful. "This isn't proper?"

"There are restaurants up in the hills—places where the

food is cooked specially for you. Not fast food but real country cooking."

"Like truffles . . . and good wine?"

His face broke into a grin. "You told me off for laughing at you. Now you're laughing at me."

"Not at all."

"You don't like Signora Bianchini, Brigadiere Ciuffi?"

"Why don't you call me Ornella?"

Trotti placed the end of a grissini into his mouth to hide his smile. "What have you got against Signora Bianchini?"

"You could never return to the hills, Piero. Not for good. You'd be lonely away from this town, away from all your friends."

"Answer the question, Ornella."

"You like to pretend you're above things—but, like all men, you're fascinated by other people, fascinated by all the gossip. You need to have your friends around you."

"I have no friends."

"Your friends in the Questura, your friends in this city you pretend to despise so much—without them you'd be lost." A little laugh of private amusement. "In Tarzi or Santa Maria, you'd be so lonely, you'd sit by the telephone and you'd spend your measly pension on phone calls." The young, mischievous eyes watched him carefully.

"I've spent enough money in my time phoning my wife in America."

The young smile vanished. "I thought you were getting divorced."

He shrugged.

"A new life, Piero."

A waiter brought the two pizzas. Trotti was no longer hungry.

A screech of tires.

"That's what you need. A new life—with children. And with a woman who can look after you."

The Alfetta pulled into the piazza. It came to a halt only a few centimeters away from the potted plants.

Pisanelli climbed out.

He ran his fingers through the long hair at the side of his head. He was grinning as he gave Trotti a little wave.

31: Raffaele Arzanti

TROTTI HELD A half-eaten grissini in his hand. "Good to see you're still alive, Pisanelli."

Pisanelli looked at Trotti and grinned. A hurried, cold glance at Ciuffi. He took a glass from a nearby table and, without being invited, sat down beside them. He poured himself some mineral water and drank thirstily.

Then he ran the back of his hand across his lips. "Feeling better?"

Pisanelli nodded.

"Good."

"Somebody in the car, Commissario, that you had better talk to."

"I am having my lunch."

"So I see." Pisanelli took another thirsty gulp. Another brief glance at Ciuffi.

"Brigadiere Ciuffi and I are not going to be free for twenty minutes. Perhaps you would care for a pizza." A thin smile. "Why don't you join us?"

"Not the time. Our friend"—a gesture towards the car—"thinks he's under arrest. I had difficulty in getting him to talk. However, if you feel . . ." Pisanelli shrugged.

"You always choose the most opportune moments."

"Just doing what I see to be my duty."

Trotti threw his napkin down. A grimace of apology to Ciuffi as he stood up. Then he followed Pisanelli to the car.

"Couldn't you have chosen a better time?"

"Commissario, I didn't know he was going to break down and cry." He added, "And I didn't know you were having a tête-à-tête with our resident policewoman."

Trotti got into the back seat.

It was hot inside the car and there was an almost tangible smell of fear. Trotti pulled the door shut. Pisanelli sat behind the wheel and put the car into gear.

"Well?"

The young man had been doubled forward as if he had received a sharp blow to the belly. He now slowly drew himself up into a sitting position. He blinked, his eyes red and unaccustomed to the light. He breathed through his mouth.

Pisanelli spoke over his shoulder. "He didn't want to speak. All he would say was that he was with Riccardo Bianchini."

The boy's eyes looked at Trotti for sympathy. "That's what he told me." There were the dry traces of tears on his cheeks. He was overweight, with pale flesh and dark, long hair that fell forward over a round, young face. The irises were colorless, except for the flecks of yellow. A tennis shirt that was new but already crumpled. He had breasts like a woman's.

Trotti said, "You've nothing to be afraid of. If you tell the truth."

Pisanelli snorted. "A little liar." He turned the car into Corso Cavour, now empty at lunchtime. "A couple of nights in the Questura and—"

"What's your name?" Trotti asked softly.

"I didn't realize . . ." A gesture of his chin. "I didn't realize the gentleman was from the police."

"Never seen a police car before?"

"Quiet, Pisanelli." Trotti felt hot and sticky. He wanted to get back to Ciuffi. "What is your name?"

"I am Raffaele. Raffaele Arzanti."

"You are a friend of Riccardo Bianchini?"

"We go to school together."

"And you are friends?"

The boy did not answer.

"Is Riccardo Bianchini your friend?"

"I don't have many friends."

"Why not?"

He shrugged. "Not many people like me."

"But Riccardo likes you?"

"Papa bought me a computer. I don't mind sharing it with Riccardo. Sometimes we get on well."

"How old are you, Raffaele?"

"Seventeen." A hesitation. "Seventeen and a half."

"And was Riccardo at your house last Saturday?"

"I live in the AGIP flats—near the river. Riccardo comes sometimes when he wants to work on the computer. He is good at programming."

"And he came round on Saturday?"

"He's supposed to be preparing his exam. But lately he's been working on a program of English verbs. He thinks he can sell it. It is quite good, actually."

Trotti had not paid attention to where they were going. Now Pisanelli pulled the car up on to the pavement and Trotti realized they were by the old moat of the castle, only a few hundred meters from the Piazza Castello. He had parked the car in the shade. There was virtually no traffic. It was still hot in the car but a breeze came through the open windows.

"Did Riccardo come round last Saturday?"

The boy's eyes seemed to glisten.

"Well?"

"I told everything to the other gentleman."

"If you can tell Pisanelli, you can tell me."

"I don't want to get anybody into trouble."

"You can get yourself into trouble by lying."

The smell of fear, of sweat—and the taste of grissini still on his tongue. The boy looked at Trotti and Trotti felt sorry for him—a boy who could have been his own son.

"You have nothing to be afraid of. Just tell me what you told Pisanelli."

"I don't want—he will be angry with me . . ."

"Riccardo?"

Raffaele nodded unhappily. The hair was now unkempt, but it had kept its straight, neat parting.

"There is nothing Riccardo Bianchini can do to you. He is in enough trouble."

"Riccardo is . . . he is my friend."

Trotti placed his hand on the boy's knee. "Lying—being deceitful—that is not the way to have friends."

"But I did it to help him."

"To help him?"

Raffaele raised one shoulder. "So that his mother wouldn't get upset. You see, he really is good at programming."

"Riccardo?"

Raffaele nodded impatiently. "But it is in the afternoon that he comes round. That's when he works on the computer—it's an Apple, and although it only has a sixty-four-K memory . . ."

"Riccardo comes in the evening?"

"In the afternoon." A hurried shake of the head. "But it's in the evening that his mother rings and that's when I say that he's busy."

"Busy doing what?"

"She worries about him and wants to know if he is coming home. Once or twice he has slept at my place." The smile broke through the pale complexion. A schoolboy sharing his guilty secret. "I tell her that he is working on a program and that he can't come to the phone."

"And where is he?"

"She always seems to believe me. It must have happened half a dozen times—and I've expected her to want to speak to him. But she never does. She just says 'all right' and then she hangs up."

"What do your parents say?"

He raised one shoulder again. "They are rarely at home."

"And where is Riccardo?"

"You see, he asked me to say that. I know it was lying—but he's older than me, and . . . and sometimes he can be very nice. Sometimes we get on very well." A little smile. "It is as if we were brothers. And sometimes he really does stay the night—and I like that. We talk late into the night."

"Where was Riccardo on Saturday night?"

A shrug.

Trotti said, "It is very important. And I know you want to help your friend."

"I like Riccardo." The heavy eyelids started to flutter. The breathing grew heavier.

"And I like Riccardo, too. That's why you must tell me."

"But I don't know."

"Raffaele," Trotti said, "it is very important."

The boy turned away, glanced at Pisanelli and then out of the window of the car. At the dancing shade of the plane trees on the empty road—at the weathered billboards on the far side of the street. At the fading graffiti, handed down from a different era.

"Raffaele, where does Riccardo go?"

The boy lowered his head.

"Well?"

"He has a girlfriend."

"The girl in Piazza Castello?"

Raffaele looked up. "Netta Vardin—the girl at school? She's a stuck-up little snob—all she's interested in is clothes and older men. And anyway . . ."

"Yes?"

Raffaele blushed, a girlish blush that ran across the pale features.

"What about her?"

"Riccardo doesn't like her. Not anymore."

"Why not?"

"Because she won't . . . because she won't go to . . ."

"Because she won't sleep with him?"

He nodded, relieved. "She says they must wait until they're married."

It was almost silent. The rustle of a light wind in the trees, the distant sounds of the somnolent city.

"Where was he on Saturday night? He wasn't with the Vardin girl?"

"Of course not."

"Then where was he?"

"He has . . ."

"Yes?"

"There is a woman. She is a lot older than him—but he likes her a lot."

"A woman?"

"He says that she is nearly forty—but he prefers mature women. He prefers older women because they understand him."

"What's her name?"

A shake of the young, large head.

"Tell me, Raffaele, who is this woman?"

"I only saw her once. I think she works as a medical secretary. And she lives near the Cairoli barracks." He added, "She has bug eyes."

32: Decision

"AND ABOVE ALL, we can't all hope to find a beautiful young wife to share the evening years of our lives."

Spadano's words ran through his head and as the car stopped in the piazza—there were the first bicycles of the afternoon and people were talking in the cool arcades—he caught sight of Ciuffi behind the potted plants. She was still sitting at the table, an empty plate in front of her and her back straight. There was about her a natural severity; yet the face was young, gentle and innocent. A beguiling freshness.

Trotti got out of the car.

Pisanelli glanced towards Ciuffi and grinned.

"I'll see you in the Questura, Pisanelli. Be there at four—I need to talk to you about Bettina."

Pisanelli placed his arm over the top of the passenger seat. "Vardin's niece, you mean?"

"You spoke to her yesterday—before she left for Ovada."

Raffaele was sitting on the back seat. The boy had lowered his head and seemed to be sleeping.

"What do you want to know?"

Trotti nodded. "Four o'clock, Pisanelli. Try and be on time for once."

"I am always on time, Commissario."

"Really?"

"Although I'd love to be able to take time off for intimate

lunches. But I'm a mere flatfoot. Beautiful women aren't interested in men like me."

"Ciao, Pisanelli." Trotti took his hand from the car window.

Pisanelli grinned; there was no humor in his eyes.

The exhaust pipe rattled. In the back seat, Raffaele looked over his shoulder and gave Trotti a wan smile. Through the rear window, his face looked old.

The car turned into Corso Cavour.

Trotti rejoined Ciuffi.

"Ah! Piero." Ciuffi looked up, unable to repress her wide smile.

Trotti made a hushing sound. "We're in a public place." As he sat down, Trotti added, "You seem to be very fond of my Christian name."

"I'm fond of you."

Trotti coughed. "He may be a phallocrat . . ."

"Who?"

"Pisanelli has the makings of a good policeman. When he puts his mind to things."

"If he puts his mind to things. He should do that rather than using mine." She turned and looked towards the interior of the pizzeria. Already many of the customers had left. Two of the waiters were talking to the cook. The dark bow ties had lost their crispness and were no longer straight. Neither waiter noticed the wave from Ciuffi. Trying to catch their eye, she said, "I told the man to keep your food warm."

"I'm not hungry."

"A man in the prime of his life, Piero. You must eat."

Trotti clicked his tongue. At the same time he smiled.

"Where did Pisanelli take you?"

"I think we had better go and see our young friend Bianchini this afternoon."

Ciuffi's face clouded. "I thought we were going to find the old man."

"Old man, Brigadiere?"

"Why don't you call me Ornella?"

"This is a public place. And a lot of people know me here."

Ornella Ciuffi smiled. A contagious smile.

Trotti asked, "Who do you want to go and see?"

"We agreed we were going to talk to Vardin."

"I need to see Bianchini."

"Why?"

"I want to know where he was on Saturday night. I need to talk to him."

"With Bianchini? Or with his mother? And eat truffles? And drink wine in the middle of the afternoon?"

"Professional objectivity, Signorina?"

"Is it professional, Piero, to—?"

"In public, my name is not Piero."

"Is it professional to get involved with people—with an attractive woman—we're investigating?"

"Is it professional to call your superior officer by his Christian name?"

For a moment there was no reaction. Then her chin seemed to tremble. The corner of her lips whitened. She took a deep breath before speaking. "You said we were going to speak to Vardin. About the gun. And about his receiving threats from Galandra."

The mask returned, the youthful freshness disappeared. Impersonal, businesslike. She was no longer looking at him.

"There's no proof that Vardin was receiving threats from Galandra."

"Then let's go and ask him, Commissario. Ask him what he's done with his gun."

"I've got no idea where Vardin is."

"He's gone fishing." She added, "You know that."

"He went fishing this morning."

"Signor Vardin's fishing near the Ponte Imperiale. Or at least he was still there ten minutes ago."

Trotti gave her an appraising stare. "How on earth do you know that?"

Her voice was devoid of emotion. "You invite me for a meal. But no sooner have you ordered a couple of pizzas than you leave me here like a discarded toy."

"But—"

"You forget all about me."

"You're not being very fair."

"You want me to read *Annabella* and look at the pictures? Is that what you want me to do while I'm waiting for you?"

"Ornella," he said. "Please . . ." His hand moved across the deep red tablecloth and Trotti found himself touching her fingers.

"A woman, Piero Trotti. But I'm also a policeman. Don't forget that."

33: Rod

EITHER CENTRALE HAD got it wrong or Ciuffi had misheard. Vardin was nowhere near the Ponte Imperiale.

Ciuffi parked the car by the side of the road and they went down the path to the edge of the river. The Po ran sluggishly, clinging to the low riverbed. Underfoot, the pebbles were pale and reflected the afternoon glare. Smooth grey branches and miscellaneous flotsam were now stranded and dry against the stones, and dark traces of tar brought down by the river from the industrial centers upstream.

Nobody, nothing.

For a moment, Trotti stood with his hands in his pockets. The city—"*A Northern city. Hard working, conservative and quietly xenophobic. But kind. And decent*"—stood on the far side of the river. The modern, AGIP condominium rose up among the terracotta roofs, an anomaly in the architecture of the LungoPò.

Yellow buses were turning into the bottom of Strada Nuova.

Trotti turned and looked at Ciuffi. "Well?"

"Well what?"

He shrugged. "I did as you asked."

"I am sure Galandra—his blackmailing—is the key to the attack on Laura Vardin. We must talk to Vardin, Commissario."

"Why?"

"Vardin hasn't been totally honest with us."

"Then we'll talk to him—but another time."

There was something of the stubborn child about her. She stood with her legs slightly apart. The reflected light from the pebbles lit up her face from below. She shook her head. "Can we first check back with Centrale?"

"It'd be more useful to go and see Bianchini."

"I'm certain Centrale said Vardin was here."

"It's Bianchini I want to see."

"Riccardo is not going to run off." She moved towards the path and the main road. She didn't look at him. "Nor is Signora Bianchini."

In the car neither spoke. They had to cross the river to get back into the city. They took the Ponte Coperto and, although Ciuffi was driving, she turned her eyes from the road to look over at the river bank below. The columns of the covered bridge—it had been totally destroyed by the Allies at the end of the war and then rebuilt a few years later—dashed past, casting light and shadows on to her drawn face.

The mask slipped. "There's somebody fishing down there." Excitement in her voice.

"Near the Ponte Imperiale, signorina?"

"I must've misheard."

"We're going in the wrong direction, if we hope to see Bianchini."

"We're not on piece work, Commissario Trotti."

"I see we are no longer on Christian name terms."

She was frowning, staring past him through the car window. "You didn't seem to enjoy it."

"You're angry with me."

"You don't want to be liked, do you, Piero?"

"What makes you think it's Vardin down there?"

"Or perhaps you can't spare five minutes to go and look?"

Back on the city side of the river, she turned right and after a hundred meters, pulled the car up on to the pavement between the trees, trees that had been planted towards the end of the Fascist era.

(The LungoPò with its wide road had been one of Mussolini's legacies to the small, provincial town—the LungoPò and the concrete barges, the hangars that had been built on the river banks for the seaplanes. And the young men Il Duce had sent to their death in Albania, in Russia and in the hills beyond the river.)

"It's him." Ciuffi grinned her joy at Trotti. She got out of the car and started running down the steps.

Almost in the shadow of the Ponte Coperto, a large boat rode at anchor. It must at one time have come upriver from the sea and now it served as a floating restaurant. Decorative rows of naked lightbulbs ran along the sides and on the aft deck, half a dozen tables were set out beneath an awning. The restaurant only functioned in the evening. In the early afternoon the boat seemed asleep, lulled by the slow and gentle movement of the river.

A gangplank ran down from the boat on to a wooden pontoon.

It was on the pontoon that Vardin sat fishing. In one hand he held a fishing rod. Beside him on the wooden planks there was another rod as well as fishing tackle.

Trotti turned his glance from Vardin to Ciuffi. He was surprised by her speed. Neat, fast steps as she went down the stairs, her body slightly to one side and the click of her heels echoing off the red-brick wall of the LungoPò.

On the other side of the river, Borgo Genovese.

The serge uniform was attractive but it did not succeed in ageing her or giving her authority beyond her years. The small, lithe body of an adolescent girl.

Trotti smiled.

At the bottom of the stairs, Ciuffi ran a hand through her hair. She walked across the pontoon and called out to Vardin.

Vardin turned.

It was as Trotti approached them that the first bullet entered the side of her body, piercing the neat weave of Ciuffi's uniform, her lungs and then her heart.

Fractionally later there was a detonation but Trotti heard nothing.

34: Phone

"PAPA, IS THAT you?"

"Pioppi."

"Papa, how are you? Are you all right?"

"Where are you phoning from, Pioppi?"

"They told me you were wounded. I've been trying to get you for the last twelve hours. Are you all right, Papa? I'm catching the next train home."

"There's no need."

"The woman said you were shot at."

"It's nothing."

"Papa, you must tell me the truth. I am worried about you."

"It's nothing, Pioppi."

"It can't be nothing if you're in the hospital. Where were you hit? And how long are you going to be there for?"

"A slight graze. I lost some blood."

"In the arm? Where were you hit?"

"I'll be out of here by tomorrow."

"Why did the woman say I couldn't speak to you?"

"There's really nothing to worry about, Pioppi."

"Of course I am worried about you."

"There is no need. You must study. How is the course? And how is Nando?"

"Nando's with me now. We're phoning from the station and I'm getting the Milan train in ten minutes."

"That's absolutely stupid."

"Nando says it's the right thing. Papa, you've been wounded. I will be there in five hours. And I phoned Mamma in America."

"In five hours I'll be out of here."

"Mamma's worried."

"Your mother has better things to worry about."

"Why are you always so stubborn? Why won't you accept any help? I am your daughter—and I want to be with you."

"It is really not necessary."

"And the girl?"

"What girl?"

"They said there was a girl with you—a policewoman."

"Yes?"

"Well, how is she?"

"She was hit."

"She will recover?"

"Listen, Pioppi. There's no need for you to come up. I am all right. I'll be out of here soon. I will ring you tomorrow. I will ring from home. And, in the meanwhile, stay in Bologna. Stay with Nando—because he needs you. I'm all right, I swear to you. Don't worry about me—and there's no need to bother your mother. Tell her I am well. Just look after yourself, Pioppi. Ciao, bella."

"But Papa . . ."

"I love you, Pioppi. Ciao."

35: Déjà vu

"COMMISSARIO?"

He was wearing an anorak and he had shaved away his mustache. He looked plumper than when Trotti had last seen him in Milan.

"Commissario?"

If Magagna had not been wearing his American sunglasses, Trotti would have had difficulty in recognizing him.

"Well?"

He had been sitting on a steel chair. He now stood up and emptied the contents of his pockets on to the bed. "I bought you these." Half a dozen packets of boiled sweets.

"A rich man."

"One of the advantages of working in the Pubblica Sicurezza—easy money and fast promotion."

Trotti smiled; then he winced in pain as they shook hands. "Unwrap one of those things for me."

"What flavor?"

"A few years in Milan and you've forgotten that rhubarb is my favorite?"

Magagna took one of the packets, removed the wrapping and placed the sweet in Trotti's mouth.

"Somebody been taking shots at you, Commissario?"

"At me—or at a young policewoman."

"Ciuffi?"

A sudden, overwhelming sense of déjà-vu. "You knew her, Magagna?"

He shook his head. "Who did it, Commissario?"

Trotti clicked the sweet against his teeth. "How did you know I was here?"

"Not every day a policewoman is murdered—and a Commissario of the Pubblica Sicurezza has his rib broken by the same bullet."

Trotti said, "I want to get out of here."

"You're in for at least a week."

"I'm going to find him."

"Who?"

"Even if it's the last thing I do."

"You know who it was?"

Trotti shrugged.

"And Ciuffi—you knew her well?"

"We worked together. She was okay."

"Then it's best if you do nothing, Commissario." He shook his head. "Personal animosity . . ."

"Even if it's the last thing I do, Magagna."

"Think about your pension." Magagna removed his sunglasses and looked at him. Dark, intelligent eyes. "Rest, Commissario. That's what you need—perhaps even a holiday."

"I can count on your support, Magagna, can't I?"

"You'll need to convalesce. You're no longer a young man—you can't afford to take risks."

"A few days, Magagna—that's all I'm asking for."

Magagna placed a sweet in his mouth. He looked at Trotti. Then with both hands, he carefully put his sunglasses back on his nose.

"You don't owe me any favors, Magagna. But now, I'm asking you for a favor."

"Any news from Pioppi, Commissario? Not married yet or anything?"

36: Warning

"I THINK I know who killed her."

He had brought roses and the nurse had placed them in a vase by Trotti's bedside. Now there were flowers everywhere. Bouquets from friends, colleagues, well-wishers. The sweet smell was strong and filled the small room.

"I'm afraid you're out of action." The Questore put his head to one side as if to emphasize the point. "For the time being."

"But I know who killed her."

"Then you must tell the investigating judge in charge of the case."

Trotti let himself drop back against the pillows and stared at his hands and the wrinkled, sunburnt skin. The hands of an old man.

"You can tell all you know to Judge d'Avorio." A shrug. "Trouble is, Trotti, we have got all the press here—not just Milan, but people up from Rome, asking stupid questions. Not good for the city—and not good for the Questura. Things are going to be uncomfortable for a few days. I know that I can count on you." The Questore raised his hand. "I would like you on the job. Rash at times, impulsive, polemic—but our Commissario Trotti usually manages to get the job done. Done well and fast." An approving smile and a glint of the regular, white teeth. "Trotti, I don't want you to think that you're not appreciated."

Trotti was silent.

"You understand?"

He stared at his hands. "And Principessa, Signor Questore?"

"I don't want you thinking your competence is being called into question."

"What are we going to do about Principessa?"

The Questore sat by the bedside. He was wearing a neat blue suit, immaculate and freshly pressed. "Principessa?" His hands lay on his lap. He raised his left hand slightly as a sign that he did not understand.

"Gino's dog."

"The doctors tell me that you should be out of here quite soon. I am relieved. You're a lucky man, Trotti. Lucky to get off with just a broken rib—and slight shock."

"Gino retires at the end of the year—and his dog is dying. Gino needs a dog to get around. And for the company."

"You are in no way responsible for what has happened. Brigadiere Ciuffi was murdered in the course of her duty. All very unfortunate. And sad. There can be no question of your being held responsible. We all know that you are not a man to risk the life of your subalterns."

"Without his job—and without the dog, Gino will have nothing to do—nothing to live for."

"Ciuffi must have stepped back at the wrong moment."

"Gino has told . . ." Trotti lifted his glance. "I beg your pardon?"

"Brigadiere Ciuffi must have stepped back at the wrong moment." A hesitant cough. "The bullet wasn't meant for her."

The smell of the flowers was now sickening. Turning his head, Trotti noticed for the first time there was a box of Swiss chocolates.

"What you need, Trotti, is a rest. Perhaps up in the hills." An indulgent smile. "Don't you have a villa on one of the lakes?"

"Lake Garda, Signor Questore."

"Get away, you need a rest. Go to the lake."

"I'm afraid . . ."

"Or perhaps you would like to go to Bologna to be with your daughter." He smiled. "Dotta e grassa—Bologna, the fat and learned city."

Trotti took the box of chocolates. A picture of the Dolomites on the lid.

"I spoke to Signorina Trotti this morning over the phone. She is very worried about you. I'm sure you would be doing her a service by staying with her."

"There are things I have to do."

A cold edge to his voice. "I don't think you have anything to do—not immediately."

"Things to do here," Trotti said. "Here in the city."

"No, Trotti—I'm afraid I can't allow that."

"Signor Questore—"

The Questore held up his small hand. "Be reasonable." He tried unsuccessfully to return the smile to his face. "I know you too well. I know you better than you know yourself, Trotti. And I know what happened between you and Leonardelli." The Questore glanced at the box of chocolates. "I have nothing but respect for you. You are an honest man."

"A chocolate, Signor Questore?"

"Honest—but rash. And at the present moment, with all of Italy watching us, I cannot allow any lapse of diplomacy."

Trotti was silent.

"You do understand, Trotti, why I'm putting Commissario Merenda in charge of the police enquiries?"

"Merenda?"

"Two months, three months. A well-deserved rest. Time enough for your rib to heal. Time enough for you to get over . . ." The Questore leaned forward, placing his arms on the neat creases of his trousers. "I understand how you feel about Ciuffi. We are all upset about her. She was a woman—but she was more than that. Brigadiere Ciuffi was one of us. A good man—one of the best. Hard-working and good-humored. And above all, she shared all the ideals that for us in the Pubblica Sicurezza are so important. She was one of the team and as her immediate superior . . ."

"Merenda in charge of the enquiry?"

"I know Merenda will get the girl's killer." The Questore took a chocolate in gold wrapping.

"It was me the murderer was aiming at. Me—not Merenda. And now Ciuffi is dead."

A nod as the Questore put the chocolate in his mouth and licked his fingertips. "Ciuffi is dead, Trotti. Nothing that you or I—"

"Ciuffi died instead of me and now I don't give a damn about you or Merenda or d'Avorio. It was me that was supposed to die—the bullets were meant for me. I'm going to find the man who killed Brigadiere Ciuffi." He touched the bandage at his ribs. "If it is the last thing I do, I'm going to find him."

37: Escape

"I'VE BROUGHT SOME clothes."

Trotti could make out her silhouette against the open doorway, the well-kept body and high-heeled shoes. It was dark and the glow of the bedside lamp did not reach the face.

"Magagna phoned you?"

"My husband is not a small man." She stepped carefully past the jars, the vases of flowers and the empty wrappings that littered the floor. She placed a brown parcel on the bed. "You might find them a bit big."

Trotti got slowly out of the bed, shivering slightly, and put on the clothes. Good-quality clothes, a silk shirt and bespoke trousers with lining. Shoes from Varese that pinched his toes.

"How's the rib?"

Trotti said nothing.

"Perhaps you ought to shave, Commissario."

"I'll shave when I get home."

The hospital was asleep.

She took him by the arm and, as they went along the empty corridors, the only sound was the squeaking of his shoes on the rubberized floor. Trotti walked slowly, aware of the pain and trying to ignore it. She supported him with her arm and he could feel the warmth of her body. At the top of the stairs they went past a young nurse who did not even raise her head to look at them.

The marble of the banister was cold beneath his hand.

She opened the doors of Surgery and they stepped out into the chill air of the September night.

"The car's over here." Signora Bianchini walked with him across the road.

"Thanks." He lowered himself into the passenger seat.

She got into the car, sitting behind the steering wheel. "The gentleman on the phone said you might be able to help me."

"Magagna?"

"You will help me?"

The light from the hospital building lit up one side of her face. She turned and faced him.

"I didn't ask Magagna to contact you."

"Where to, Commissario?"

The engine came alive with the soft rumble of German engineering. The outside world was dark through the tinted glass of the windscreen. Trotti closed his eyes and, leaning back, placed his head against the rest.

"Take me home."

"I don't know where you live."

"Via Milano."

She drove the car through the bright pool of neon light at the hospital entrance. The man on the gate came out of his cubicle, lifted the barrier in silence and then returned to where a portable television was flickering.

They left the Policlinico San Matteo, and went over the railway bridge.

Trotti laughed noiselessly. His eyes were still closed.

"What's funny?"

"A lot of people are going to be rather unhappy about my leaving the hospital."

"You don't often laugh."

"I don't have much to laugh about."

"You need to rest, Commissario."

"I haven't got the time."

"I will look after you."

Trotti opened his eyes. "Did Magagna say anything, signora?"

"Magagna?"

"The policeman on the phone. He didn't say that he was going to help?"

"Help who?"

"He is a friend of mine. He used to work in the Questura a few years ago. Now he's with Buoncostume in Milan. I'm going to need all the help I can get if I'm going to find the murderer . . ."

"You're not well—look, you're shivering."

"What did Magagna say?"

Her eyes were on the road. "He just said that you needed clothes."

They went over the canal, past Piazza Castello, which was almost empty, despite the bright cinema lights and the street lamps, towards the Città Giardino.

"Turn left, signora."

Signora Bianchini turned right.

"I said left."

A low, swirling mist clung close to the cobbled surface of the street.

An empty bus went by in the opposite direction.

"You're going the wrong way, Signora Bianchini?

The headlamps of the Audi were reflected in the window of the florist's shop in via Petrarca.

She looked at Trotti. "My husband's clothes suit you, Commissario Trotti."

38: Pisanelli

"NICE PLACE."

"Glad you like it, Pisanelli."

"And a charming lady. I'm sure you must be very happy."

"I won't be happy until I've found the murderer."

"We're all working on it, Commissario."

"All?"

"Everybody." Pisanelli nodded. "And Merenda—"

"I don't give a damn about Merenda." Trotti pulled himself into a sitting position. "I need you, Pisanelli. You can help me find the man."

Pisanelli was carrying his suede jacket over his shoulder. He let it drop over the back of a chair and he sat down on the edge of the bed. The empty coffee cup rattled on the tray.

"Oh, this is for you." He held out a bunch of flowers.

"Did you bring me some clothes?" He held up a brown parcel as he looked around the room. "Where do I put these things?"

"I'm counting on you."

"You don't seem too excited by the flowers."

"I'm excited at the thought of having clothes that'll fit me. Listen, Pisanelli, I'm counting on your support."

Pisanelli placed the parcel on the floor.

"I'm not sure that's a good idea." He dropped the flowers— tight-budded roses of delicate pinks and reds—on to the tray.

"You've always worked with me."

"As far as the Questore is concerned, Commissario, you are out of things."

"Why on earth should I be out of things?"

"You're injured and he wants you to rest."

"There's nothing wrong with me."

Pisanelli tried to smile. "A lot of people think it would be better if you stayed away from the Questura for a few weeks." The face was taut, the eyes without amusement.

"I've got a job to do."

"Commissario . . ."

"Pisanelli, I'm counting on you."

A sudden gesture of impatience. "No."

"But you can tell me what's happening in the Questura."

"I've told you. Merenda's in charge. An all-out search for Ciuffi's murderer."

"But where have you got with the enquiry?"

"I don't know."

"Don't lie to me."

"Commissario, I tell you I don't know."

"The bullet's been identified, for God's sake?"

"Perhaps."

"What do you mean, perhaps?"

Pisanelli stared at the counterpane.

Signora Bianchini had drawn the curtains apart when she had brought Trotti breakfast. Beyond the window, the foothills of the Apennines were turning brown. The air was warm.

"What exactly do you mean, Pisanelli?"

Pisanelli continued to stare at the bed. "You're better off here, Commissario. Stay here and rest. Let the charming lady look after you—she seems to like having you here." He shook his head and the long hair rose slightly from his temples. "Don't you understand that you worry too much? And by worrying, you're not going to solve anything?"

"Galandra killed her."

Pisanelli looked at him. "Galandra?"

Trotti could not repress the triumph in his own voice. "With-out me, you know nothing. You and Merenda and all the others—you don't know what Ciuffi and I were working on, you don't know why we were seeing the old man. How can you conduct your enquiries when you don't know anything about the case?"

"Who's Galandra?"

"The man who watered down the plasma at the hospital. It was thanks to Vardin's testimony that he and his wife were sent to jail." Trotti raised a shoulder—and immediately felt the jab of pain in his ribs. "He got out of jail a few months ago. While you were running up and down the hospital, Ciuffi was putting a file together."

Pisanelli's face seemed to harden, little wrinkles formed around his eyes. "There was a reason for my going to the hospital."

"Galandra threatened Vardin—and knifing his daughter was part of the revenge. Only it wasn't enough."

"Enough, Commissario?"

"Galandra's the murderer—of that I am now sure. Because he had the motive. The motive to hate Vardin enough—to hurt his daughter and then to shoot at him. Only he didn't hit Vardin. He hit the girl."

"But Commissario, there were people in Borgo Genovese."

"Eyewitnesses?"

"After a fashion."

"Where were they?"

"On the other side of the river."

"And what did they see?"

"Nobody heard the gunfire—or rather those people who did hear something just thought it was a car backfiring. But you know Borgo Genovese, the road that runs along the river is a cul-de-sac. It turns into a path."

"What did these people see?"

"Nothing."

"My God." Trotti thumped his hand down on to the bed and the cup jumped, toppled and the dregs of the coffee ran on to the stalks of the roses. "What eyewitnesses are they supposed to be if they didn't see anything?"

"But that's the point."

"Don't talk in riddles."

"A man would have been noticed. Anybody going to Borgo Genovese would have had to go past several houses. And all the witnesses are agreed that they saw nobody."

"The gunman must have run off in the other direction . . . along the path."

"Possible." Pisanelli shrugged. "But not very likely. Where would he have left his car? Or do you think that he would have left his car a kilometer away and walked all the way along the river? With a rifle under his arm?"

Trotti shook his head.

Pisanelli lifted the bunch of flowers and carefully wiped their stalks with a soggy paper napkin.

"I know Galandra killed Ciuffi—and I'm going to find him. And I need you, Pisanelli. I can't drive in this state and I've got to go to Verona."

"Why Verona?"

"That's where Galandra was in jail."

"Some rest, Commissario—that's what you need."

"Don't you care about Ciuffi? Don't you care that she was slaughtered like an animal?"

"You must rest."

"You never did like Ciuffi, did you?"

"You're not acting rationally, Commissario."

"Galandra attacked the child. Of that I am sure. And in trying to kill Vardin, he murdered Ciuffi. And nearly murdered me."

Pisanelli shook his head. "No."

"Pisanelli, I need you."

"Galandra never attacked anybody."

"All part of his revenge against Vardin."

"Yesterday, Colonello Vincenzo had one of his men arrested. A conscript with a record of rape and physical violence on women."

"Not possible."

"And they found the knife he used on the little Vardin girl. It was under his mattress in the Cairoli barracks."

39: Meeting

"YOU SHOULDN'T HAVE lied."

"I didn't lie."

They were sitting in the public gardens behind the civic museum.

Little children played on the grass and in the balding sandpit. Mothers watched or talked or read photo romances.

Signorina Podestà had crossed her ankles and was looking at her shoes. She did not wear stockings and her legs were very white. Red spots showed where she had taken a razor to the leg hairs.

"Signorina, you were not attacked. There was no rapist."

She turned her head. "What do you know?"

"Still not enough. That is why I am trying to get at the truth."

"I can't help you."

"I know that you can."

"Leave me alone, can't you? Why did you send that woman to find me? And why are we talking here?"

"Because I wanted to save you the embarrassment of being interrogated in front of your colleagues in the insurance office."

"I would have come to the Questura."

"It's now that I have to speak to you. I can't wait—or perhaps you don't understand."

"I understand that you are accusing me of lying. You are intimidating me. You are preventing me from getting on with my job. I don't like your attitude. I am a woman of the twentieth century and I am not going to put up with this kind of bullying from a man."

"The young policewoman who interrogated you is now dead."

Signorina Podestà blinked her bulging eyes.

"Murdered, signorina. Murdered in cold blood."

"I must get back to the office."

A squirrel had come out from hiding behind the granite memorial to Garibaldi and was worrying at a twig. It looked at Trotti with small brown eyes and twitched its nose in disapproval.

"Are you going to answer my questions?"

"You can't make me."

"Or do you want to be involved in a murder enquiry?"

Trotti was surprised to see that there was a hint of rouge on the pale cheeks.

"There's nothing I can tell you."

"How long have you been sleeping with him?"

She did not answer. "How long have you been sleeping with Riccardo?"

She had started to blush—a deep crimson blush that moved upwards over the pale face. "Mind your own business."

"Riccardo Bianchini."

A moment of hesitation, the eyes blinking. "I know nobody of that name."

"He has been sleeping with you these last few nights, hasn't he?"

She looked down at her hands, loosely clasping the handbag.

"It doesn't worry you that his own mother doesn't know where he is—that she worries because he no longer comes home?"

"My private life has nothing to do with you."

"Or perhaps you really believe that it is love."

"Love?"

"Perhaps you really believe that there is something between you and a boy half your age. Perhaps you really believe that there is a future for you—and that is why you are willing to perjure yourself, perhaps even risk a jail sentence."

"Riccardo . . ."

"Riccardo is still a child—he is only just eighteen."

"Eighteen and no longer a minor."

"You admit you know him?"

"I admit nothing. And I don't like the way—"

"I don't give a damn. Believe me, I don't give a damn what you do or what you think or who you are in love with, who you want to sleep with. But I do give a damn about Signorina Ciuffi—because she was a friend of mine and because she is now dead." He added, "Murdered."

Trotti caught his breath and then they sat in silence on the cold stone bench. It was nearly four o'clock and the sun had lost much of its harshness. A couple of wool-like clouds in the sky. Garibaldi stood with a foot forward and his eyes staring towards the city, his red shirt transformed into a dark grey granite.

Two little boys were shrieking in the sandpit, while a dog watched them in silent envy. The distant hum of traffic.

Beyond the park gate, Trotti could just make out the white Audi.

"The lady who came to fetch you in your office—she is Riccardo's mother."

"Riccardo is an adult."

His ribs hurt—a dull, sullen pain. "He is her only child."

"Riccardo loves me." She turned her head and Trotti was surprised by the calmness that the woman showed. "You can't understand that, can you, Commissario? You can't understand how a young man can be interested in an older woman. But Riccardo is. Riccardo loves me, you see. And I love him."

"And that is why you lied? That is why you invented your rapist?"

"We are going to get married."

"I am pleased for you."

Signorina Podestà blinked.

"But I don't think you can have much faith in him if you feel you have to lie."

"Riccardo is in love with me."

"You know that he used to be friends with the Vardin girl. And you don't trust him. You love him, but you don't trust him."

"Of course I trust him."

"Then why the lies?"

"Lies, Commissario?"

"It is precisely because you think he attacked the girl that you try to protect him. And the best way of protecting Riccardo is by creating another rapist."

"I love Riccardo."

"I don't care who you love or what you do or anything. Do you understand? I don't care. I just don't want you to lie to me."

"I never lied. I am a woman of my word."

"Of course you lied."

"I love Riccardo, Commissario."

"And where is he now?"

"Are you looking for the girl's killer—or Riccardo?"

"I need to know why you felt you had to protect him."

"Riccardo is impetuous."

"You read about the little girl in the *Provincia*—and you must have known that Riccardo had been seeing her sister. But why go to all the length of inventing your little story."

"Commissario, I am entering my fifth decade. I am no longer the young and dynamic woman that I once was. Even though I consider myself as a woman of my epoch, I have made mistakes and I cannot afford to waste any more time. Before long, I will be losing my beauty—you know that life is not kind to women. Perhaps Riccardo is young, perhaps he has still to grow up. But he loves me. He is old enough and intelligent enough to see in me a woman of her century—an emancipated and intelligent woman."

Trotti nodded.

"His love is something that I cannot afford to throw away."

"You suspect him of attacking the little girl?"

"Don't ask me that question, Commissario."

Sitting on the bench in the municipal gardens, the spinster with the bulging eyes had started to cry.

40: Road

"WITH HER?"

"Why not?"

"But the Podestà woman's not even attractive."

"At Riccardo's age, I don't think a man really cares."

"But . . ."

"She's ugly, perhaps—but she will do anything for him. And she will sleep with him."

"You are disgusting."

"Realistic, Signora Bianchini."

"You are disgusting. I know Riccardo and I know he is a good boy. And at least the Vardin child is of his own age. For all her vulgarity, Netta Vardin has got a pretty little face. A pretty, stupid little face."

Trotti made a gesture with two outstretched fingers. "But she won't screw."

Signora Bianchini took her foot off the accelerator and pulled the Audi on to the shoulder of the highway. The car came to a standstill near one of the blue Fiat road signs, indicating that Milan was forty-three kilometers behind them to the west. "You can get out of this car."

"That won't help."

"Get out."

"No."

"I do not appreciate obscenity and I will not have you insult my son. He is not an animal." The corner of her lip quivered. "And he is not interested in such . . . such carnal things."

"I'm in a hurry to get to Verona."

The traffic rumbled past, the articulated trucks shaking the Audi as they ploughed their way towards Brescia, Verona and Venice, the Adriatic and Yugoslavia. The blue-grey fumes of unburnt petrol hung over the road and the polluted edges of the fields of maize.

Somewhere in the distance, beyond the fields and the motionless plane trees, there stood the green cupola of a village church.

In a voice that was little more than a whisper, the woman asked, "Why are you so spiteful, Commissario?"

"I am honest."

"Have I not helped you? Did I not take you to my place, let you rest? Did I not give you food and attention?"

"I never asked to go to your house."

"And am I not driving you to Verona?"

"Perhaps you haven't got anything better to do."

"You are ungrateful."

"Cynical. I have been a police officer for too long to believe in disinterested generosity. You need me—because I can be useful to you."

"I want to help you—and I want to help Riccardo. But believe me, there's no pleasure for me in taking you to Verona."

"I think there is."

She did not look at him. "You are a powerful man, Commissario, with a lot of people working for you. Why ask me to take you? Why not go with one of your policemen?"

"Symbiosis—we can be mutually useful to each other."

"You are devoid of feeling."

"Tell me, signora, why you try to convince yourself that your son did not attack the little Vardin girl."

"You know as well as I do that Riccardo didn't attack her, Commissario."

"I know that Signorina Podestà has been trying to protect him. She thought he attacked the girl, and that's why she invented another rapist—to put us off the track."

"Riccardo wouldn't hurt anybody."

"Then why doesn't he talk to me?"

"Perhaps . . ."

"Why is he hiding? Why hasn't he been home these last few days?"

"Hiding?"

She was wearing the sunglasses and he was struck by the beauty of her face. Beautiful but distant, the beauty of a doll. Again the memory of Ciuffi jabbed like a cold syringe at his heart.

Signora Bianchini turned. "You are not really interested in Riccardo, Commissario. You know he never touched the girl. The interview with the ugly woman—it's all a trick, isn't it?"

Trotti remained silent.

"Why did you ask me to take you to Verona?"

"There is somebody I must see."

"It's not Riccardo you're interested in at all."

He looked through the tinted glass at the endless stream of passing vehicles. In the opposite direction, beyond the skimpy barrier of blighted oleander, a Carabinieri Alfa Romeo flashed past, its siren squealing and the blue light revolving urgently.

With a sigh, Signora Bianchini put the car into gear. After waiting for a gap in the flow of traffic, she pulled out on to the autostrada.

"And I know it's not me you're interested in, Commissario. You don't find me attractive."

41: The Lake

IT WAS LATE and yet Trotti insisted that they leave the auto-strada and take the smooth road down to Desenzano and Lake Garda.

It was nearly a year since Trotti had been back to the lake, and he found himself excited just at the thought of seeing it again.

Lights had come on along the lakeside and were reflected in the rippleless water. To the north, the pre-Alps and Monte Baldo were lost in the failing light. As the Audi followed the long line of cypress trees, Trotti saw a motor launch making its steady way towards Sirmione.

Garda.

Self-pity, perhaps, or just the sense that he was growing old while Lake Garda remained unchanged, timeless. Whatever the reason, Trotti resented the pang of sharp regret that rose in his throat with an almost physical reality.

For a moment he was tempted to tell Signora Bianchini to turn the car around, to take them to Gardesana and the Villa Ondina. They would sit on the wooden pontoon and look out over the water at the shadow of Monte Baldo. And he would feel—for a moment, or for an evening—that he, too, like the lake, was untouched by time.

Trotti wanted to say something but then it was too late and they were entering the outskirts of Verona.

"Where are we going to spend the night?"

"We, Signora Bianchini?"

She turned and looked him. "Now we've arrived, you're sending the chauffeur back home?"

It was the end of the opera season and as they got closer to the city center and the Roman arena, the more pedestrians there seemed to be. Women with silver handbags and flowing evening robes, men in bow ties and tortoise-shell glasses. Some carried instrument cases. The gelaterias and the neon-lit cafes were all doing brisk business. Carabinieri in khaki uniform and riding boots walked along the pavement, heedless of the admiring glances that they attracted. There were other policemen on horseback.

Signora Bianchini found a parking place near the Ponte Nuovo and together they went for supper.

"You still haven't answered my question, Commissario."

"Question?"

"Where are we spending the night? I imagine you have friends in the Questura here . . . ?"

"I phoned before leaving. There is a hotel in via Pigna."

"A hotel?"

"You don't mind, I hope. It's not the most expensive, but it's clean."

"And where am I sleeping? We're not sleeping in the same room?"

Trotti laughed. "The idea frightens you."

"What sort of woman do you take me for?"

"In the car you said that I wasn't interested in you."

"I wonder if all policemen are the same."

"The same in what way?"

"You are a cold man."

He put down his knife and fork and sipped some mineral water.

Embedded in one wall was a natural fountain that poured an unending stream of water into a thick, carved marble basin. The Ristorante Fontanella was small, and reluctantly Trotti had agreed to an indoor table because all the tables on the terrace had been taken by Scandinavian tourists—blond young men and women in pastel clothes.

She sat back—Signora Bianchini had eaten the spaghetti alla veronese with considerable appetite—and looked at him. The wall-lighting made shadows that softened her face, that accentuated her appearance of youth. "Why did you bring me here?"

Thirty-eight years old. A beautiful woman in the bloom of her life. Trotti looked admiringly at the long, delicate fingers on the tablecloth. He smiled. "You're the chauffeur."

"You think that I'm involved, don't you?"

"I don't think anything."

"You think I'm trying to protect my son."

"That would be quite normal."

"And you think that somehow I am connected with the death of the girl."

"Why do you say that?"

"Don't you, Commissario?"

"Don't I what?"

"You believe I won't stop at anything to protect my son."

Trotti shrugged.

"Well?"

"Riccardo is all that you have."

"You think that I knew about the shooting down on the river."

"Listen—you came to the hospital. You took me to your house. I didn't ask for that. I never asked Magagna to contact you—and there was no reason for you to want to help me."

"You never give a straight answer, Commissario."

The serving girl came to take their plates.

With an empty table between them, neither Trotti nor Signora Bianchini spoke for several minutes. He looked at her graceful hands.

"What is it you want, Commissario?"

He smiled, feeling the muscles pulling at his eyes. "I have been asked to take a holiday."

"You need rest. I can understand that."

"Mine is not an official enquiry. At this moment, I should be lying in bed, watching twenty different channels on my TV."

She had raised one hand to her throat.

"The Questore doesn't want me interfering with the enquiry into Ciuffi's death."

"But why Verona?"

"Somebody that I have got to see—somebody who can help me find Ciuffi's murderer."

"Then I really am just the chauffeur?"

Trotti looked into the almond eyes.

42: Melbourne University

"NEVER REALLY LIKED Italian opera—too much shouting."

"Then what do you like?"

The journalist shrugged but did not reply.

MacSmith had aged since Trotti had last seen him, and put on weight. More flesh to the chin, the long hair had started to go grey and the bags under the eyes bore witness to too much alcohol and too many cigarettes.

"You smoke, Trotti?"

Trotti shook his head. "I gave it up."

"Lucky man." MacSmith grinned, letting the smoke of the Marlboro flood through his nostrils. "What are you drinking?" He nodded towards the empty coffee cup.

He was an Australian. Many years previously he had taught English in a language school. Then there had been a strike of the teachers and MacSmith had submitted a series of articles to a London-based educational newspaper. The start of a career as a foreign correspondent. Now he was the stringer for several Australian and American newspapers. Over the years he had moved away from education, specializing in crime. Political crime, industrial espionage, the Mafia, the Years of Lead and carbonized corpses—English-speaking readers had an insatiable appetite for Italian violence. MacSmith had slowly built up the reputation as a reliable, well-informed journalist. He had developed a wide circle of contacts. He had worked in Sardinia and Sicily. He had even gotten to be friends with a killer in Palermo. The resulting article had won a prize in New York.

(It was believed that in 1977 there had been an attempt on his life. Shots were fired through his front door at a time when MacSmith was researching into a leak of toxic gas from a Swiss-owned factory in the Brianza. MacSmith gave a dossier to his lawyer with the instructions that it should be sent to the newspapers in the event of his untimely death. There were no more shootings, but on two separate occasions MacSmith was refused entry into Switzerland.)

MacSmith had an easy manner and a slow, stumbling way of speaking Italian that belied a sharp mind and an impressive memory.

Trotti had first met MacSmith in Bologna. In those days, MacSmith had been thin, poor and poorly dressed. Now he had a large belly that pushed at the buckle of his corduroy trousers. His clothes were of good quality, although they had acquired a look of shabbiness.

"Another coffee, Trotti?"

"No thanks."

"Or you'll join me in a grappa?"

Trotti shook his head.

MacSmith called the thin waiter, who removed the dirty cups.

"And how's the family? Your daughter must be quite a big girl now." He smiled. "I can never remember that strange name of hers."

"Pioppi's studying in Bologna."

"Married?"

A toneless voice, "She has a boyfriend."

"She was a delightful little girl. So fond of her father. So proud of him."

"My wife has left me. She's now living in America."

"Sorry to hear that." MacSmith took the cigarette from his mouth. "You get back to Bologna ever?"

"Don't have the time."

"A city I miss—the food, the people. I miss the Emilia."

"You're better off here in Verona."

"Verona?" More smoke from his nostrils. "Not my favorite city."

"An attractive place."

"If you don't have to live here."

"I find it very civilized."

"Verona must be the only city in Italy without a pedestrian precinct."

Trotti laughed. "That's important?"

MacSmith raised an eyebrow. "Do you still cycle to work, Trotti?"

"I'm getting old—and fat."

"After Peking, Parma has the highest number of bicycles per inhabitant." There was an awkward silence. "But Parma is in Emilia—and here we are in the Veneto. I miss Emilia—Bologna, Modena, Parma—even Piacenza which has now become little more than a suburb of Milan. The Emilians are lively, full-blooded. But here in the Veneto, the people are mean and hypocritical. Fervent church-goers, mind, and anti-Communist. Wealthy peasants." The Australian took the cigarette from his mouth. "Culture, the opera, the tradition of music? A shopping mall. That's what Verona is really. Culture? An endless string of shoe shops and boutiques. Benetton and Timberland."

"All good for business."

MacSmith laughed. "You know the business of Verona?"

"An international opera? It must bring in a lot of money."

"Drugs, Commissario. We have the highest percentage of addicts in the entire peninsula. And the easy money you see—it's not from the opera." He gestured with his thumb. "Go down to the river at night—and you can see them, the addicts, huddling together for warmth."

"As in any other Italian city."

"The kids of the wealthy—that's okay. Their parents can get them into clinics and have them looked after. But there are the rest, too. Working-class people, out of work and with no future—other than hepatitis, or an overdose. Or AIDS." There was no humor in his brown, tired eyes. He looked at Trotti, his head to one side and the smoke rising from the cigarette towards the dark awning of the terrace.

"It gives you something to write about."

MacSmith stubbed out his cigarette. "What can I do for you, Trotti?"

Piazza delle Erbe, ten o'clock in the morning.

The winged lion of the Venetian republic—*la Serenissima*—stood proudly atop its column, a rain-stained paw placed on the open book. Behind it, the Palazzo Maffei was being restored and cleaned. Scaffolding had been set up and a green net—it looked like a mosquito net—spread the length of the scaffolding to retain the dust and rubble.

Reaching towards the sky, like a sturdy tree determined to survive, the Gardello tower rose above the green netting.

The waiter brought MacSmith's drink.

"Sure you don't want some grappa, Trotti?"

"I had breakfast in the hotel."

The sound of a pneumatic drill was hardly audible against the noise in the piazza. Permanent canvas roofs protected the various stands—sausages, cheeses, wines, old detective magazines, doughnuts. Tourists wandered aimlessly backwards and forward, mixing with the Veronese housewives and the amiable merchants.

"Where are you staying?"

"Via Pigna."

"You could've stayed at my place."

"I'm with a friend."

"A lady friend?" MacSmith raised an eyebrow. "Congratulations." He swallowed a thirsty gulp of grappa.

"You were married once, I seem to remember."

The dark eyes watered. "What do you want from me, Trotti?"

"You heard about the murdered policewoman?"

"I got your message."

"A man called Galandra. I think he may be involved directly or indirectly in the girl's death."

"Galandra?"

"He got seven years for watering down blood and selling it at the Policlinico San Matteo."

"In your city?"

Trotti nodded.

"What's that got to do with me—or with Verona?"

"He was in prison here."

"So what?" A tone of aggression had crept into MacSmith's Australian accent.

"You can help me."

He held up the glass. "You're paying for the drinks?"

"Official channels are temporarily closed to me."

MacSmith laughed unexpectedly and the bags beneath his eyes seemed to have a movement of their own.

From the Piazza dei Signori came the sound of a church bell.

43: Dresden

SHE HAD PUT a woollen shawl over the gently tanned skin.

"I thought Pisanelli was a friend."

"Who's Pisanelli?"

"He works with me in the Questura."

"Have I met him?"

"He came to your house, signora. He brought the flowers."

"He was the same man who phoned me?"

"No—that was Magagna."

The arena was always full for the operas, particularly the Puccini and Verdi. Now only the bank of seats directly opposite the stage was filled. All the scenery from *Aida* had been removed—sphinxes that sprawled nonchalantly into the streets around the arena—and in its place five columns supported a strange, undulating canopy that appeared to be made out of polystyrene foam. Beneath this temporary roof, the chairs in the bright light were empty, awaiting the arrival of the orchestra. The music stands were barren, like skeletons, without their scores.

An atmosphere of expectation.

Old men were selling cushions to the latecomers. The ancient, weather-worn tiers of steps where Trotti and Signora Bianchini sat were hard. Without a cushion, the stone was cold. There was more comfortable seating nearer the stage. Chairs—and even armchairs—in the stalls, to which the elegant concert-goers were escorted by officials in tails and bow ties. Red carpets that silenced the discreet footfalls.

"What do you want from Pisanelli?"

"From Pisanelli, I expect help."

"But you yourself say that your enquiry is not official. I imagine he has other things to do."

"That doesn't mean he has to work with Merenda."

"Who's Merenda?"

"Pisanelli has been with me for more than five years—and we get on well together. Merenda is only—"

"If Pisanelli has a job to do, you can't really expect him—"

"Pisanelli knows how I feel about Ciuffi."

"And Merenda is in charge of the official enquiry?"

"Yes."

"Then is there any need for Pisanelli to help you?"

"Pisanelli and I have always worked together."

"You are not working now, Commissario."

"I need his help."

The lights around the arena began to dim; spotlights turned towards the orchestra. There was clapping and then the musicians filed like penguins into the floodlit oasis beneath the strange roof.

"I left a message for him to contact me in the hotel."

"And?"

"Nothing."

The Dresden Orchestra.

Schubert's *Unfinished Symphony* and, beside him, Trotti felt Signora Bianchini's body swaying gently with the rhythm. Overhead in a now cloudless sky, the stars glittered. The smell of Signora Bianchini's perfume seemed to be an extension of the music, part of it.

Applause.

A woman with an English name came on to the stage. The conductor held her hand and there was more clapping. The woman faced the audience and sang. Strauss, the last lieder. Music both beautiful and sad.

Trotti could sense a change in Signora Bianchini and he found his own thoughts returning to the pain in his ribs. Instead of the

German orchestra, before his eyes, he saw the image of Ciuffi's face.

The lights came on.

When Signora Bianchini turned to look at him, she was frowning.

"You are not listening, are you, Commissario?"

"Of course."

"Let's go."

"You do not like the music?"

"Let's go."

They climbed up the several rows of seating—twice she turned to look over her shoulder—and then they took the long, broad stairs that carried them out on to the piazza.

"You want to go back to the hotel?"

"Ponderous German music." She slipped her arm through his.

"The hotel—or perhaps a nightcap in Piazza delle Erbe?"

They went past the brightly lit shops in Corso Mazzini, pushing and jostling their way through tourists strolling, window shopping, eating ices and enjoying the cool evening air.

Suddenly she stopped outside a bookshop and stepped into the small portico. Signora Bianchini bent forward and for a moment he thought she was studying the book display—several photographs of Umbria, advertising a guidebook of the Touring Club Italiano.

She had not released his arm.

"We must hurry. The bars in Piazza delle Erbe will be closing."

"You can't feel it, Commissario Trotti?"

"Feel what?"

Instinctively she rubbed at her shoulders. "Feel it in your back."

"What?"

Her voice was very low but hoarse. "We're being watched. In the audience—there was somebody behind us and he was watching us."

"Who?"

"Watching us—and he followed us out of the arena when we left."

44: Room

"I CAN'T SLEEP."

For a moment, Trotti hesitated. Then he stepped back. "You'd better come in."

She was wearing the shawl over her nightdress. A brief smile. "You do understand, don't you, Commissario?"

"I had just dozed off."

"By myself I'm afraid."

"I have a lot of things to do tomorrow."

"You must think I am a foolish woman."

He shrugged. "You can use the other bed if you wish, signora." He closed the door and turned the key. Signora Bianchini watched Trotti in silence.

There was a folded blanket in the wardrobe. He took the blanket and, opening it, placed it on the smooth bedsheets.

"Afraid I'm going to be cold?"

"I sleep with the window open."

"You think this is all a trick, don't you? You think I just want to sleep with you."

"An old man with a broken rib?"

"I don't like that room—and I don't like being alone."

"There's nothing to be afraid of."

"There was a man—of that I am certain." She pulled the shawl to her throat. "I saw him in the Roman arena. He had a program in front of his face but he was watching us. It was like a gimlet in my back. And when we left, I am certain he followed us."

"Nobody knows we're here."

She climbed into bed.

Trotti waited until she had pulled the blanket up over her shoulders before turning out the bedside lamp.

Outside the occasional car and the permanent, lulling rush of the Adige, swollen with the first autumnal rains, running towards the sea.

Signora Bianchini spoke. She had turned in the opposite direction and her voice was muffled.

"Please try to sleep, signora."

"I'm not scared here." She moved her head on the pillow. "Not here with you."

Trotti stared at the ceiling, at the reflected lights of the city moving towards the lightbulb.

"It is kind of you to put up with me like this." A light laugh. "There are times when you are almost human."

"Thanks."

"And then there are times when you are worse than a monster."

"I should like to sleep, signora."

"That's what you need . . ." Her voice part muffled by the pillow. "You need someone to look after you."

"Signora . . ."

"You've never thought of getting married again, Commissario?"

"There will be time enough in the morning for matrimonial counselling."

"Perhaps I was wrong. Perhaps you are interested in me as a woman but—"

"Interested in getting some rest."

"You really don't like me?"

He turned his head.

"You don't like me, do you, Commissario?"

He could see the whiteness of her face and the shadows of her eyes.

"That's not what Brigadiere Ciuffi thought."

"The dead girl?"

"Ciuffi didn't like the way I ate your truffles." He propped himself up on an elbow and switched on the bedside lamp. It threw its pink glow over the neat hotel room.

Signora Bianchini was smiling.

"Please, signora, let me get some sleep."

"You talk like an old man."

"If it is necessary, I will go and sleep in your bedroom."

"Stay with me, Commissario. I am scared."

"You must keep quiet." He switched off the lamp. "Goodnight, signora."

"I am cold."

A sigh of exasperation. "I will close the window."

"You don't understand."

"It's nearly two o'clock in the morning."

"You see people as enigmas—or as numbers. But you don't see them as human beings. A woman is not a machine—a woman is a human being who needs affection."

"Goodnight, Signora Bianchini."

"Why did you bring me here, Commissario? Two days in your company—and I still don't know what you want."

"I want to sleep."

"A stubborn man." Signora Bianchini sat up in her bed. "You are not making things any easier for me. Can't I—"

There was a light knocking on the hotel door.

Signora Bianchini held the bedsheet to her throat.

A man's voice. "Are you there, Trotti?"

45: Man

"A TURD."

"Why?"

Soldati laughed. Not a pleasant laugh but a laugh that turned down the corners of the small, bruised mouth. Short lips, dark stubble and furtive eyes whose glance, behind the smudged glass, darted from Trotti's face to the continual flow of customers.

"Why is Galandra a turd?" Trotti glanced down. The digital readout registered two units.

"Haven't seen him in more than three years."

"You didn't like him?"

"At first he was all right—but that was when he was new in Santa Cecilia." A grim smile behind the glass. "That was before I found out what he was really like."

"What sort of person is he?"

"A turd."

Trotti tightened his hold on the mouthpiece. "Why didn't you like him?"

"I just told you that at first he was okay."

"Then what happened?"

A pause.

Trotti repeated his question. "What happened?"

"The English journalist said you were going to pay me."

"Of course."

"Three hundred and fifty."

"Tell me about Galandra, Soldati."

"You're going to pay me?"

"If you don't give the information, I won't pay anything."

"I can tell you all that you need to know."

"Hurry up, Soldati," Trotti said tersely. "I'm paying for this call."

A harsh, rasping laugh. "The Pubblica Sicurezza can afford that, I think."

From the other side of the glass, Trotti saw the man's eyes wrinkle in amusement. A face that was neither cunning nor stupid. A face that was pale from a life spent indoors.

Trotti waited, but there was just the crackle over the line.

"You shared a cell with him, Soldati?"

"Too damned cramped."

"How long were you together?"

"Together?"

"You and Galandra?"

"We got on well—until the fight."

"How long were you in the same cell?"

"On and off for over two years."

"What was the fight about?"

"I cut him a bit."

Three units and the colons blinked with each second.

"What for?"

"Nothing serious. But he deserved it." The same laugh. "I didn't even leave a scar."

"Why did you fight with Galandra, Soldati?"

"My name is Signor Soldati."

Although the two cabins were less than five meters apart, the line was far from good and it was only by looking at Soldati and seeing the movement of his lips that Trotti could understand what the man was saying.

"Signor Soldati, why did you fight with Galandra?"

"At least he wasn't a queer." A derisive gesture of the free hand to his ear. "Then I'd've cut his balls off."

"Why did you fight?"

"Because he was a two-faced bastard, that's why."

"What did he do to you?"

"No more than what he did to everybody else." A spitting sound. "A bastard, a sly bastard."

"Did Galandra tell you about the plasma—about how he'd been watering down blood at the Policlinico?"

"He said it was a frame-up."

"And you believed him?"

"I told you—Galandra was a turd."

Four units, in a blinking quartz green.

"Did Galandra ever mention Vardin?"

"Who?"

"Vardin? The porter at the AVIS institute?"

"You mean the plasma thing?"

Trotti nodded.

People—young men in their uniform tight jeans and several tourists in bright summer clothes—were forming a queue at the cash counter. Trotti's view of the other man was blocked. "Yes, the plasma thing."

"He said it was a frame-up."

"What was a frame-up?"

"He was going to get his revenge."

The queue at the counter moved forward, letting Trotti catch sight of Soldati again. The pale face was looking at Trotti.

"Galandra told you he was going to get his revenge?"

"After the riot, I didn't believe anything he said." A pause. "A turd and a liar."

"But he told you about Vardin?"

"After the riot there were a lot of people who wanted to get even with your friend."

Trotti said, "Galandra is not my friend."

"Policemen are turds."

"A different class of turd, Signor Soldati."

"But still turds."

"You want the money?"

A cough.

"The choice is yours—three hundred and fifty or else I put this telephone down."

"The journalist said you would pay me." He added lamely, "I need that money."

"You must tell me the truth."

"Not my fault if I hate the bastard. He would use anybody if there was something in it for him. He'd sell his own mother." A click of the tongue. "Galandra's a turd."

"What did Galandra say about Vardin?"

"You've got the three hundred and fifty thousand lire?" The voice was ingratiating.

"Of course."

"The journalist didn't say you were with the Pubblica Sicurezza. Not that I care, of course—but it's just that—"

"You'll be paid. Just tell me what you know."

"He always lied."

"Galandra?"

A nod from the other side of the glass. "We thought that he was with us. When there was first talk of a demonstration—you ever been inside, you know what the food is like? But I keep forgetting you're a turd of a cop."

"A turd with money in his pocket."

"Things were getting impossible at Santa Cecilia, people were falling ill because they weren't getting a decent meal. And when there was talk of taking action, Galandra was in the front line." A dry laugh. "Oh, yes—he was all for doing something. He was good at talking. And after talking to us, he talked to the warders. Galandra was the one who kept the warders informed." He placed his hand on the glass window—pale, outspread fingers. "If you see Signor Galandra, you can tell him from me that he'd better keep out of my way. My way and the way of thirty or forty other old friends from Santa Cecilia."

"He rioted?"

"Of course not—it was just part of his plan. What better way to get remission than by spying on his fellow prisoners?"

"And it worked?"

"He made a lot of enemies."

"When did Galandra leave?"

"I was given an extra six months. You realize that? And you think it's easy for a man to find a job after that?"

"When did Galandra get out?"

"He was hoping for remission—but I don't know if he got it. After the riot, they sent him to Modena—he wasn't safe at Santa Cecilia. The last I saw of him was about three years ago. And the extra six months—it was his fault."

"Before you quarreled, what did he tell you about himself?"

"We didn't quarrel—I didn't see him after the riot. Because if I did, I would have perforated his rectum."

"Did Galandra ever say what he was going to do once he got out?"

"A divorce." The man had turned his back and was now speaking into the phone, with his shoulders hunched. The shoulders moved with amusement.

"But he didn't say where he was going?"

"He's got a sister, hasn't he?"

"Where?"

"Get even on the bastard that had put him away. And then hole up with his sister in Bergamo. That's what he said he would do. Get back some of the money he was owed."

"Money he was owed?"

"They'd been working together. It was a business arrangement."

"Who?"

"You knew that, didn't you? They'd been working together."

"Who was working with Galandra?"

"Working together and then the porter got greedy—or perhaps just plain scared. Either way, Galandra was set up. The bastard handed Galandra over, hook, line and sinker." A laugh and a movement of the shoulders. "Unreliable—a liar and a spy, Galandra, and he would use anybody—but when the porter at the AVIS did the same thing to him, then he was furious. His so-called business associate." More laughter. "God knows why you want to see Galandra." A sound of spitting into the telephone. "One of the Creator's mistakes."

"Worse even than a cop?"

"A turd. A real turd."

46: Vermouth

"VERMOUTH?"

Trotti shook his head.

MacSmith shrugged his narrow shoulders, poured two glasses, then returned the cap to the sugar-encrusted bottle-top.

He drank. "So what are you going to do?"

"See Vardin."

"Go back and you'll be out of action. The Questore will see to that. He'll make sure you stay put." It was Spadano who spoke. He sat back in the leather armchair. He held his glass of vermouth in one hand. A cloud of smoke rose from the stub of his cigar. "The Questore's not overjoyed by the way you've disappeared, Trotti."

"What am I supposed to do?"

Spadano laughed.

"Vardin lied," Trotti said.

"So what?"

"All along Vardin knew who was behind the attack on his daughter."

"Why does it bother you, Trotti?"

"It bothered Ciuffi."

"Ciuffi's dead."

"I don't like being lied to."

"You're not going to bring Ciuffi back to life."

"Vardin is responsible for Ciuffi's death. Because of his lies."

Spadano shrugged.

"If I had had just the slightest inkling of what was happening, Ciuffi would be alive today." Trotti turned from Spadano to MacSmith. "You can understand that?"

"You expect Vardin to tell you that he had collaborated with Galandra? Collaborated with a man who had just spent more than seven years in jail?"

"Vardin knew who attacked his child. He knew it was Galandra."

"You're not being realistic."

"Ciuffi would still be alive."

"Not realistic and enjoying wallowing in your guilt."

"Ciuffi was killed because she was working for me."

"How could you have known that Galandra was going to take a shot at Vardin?"

"I should've guessed."

Spadano took the cigar from his mouth, blew smoke from his lips and then swallowed the remaining vermouth. His eyes remained on Trotti. "How were you supposed to know that Galandra would start shooting the minute you and Ciuffi turned up?"

Trotti stood up and went to the window, breathing in the fresh air.

MacSmith's apartment was at the top of an old building and the small attic window gave on to the red roofs of Verona, a network of nearly deserted streets and the hurrying, muddy Adige.

It was mid-morning, but already the atmosphere in the room was thick with the smoke of MacSmith's Marlboro and Spadano's Toscani cigars. A small room, almost claustrophobic with its stacked, sagging bookshelves and the dusty, engraved prints on the walls. Old Piranesi prints and maps in Latin of the Americas. Everything in the room appeared old—even antique—except for the red telephone on the desk, and next to it, the portable computer.

"You checked for me?" Trotti turned to face Spadano.

"Checked?"

"On Primula Rosa. Isn't that why you came knocking on the door after midnight?"

"You asked me for a favor, Trotti."

"I don't imagine you came to see who I was sleeping with."

A smile that seemed to run parallel to the line of his crew-cut. Short, grey, well-cut hair. "I liked what I saw. Nice tits. And broad hips."

"Primula Rosa, Spadano?" Trotti said.

"I haven't been able to find anything on Primula Rosa."

"Thanks for the favor."

"The deaths at Santa Maria are coincidental, whatever the priest likes to think. Even if we do find this Primula Rosa of yours, it's not going to change anything."

Trotti looked out over the roofs. He could just make out the grey walls of the arena. "You know, when I took the train at Voghera, I'm pretty certain I saw Signora Bianchini in the station bar."

"You've had ample time to ask Signora Bianchini about these things. Ample time—and where better than in bed?"

Trotti spun round. "You saw her?"

"A beautiful woman."

"How did you know I was with Signora Bianchini?"

"You're a lucky man, Trotti."

"You've been following me."

Spadano smiled enigmatically.

"Why have you been following us?"

"I must be jealous of your success, Trotti."

"It was you who followed us to the opera?"

"You go to the opera, Trotti?"

"You were following us. I went with Signora Bianchini to the arena and you were following us."

"Not very likely. I didn't get into Verona until midnight."

"What game are you playing, Spadano?"

"Trying to help you, Trotti."

"We were followed last night. That's why she was scared—that's why Signora Bianchini came into my bedroom. You scared her with your silly games."

MacSmith had been sitting back with his head on the worn leather of the armchair, staring at the ceiling. In one hand he held his small glass; in the other, the bottle of vermouth. "You gave the money to Soldati?"

Trotti turned his glance from Spadano.

"I told him you would pay him."

Trotti nodded. "At the SIP there are all the telephone directories. I put the money in the Isernia directory and waited until I saw him picking it up."

"Perhaps it was Soldati checking you out last night," Mac-Smith said. "He wanted to see what you were like—wanted to check you before the meeting at the telephone exchange."

"You told him I was going to the arena?"

"No."

"You told him which hotel I was at?"

"No."

"Then it wasn't Soldati."

Spadano laughed. "You're a strange man, Trotti."

"I want to find out who murdered Brigadiere Ciuffi. If you find that strange . . ."

"I find you strange."

"I asked you for a favor, Spadano. I asked you about Primula Rosa. The Carabinieri have been making their enquiries, you have access—"

"Strange, Trotti, because you know that Primula Rosa is a dead end. Strange because you're now looking for the girl's murderer and yet you keep worrying about those deaths up in the hills."

"Perhaps there's a connection."

"Connection between Ciuffi's death and the muddled lucubrations of an old partisan priest?"

"Signora Bianchini—"

"You saw her at the station in Voghera? So what, Trotti? So what?"

"Then what the hell are you doing here, Spadano?"

"I told you."

"Told me what?" Trotti had raised his voice and he could feel that his face had flushed.

"I am paying back a few favors."

"What favors do you owe me?"

Spadano drank the vermouth. "Sometimes I wonder."

Someone whistling in the street below; the distant sounds of the city.

"I didn't have to come down to Verona, Trotti. And if I had known the reception I was going to get, believe me, I wouldn't have bothered. I would have let you get on with it. Instead of phoning through to the hotels to locate you, I could have stayed home in the barracks." He put the glass down. "I don't have to help you."

"What help?"

"You need my help. Because you're not going to get any from the Pubblica Sicurezza. You're certainly not going to get it from Merenda, who hates your guts. Or from Pisanelli, whom you've alienated by treating him like a child. Or from Magagna, who you kicked off to Milan once he wanted promotion."

"What are you trying to say Spadano?"

"Something that you should have realized a long time ago, Trotti—that you put people's backs up. That you make it hard for them to work for you."

"Then leave me alone."

"I'm saying that people who like you, who respect you because they know you are honest, because they know you are a good policeman—even they find it impossible to work with you."

"That's what you drove down to Verona to tell me, Spadano?"

Silence.

"Thanks."

"There are times, Trotti . . ."

"Thanks, Spadano. Now drink up your vermouth. Thanks again—it's all very helpful." Trotti turned back to the window. "But it doesn't bring me any nearer to finding the girl's killer."

"Chiasso, Trotti."

"What about Chiasso?"

"I'm telling you something that even Merenda doesn't know yet."

"What?"

"The customs post at Chiasso is run by the Carabinieri and that's why I wanted you to know. I wanted you to know before

Merenda. I wanted you to know last night. I came to your hotel and you sent me away."

"Know what?"

"A car with German registration plates was stopped for a random routine check. And beneath a false bottom to the boot, one of our men found a gun."

"Well?"

"Still too early for thorough ballistic tests. But it would seem we have located the gun that was used to kill Signorina Ciuffi."

47: Truth

"WHERE TO?"

"We'll take the autostrada."

"Where are we going, Commissario?"

"Como."

"This morning you said we were going to Bergamo—to see a woman."

"The same direction." Trotti shrugged. "I can see Galandra's sister later."

"Why do you want to see Galandra's sister?"

He did not reply.

"A stupid woman asking stupid questions?"

Trotti glanced at his watch.

Signora Bianchini raised an eyebrow. "You can't be an easy person to live with."

"Who's asking you to live with me?"

"Thank you."

Trotti bit his lip. "I'm seeing a man the Carabinieri arrested at Chiasso. They're now holding him in Como."

"You're angry, Commissario?"

"No."

"You're angry with me. I shouldn't have asked you to let me sleep with you."

"You didn't sleep with me."

"We slept in the same room."

Trotti gave her a brief glance.

"At the Ristorante Fontanella you seemed very worried at the prospect of having to share the same room."

The tinted window of the Audi cut out much of the September mist that was hanging over the fields of maize.

Her voice was bantering. "I hope you're grateful."

"Grateful for being kept awake?"

"Grateful for all the driving."

"I've already thanked you for your help."

"But you don't trust me?"

"No."

"At least you're honest."

"I've reached an age where I can no longer be bothered to lie."

It was lunchtime and the autostrada was virtually empty except for a few trucks in the slow lane.

They drove past a Pavesi restaurant, where the adjoining parking lot was full of cars and neatly parked articulated trucks. The smell of hot oil and tomatoes.

It was hot inside the Audi.

She was no longer smiling. "Why don't you trust me?"

Trotti lowered the window. "For God's sake."

She banged her hands against the steering wheel, her face pale with sudden anger. "Riccardo is innocent. You know that. You know it was Galandra who did it, you know that he wanted his revenge on Vardin."

"What do you know about Galandra?"

"Why don't you want to trust me?"

"What do you know about Galandra, Signora Bianchini?"

"At least your journalist friend is a gentleman." She did not hide her bitterness. "He knows that I have been worried about my son—it's only natural, isn't it?"

"MacSmith?"

"Your friend had the kindness to tell me things you've been hiding from me."

"MacSmith talks too much."

"He can see my son is innocent."

"I have no proof of your son's innocence."

"You still think I'm lying? When you've got virtual proof of Galandra's guilt? You still think that I'm covering up for Riccardo? That I'm using my feminine wiles to save my son?" She banged the horn noisily at a rusty Austin Innocenti which had pulled out into the fast lane. Trotti glanced at the speedometer; they were traveling at well over a hundred kilometers an hour.

She lowered her voice. "You still think I'm lying?"

"I don't know."

"I didn't ask to be your chauffeur."

"I didn't ask you to rescue me from the hospital."

"I felt sorry for you."

"For me? Or for your son?"

"Of course I must try to protect my son. I am a mother. And a woman."

"You are a married woman."

She took her eyes off the road to put her head back. "Married," she said, letting the air escape through her nose.

"You have a husband."

"You don't seem to consider yourself married," she replied hotly. "Yet you have a wife."

"We're not discussing me, signora."

"But can't you understand, Trotti?"

"Understand what?"

A hand through her hair in a gesture of exasperation. "Can't you understand? I like you."

"Good."

"Is that all you've got to say?"

"About what?"

"I like you, Commissario Trotti. I like you. You are a good man."

"I am pleased."

"I am attracted to you. As a man, as a human being."

"A flatfoot in off-the-peg clothes, signora?"

"I'm not used to making declarations."

"You're not used to telling the truth."

Her eyes widened.

Trotti looked through the open window. The wind pulled at his hair.

"I'm lying?"

"That you like me?" Trotti shrugged. "You've lied before."

"When?"

"Signora Bianchini, you yourself told me about your past, about how you came to meet your husband."

"So what?"

"The poor girl from the south. Alone and frightened in the big city."

"It was wrong to use my good looks? Is that what you're saying?"

"You have considerable charm. And you make use of it."

"And in finding a husband, I was just acting like any prostitute?"

Trotti shrugged.

"So you think I'm doing the same thing now?"

"You're a beautiful woman, Signora Bianchini."

"I'm twenty years older and my looks have gone."

"You are very attractive."

"For you I am ugly?"

"Not at all."

"You dislike me?"

Trotti was silent.

Her right hand left the steering wheel and she lightly touched his sleeve. "It is not easy for a woman to tell a man that she likes him."

"Where is your son, signora?"

As if stung, she withdrew her hand. "What do you want from me, Trotti?"

"The truth."

"I tell you I don't know where Riccardo is—and it is not important."

"For me it's important."

"I think I understand why your wife left you."

"Thank you."

"Too many wretched questions. You are like a dog, worrying at a bone—at a bone that doesn't exist."

"What were you doing in Voghera, signora?"

"Voghera?"

"The day you took me up to the hills—up to Santa Maria."

"Voghera?"

"At the railway station. You were seen talking to a man. In the station bar."

For a moment, Trotti thought she was going to smile. Then she put her hand to her mouth.

48: Guzzi

IT WAS ONE of the old Guzzi motorcycles. A single piston and still in fairly good condition thanks to careful maintenance.

Signora Bianchini took her foot off the accelerator.

The traffic policeman stood near the road. He had parked his machine against a billboard advertising pressure cookers. In his hand, he held a stick with a red roundel. With the other hand, he indicated to the Audi to pull into the verge.

He was small and his riding boots had been carefully polished.

She was a careful driver and by the time they pulled off the autostrada she was going no faster than fifteen kilometers an hour. The car bumped up on to the verge and the policeman stood back.

As he lowered the window, Trotti wondered why a traffic cop should carry a sub-machine gun over his shoulder.

"Commissario Trotti?" The man gave a brisk salute. Flat, soulless features beneath the pudding-bowl helmet. A pale face and wrinkles at the eyes.

"Yes?"

"Can I ask you to open the rear door, Commissario?"

"Why?"

"Please open the rear door."

Trotti leaned over the back of the seat and was about to unlock the door when he turned to glance at Signora Bianchini.

Fright in her eyes.

Trotti's hand stopped, hovered in mid-air.

The policeman slipped his finger on to the trigger of the gun.

The car surged forward, the engine roaring in bottom gear, and the woman holding the accelerator hard down on the floor.

"Christ!"

Trotti was thrown back against the seat. "What the hell are you doing?"

She was leaning forward in her seat, her hands grasping the wheel.

The Audi ran along the verge and then pulled out on to the empty autostrada. A few cars. A Mazda had to brake sharply, letting the Audi pull into the inside lane.

Trotti managed to turn his head and look out of the rear window. His view of the policeman was impeded by the Mazda.

"He was going to kill us." She changed gears noisily. The car gathered speed.

"You are mad."

"Traffic cops don't carry guns."

Trotti looked at her, glanced at the rearview mirror. It was then that he saw the Lancia.

"Slow down."

It must have been parked, not far from the motorcycle. A small, rising cloud of burning rubber from the rear wheels.

Signora Bianchini shook her head without looking at him.

Trotti turned again, the seatbelt impeding his free movement.

The Lancia overtook the Mazda, flashing its lights.

"Slow down, they're police."

Signora Bianchini hesitated.

The Lancia was catching up, getting bigger.

They were now traveling at a hundred and twenty kilometers an hour.

The road was virtually empty. The surface was poor, runnelled by years of heavy traffic.

The car rocked as the suspension coped with the uneven surface.

"Let them overtake, signora."

Her face was white, taut.

"Let them overtake."

She hesitated, then released the pressure on the accelerator. The Audi moved to the right.

The Lancia pushed past and then pulled in sharply, fishtailing the Audi.

She had no choice.

Signora Bianchini pulled hard on the steering wheel.

The seatbelt bit into Trotti's shoulder as the car went onto the shoulder, where the nearside hit a billboard.

Over a hundred kilometers an hour as the wheels on the left-hand side lost their adherence.

The engine roared. The wheels left the ground.

The Audi went into a spin.

49: Recovery

"BIANCHINI?"

It was hot.

"Who is Primula Rosa?"

"Bianchini?"

Trotti was sweating. He tried to concentrate. His eyes hurt. "Where is Signora Bianchini?"

"The Commissario needs rest. He needs care. He is very sick."

Trotti could smell Bianchini's perfume. He could also smell spilled petrol.

A seagull.

"Let him sleep. He is very sick."

Then the hush of whiteness, restful and undemanding.

"Doctor!"

Trotti opened his eyes. "Where am I?"

A white figure with a necklace about the long neck. "You must sleep."

Trotti tried to sit up several times, tried to reach out but there was a cold hand on his forehead and he was engulfed within the rising darkness.

"Sleep."

Trotti moaned.

"Please sleep."

Yellow flowers. Bright roses. A clear blue jar. A crocheted mat and a crucifix. Clean and white.

His vision disintegrated.

When Trotti next woke, his eyes hurt and he blinked against the harsh light. A nurse had brought him a drink of camomile. A nun with gull wings on her head. She watched with satisfaction as Trotti drank. She then went away, leaving him alone.

Trotti kept blinking.

A bright room. Sunshine poured through the high window, past the iron bars. The window frame was open. Air rustled the flowers in the blue jar.

Through the windows came the sound of life. The distant rumble of occasional traffic and the singing of birds.

His head ached but now he was no longer blinking. The smell of petrol had gone from his nostrils.

Trotti placed his bare feet on the small carpet. He tried to stand. His knees buckled and he fell forward on to the bedside chair.

On to the floor, with the chair on top of him and a cheek against the cool tiles. It was nice there. Cool and very nice. He wanted to sleep, to sleep forever. He closed his eyes.

The stocky nurse was pulling at his arms.

Sensibly, without any fuss, her shoes on the tiled floor, her strong calves bulging, she heaved him back on to the bed. His feet were cold and poked against the plump pillow. She dragged him around. His head brushed against the ample chest, against the nylon weave of her white apron.

His eyes closed again and, when Trotti opened them, there was the other figure—the figure in white. The figure leaned over him and clamped his arm. A pin-prick—a little pain in a sea of calm—and the room swirled away down the white, bottomless well.

Peace.

Night came and Trotti awoke. He tried to speak, but mumbled like a patient in the dentist's chair. "Where am I?"

"You are safe."

"Will Signora Bianchini die?"

"I will prop you up." The nurse helped him move against the pillows. "You will need a lot of rest."

"What's wrong with me?"

She shook her head.

Trotti smiled and fell asleep.

The nurse was still there when Trotti came awake. Her face was immobile, like a sculpted madonna.

"How long have I been here?"

"You've had a running fever."

"Where is Signora Bianchini?"

"You've been talking in your sleep."

"What did I say?"

She did not reply.

"What did I say, nurse?"

"You'll be better soon."

"Where is Signora Bianchini? Is she hurt?"

She fussed at the bedsheets, pulling the blanket up against his chest. "You are being well looked after."

"Where am I?"

"San Matteo, Signor Commissario," she said, smiling with faint surprise.

He caught her arm. "Nurse, how is the woman?"

"What woman?"

"Is she all right? Is Signora Bianchini all right? She was in the car with me. She was driving."

"I am afraid your friend was badly hurt. But she has ceased to suffer."

"She is dead?"

The nurse raised her shoulders. "Now please rest."

When Trotti next awoke, it was early morning and his head had lost its fogginess. He got out of bed and this time he did not collapse. His knees were weak but they held his weight. Trotti tried the door. It was locked. He placed a shoulder against the wooden frame but the door would not move.

Trotti went to the window. Somewhere a cock was announcing the new day. The room gave on to the fields beyond the hospital. In the distance the sky was still dark with the memory of night. Even the sound of traffic was faint, as though anaesthetized.

Signora Bianchini was dead, and it was his fault.

He went back to bed where he stared at the ceiling until the nurse brought breakfast. He nibbled at the rolls and the floury bread. He drank the coffee.

When the nurse had left, Trotti placed two fingers down his throat and retched like an animal. Masticated dough flooded into his mouth and poured in a thick stream into the sink. Bile burnt at his lips, his eyes watered. The acid smell was pungent and unpleasant. He watched the grey vomit caught in the vortex of clean water as it was pulled out of the sink.

Trotti washed out his mouth.

It must have been eight o'clock when the doctor arrived. The white coat, the stethoscope and hands that smelled of carbolic soap.

The nurse closed the door and went to the window. Trotti studied her sturdy silhouette through his half-closed eyes as the doctor took his pulse. Trotti could feel the man's breath on his cheeks.

"Nurse," he said, "the pulse has accelerated—are you sure . . . ?" There was a slight nasal accent and Trotti caught him on the side of the neck.

Disbelief in the cold eyes and Trotti hit him again, as hard as he could.

50: Policlinico

THE DOCTOR CRUMPLED to the ground with a slight murmur.

Trotti was expecting the nurse to scream.

He moved out of the bed. A sheet caught at his ankle and he tumbled into the sturdy body. The nurse staggered and fell backwards, a cry of surprise caught in her throat as Trotti reached out for the mouth and tried to close it.

She bit his hand. She was a strong woman. Her arms tried to push him away. Her knee came up fast and pain flooded through his groin.

Trotti held her arms and she pulled.

She was stronger than Trotti.

They were caught in a silent embrace of hatred. Saliva looped in thin threads behind her teeth. Trotti saw her throat swell and he put his hand to her neck. Her body seemed to relax. Then she suddenly moved away and banged rapid blows into his ribs.

He screamed his pain but managed to remain on top.

Trotti punched. He punched hard, knowing that he was losing his strength, aware that her hands were moving down his body, moving towards his groin.

Blood began to pour from the open mouth.

Trotti hit her hard with the flat of his hand, banging her head against the floor. Trotti hit the face again and the woman went limp. The eyes closed and the head rolled to one side.

Trotti climbed to his feet.

His head was spinning; it was hard to think, hard to concentrate.

He went back to the man. He took the coat and the stethoscope.

Trotti did not look like a doctor. The lab coat could not hide the bare feet, the pajamas or the growth of beard. Or the awkward, painful walk.

Trotti opened the door carefully and moved out on to a small landing. Stone stairs ran downwards, flanked by potted plants. He locked the door and went down the stairs.

Pain flooding through his chest.

The mist was returning to his eyes. Trotti went slowly, holding the banisters. Nobody about.

He reached the bottom of the stairs.

He found himself in a large, smoky room with onions hanging from the wooden ceiling and a smoldering log fire in the hearth. An old woman was slicing runner beans. She caught sight of him and put a hand to her toothless mouth.

The knife glinted as the woman screamed and Trotti broke into a clumsy run.

Limping as fast as he could, Trotti went through the open door and out into a courtyard. Chickens scattered before him.

He ran towards a tractor.

An old man headed him off. Trotti ducked sideways. In surprise, the old man watched, as if nailed to the ground by his shapeless boots.

A pig squealed, flustered hens flapped away. Trotti went past a dung heap. Several dogs yapped at his heels. He ran unsteadily, breathing hard. There was no strength in his legs, no power in his muscles.

Trotti stumbled forward, lost balance and fell.

The dogs gathered about him, suddenly docile. One dog licked his face. It shied away as Trotti pulled himself to his feet.

Naked, cold feet.

Trotti ran out of the farmyard, down an embankment and the dogs lost interest in him. He headed towards the open fields.

He heard a car horn and stumbled on. There was a small river that cut through the fields. His chest hurt and he wanted to slow down, but he was afraid of the shouting that came from behind him.

His vision was turning red.

Trotti stopped, exhausted.

He leaned against a tree. The bark was gnarled and cold beneath his forearm. His hands were hot, there was a spreading pain in his side.

Trotti tried to run forward, towards the stream, towards a dusty cart track.

It seemed to recede as Trotti approached.

The driver saw him. The red taillight blinked as the car went into reverse. Trotti zigzagged away, running off in the opposite direction, looking over his shoulder and bent double.

The pain in his side was now unbearable.

Two yapping dogs accompanied him.

The car turned and was catching up.

Above his breathing, the sound of the wheels on the cart track.

Trotti headed for the grass ditch.

"Get inside."

Trotti shook his head.

"Don't be a fool. They'll kill you."

"I don't trust you."

"You have no choice." She leaned over to open the door.

Trotti flopped into the passenger seat of the white Audi.

51: Khaki Shirt

"I THOUGHT SHE was dead."

Spadano laughed. "She saved your life, Trotti."

"I don't trust her."

"She likes you."

"I still don't trust her. She has been playing with me . . . using me."

"That's not the impression I get." Spadano ran a hand through his short hair.

"They told me she was killed in the accident."

"Clearly she wasn't."

"She was working for them. She was in on the whole thing."

"She spent two days looking for you."

"Why wasn't the car damaged?"

Spadano shrugged. "A bit of paint scraped off the side. But you know how the Germans build their cars. Teutonic thoroughness." The shoulders of his khaki shirt rose. "And Turkish workers."

"I was there. I was in the car when it went off the road." Trotti touched his face. "And I got hurt."

"Good job you were wearing your seatbelt."

"What happened to Signora Bianchini?"

"She pretended she had lost consciousness—and when they took you from the car, she saw their number plate . . . with the name of the Vimercate Lancia dealership."

"You believe her?"

"She contacted me personally. The barracks in Verona sent a man for me."

"And then?"

"And then?" Spadano took a packet of Toscani from the glovebox and lit one. The acrid smell filled the car. "Then she spent the last two days driving between Monza and Vimercate. She was convinced you were somewhere in the area—and she did everything to convince me."

Trotti coughed. His ribs hurt worse than ever. "Those things stink, Spadano."

"Consider yourself lucky to be alive." There was a cold glint in his eyes as Spadano glanced at Trotti. "Open the window if you wish."

Trotti opened the window.

"She cares for you—as soon as she picked you up running half-naked across the fields, she drove you to the hospital in Monza—and insisted on their taking x-rays."

"Where are we going, Spadano?"

"It's been difficult holding the German. The consulate has only just been informed. But it was agreed that we shouldn't do anything until you'd seen him. In Como." A shrug. "Only you decided to disappear for thirty-six hours."

"Against my will."

Spadano laughed. "And your rib?"

"Do you really have to smoke that thing, Spadano? I think I'm going to vomit."

The Carabiniere threw the smoldering cigar through the window.

"You've picked them up?"

"I beg your pardon."

Trotti repeated the question. "The people at the farm—the doctor and his nurse—have you picked them up?"

"You shouldn't have hit Signora Galandra so hard, Trotti. Wouldn't be surprised if she took action against you."

Trotti could not hide the surprise. "Signora Galandra?"

Despite the white hair at the temples, Spadano looked boyish.

"How did you know it was the Galandras? Galandra no longer looks like the photograph on our records."

"Galandra was the doctor?"

"I am impressed, Trotti. You couldn't have been feeling too well after all you'd been through. They'd been pumping you with drugs for nearly thirty-six hours. Yet you managed to see through the disguise."

Trotti was silent.

"How did you know it was Galandra?"

"It wasn't the Policlinico." Another silence before Trotti continued, "The Policlinico may not be a wonderful hospital—no Italian hospital is, with beds in the corridors and doctors who can't read—but San Matteo's one of the best in the country. And I know how doctors act, how they work. And anyway there was no reason for taking me to San Matteo."

"And that's why you fought?" Spadano laughed. "You fractured the poor woman's jaw."

"One vase of flowers. When I was at San Matteo, there were flowers everywhere. And chocolates. And a few remaining friends."

"Some people must like you."

"Signora Galandra doesn't. I fractured her jaw?"

"At least something remains of your training from Padua."

"She'll recover?"

"I wouldn't worry about her. On a kidnapping charge, she and Galandra face at least five years. And by the time she comes out, her jaw'll have healed. She should've forgiven you by then."

52: Tedious

"WE WERE WORRIED, Commissario."

The warm afternoon air had turned chill. Now it was evening, and Como was like any northern town, preparing for the September night.

A light wind from Switzerland blew across the lake. Clouds were moving southwards, carrying the threat of a rainy night. The vast surface of water was dark and ruffled. There were not many people along the lakeside. A few late and isolated fishermen, dark silhouettes, stared out at their long, immobile rods.

"I beg your pardon."

A smell of roasting coffee in the evening air, and the neon lights of the bars looked inviting. Trotti felt tired. He knew that it would be some time before the chemicals worked their way out of his system. He resented the pain in his ribs.

"I am not alone in having missed you in the Questura. You disappear for several days." Pisanelli shrugged self-consciously. "We were worried about you."

Trotti noticed the blush as Pisanelli glanced at Spadano. Spadano kept his eyes on the road. The tip of his Toscani cigar glinted.

"Several of us were afraid that you might be dead."

Trotti took a packet of sweets from his pocket. "After all these years with the PS paying towards my pension?"

"You must be careful, Commissario."

"Why the concern, Pisanelli?" Trotti frowned. "It's all very sudden."

The young policeman shook his head slowly. They were sitting together in the back seat of the car.

Spadano seemed to take no notice of their whispered conversation.

"Your disappearance coming as it did so soon after the girl's death."

"Don't tell me you're feeling guilty about Ciuffi. If anybody is responsible for what happened to her, it's me." Trotti unwrapped the sweet.

"Not easy coming to terms with the loss of Ciuffi." Although Pisanelli looked tired and was in need of a shave, he had the fresh smell of soap. He coughed. "The way she was killed has been hard on us all."

Spadano turned left at the end of Corso Argentina; the green of the traffic lights stood out against the failing light. The smell of petrol fumes and the angry noise of accelerating Vespas.

Trotti placed the lemon-flavored sweet in his mouth. "She is dead, Pisanelli. She was murdered and now she is dead and there's nothing we can do about it."

"But she was special."

"Ciuffi was special for us all."

"Special for me in particular."

The Carabinieri barracks were in the center of the town. Concrete slabs had been set up as a protection against possible terrorist attacks. Spotlights lit up the barbed wire along the high walls.

"You didn't always treat her very well, Pisanelli."

"We teased her—we all did. But we were proud of her. Really proud. We liked to joke at her—telling her that she was only a woman and giving her all the niggling jobs where she would be out on her feet or taking tedious notes in her notebook."

"Not much of a joke."

There was something sheepish about Pisanelli's smile. "It was just teasing—like school children."

"You were hard on her."

"You're hard with us, Commissario."

"You're a man, Pisanelli. And you're going to spend all your life in the PS. You're not going to go off after several years to have a family."

"It was Schipisi and Cardano who were hard on her."

"You were unkind, Pisanelli."

The car entered the courtyard.

"You left her to get on with the Vardin dossier while you were hanging out in the hospital."

"I was helping Merenda."

"Merenda? You were flirting with the nurses."

"No." The vehemence with which Pisanelli shook his head took Trotti by surprise. "No, I wasn't flirting."

"'A man who understands women'—that's what the woman doctor in Ostetrica said about you."

Again Pisanelli shook his head—he was holding his suede jacket on his lap—and the long hair at his ears rose with the centrifugal force. "I don't understand women."

"You should. Pisanelli, you've been engaged at least three times in the last four years."

Spadano parked the car and turned off the engine. "We have arrived, gentlemen."

Pisanelli looked at Trotti. "Ornella—it was Ornella who I liked."

"Ciuffi?"

"She was special."

"I didn't know you were on Christian-name terms."

"More than just like. It was stronger than that." Pisanelli sucked his teeth. "I shouldn't have teased her. And yet, Commissario, at the time I wanted her to notice me. I wanted her to see that I existed. I felt that by creating a bit of distance, by being a bit stand-offish . . . I thought that perhaps, well, that she would notice. You know what women are like, how they don't like weak men . . ."

"They don't like phallocrats, either."

Pisanelli sounded hurt. "Phallocrat?" he repeated and then fell silent.

"A woman is a flower, Pisanelli."

Pisanelli stared at the jacket on his knees. After a while, he shrugged as if talking to himself.

"Pisanelli, are you going to get out of this car?"

"If only Ciuffi were still here." Pisanelli raised his eyes and gave Trotti another of his smiles. "If only it were possible to tell her that I'm sorry—that I think about her all the time."

53: Como

HE COULD FEEL Spadano's irritation at having to wait.

It hurt Trotti to walk. They had bandaged his ribs at the hospital in Monza and now he was grateful to have Pisanelli with him. He walked slowly.

"And the Questura?"

"I beg your pardon, Commissario?"

"What's the news from the Questura, Pisanelli?"

"No news."

They stepped into an elevator.

Spadano looked at the two men from the Pubblica Sicurezza. A smile hovered at the corner of his lips.

"How's Merenda coming along?"

"I told you, Commissario—we're all missing you."

"Has Merenda found Ciuffi's murderer?"

Pisanelli bit his lip. "The dog went."

"The dog?"

"Gino's dog. Principessa."

"She went?"

"Merenda said that it was inadmissible."

"What was inadmissible?"

Pisanelli gave an apologetic shrug, "The smell—the smell of Principessa."

"Merenda doesn't work on the third floor. What the hell's the dog got to do with him?"

"Schipisi complained."

"Gino's retiring at the end of the year." The elevator halted and Trotti winced. "For God's sake."

"He said the dog had to go."

Trotti clicked his tongue. "And Ciuffi's murderer?"

"Nothing so far."

"How's Gino taken it?"

The doors of the lift slid open.

"Well?"

"He hasn't been in for a couple of days."

They stepped out of the elevator and went down a corridor. Clean walls, blue-tinted neon lighting and the occasional sound of machinery from behind the glass doors. More like the headquarters of a big newspaper than Carabinieri barracks.

Yet again, faced with the organization of the Carabinieri, Trotti found himself resentful. And jealous.

An officer saluted.

"What news, Tenente?"

"The Embassy on the phone a couple of times." A grin. "Very German, very efficient."

"What did they want?" Spadano asked.

The man had an intelligent face. "If we were going to press charges against Herr Schuhmaker."

"Taking an unregistered firearm out of the country? You can tell our German friends that their Herr Schuhmaker can count on a minimum of two years in an Italian jail."

"They want to know why he's being held incommunicado."

"Don't they have their own terrorists, the Germans?" Spadano gestured towards Trotti. "I'm hoping our friend from the PS can help us."

Trotti said, "I don't know any Germans."

Pisanelli ran a nervous hand through the long hair at the side of his head.

Spadano put the stub of a cigar in his mouth and lit it. "Let's go and see Herr Schuhmaker."

They returned to the elevator. The Carabiniere accompanied

them. The smell of his aftershave lotion competed with the acrid smell of Spadano's Toscani cigar.

"Incidentally, Trotti, I forgot to tell you."

"What?"

"I managed to find him."

"Him?"

"Primula Rosa—the man your mad priest was looking for."

"What did he tell you?"

"Find in a manner of speaking, that is." A cloud of cigar smoke.

"Do you have to smoke that thing in an enclosed space?"

Spadano shrugged. "Found him a bit too late."

"Why?"

"He died in a road accident about seven years ago."

Trotti fell silent.

The passage of time.

His mind turned back to the months at the end of the war. Bloodshed—there had been a lot of bloodshed; yet, in those days, things had appeared simple. And that simplicity—like Primula Rosa, with his one good hand—belonged to the past. The end of the civil war, Reconstruction—the hopes and the expectations for the future, for himself, for Italy . . .

Trotti glanced at Spadano, and he was overcome with a sense of bitter nostalgia.

"Primula Rosa won't be helping your priest."

Nobody spoke in the elevator.

Three floors. They stepped out on to another corridor, this time slightly cooler. They were beneath ground level. No windows and the air was damp.

"This way please."

Although Spadano had lived in the north for most of his life, he had not lost his Palermo accent.

Trotti and Pisanelli followed, a step behind the small muscular back and the thick neck. Hair that showed no sign of thinning. For a man well into his late fifties, Spadano had aged well.

Primula Rosa was dead.

"Here." Spadano hammered at the grey door, the sound feeble

against the thick, riveted steel. A scraping noise of a bolt being pulled back. The door opened outwards and, following Spadano, the two officers from the Pubblica Sicurezza entered into a flood of blinding neon light.

The man sat on a bench.

The room smelled of despair. Elsewhere somebody was shouting and banging a utensil against the bars of a cell. The muffled sound came through the brick wall. It was followed by a brisk shout of command.

Silence and the man raised his head to look at the visitors.

Trotti had turned pale, staring at the German.

"Jesus."

A tired face, bags under the eyes. A narrow chin and a bald head that caught the reflected light. Thin lips and dark, hurt eyes.

"Trotti—Italo Trotti."

54: Woman

"WELL?" THE BARONESSA said sharply.

They were like an old couple, Trotti thought. Fond of each other, yet continually bickering.

"For all these years you've lied to me."

"How could I expect you to understand the truth?"

"But you lied." Fra Gianni screwed up his eyes and his voice could not hide that he was hurt.

"You're an old fool, Gianni. You have never been in love. You don't know what love means."

Velvet curtains and dark-red wallpaper.

"A little something to drink, Commissario?" A conspiratorial glance at Trotti. "This awful priest doesn't like me drinking alcohol. He would have made a terrible husband." Her repeated jibe about Fra Gianni gave Trotti the impression that she was putting on an act for him. She went to the dark mahogany cabinet and produced a bottle. "Schnapps, perhaps—nothing better to warm an old heart." She laughed to herself.

"Where did you learn to use a rifle?"

"Let us drink something and then we can talk like civilized people." She gestured Trotti to one of the deep armchairs. "Nowadays, people are always in such a hurry."

"What rifle?" Fra Gianni remained standing, a solitary old man caught in the yellow light of the doorway. His eyes watched the Baronessa attentively.

The woman poured two glasses and held one out to Trotti. "I like to tease Gianni—you do understand?"

Trotti refused the proffered glass. "Why do you want to murder me?"

She looked at him with her head tilted. The smile was almost coquettish. She sat down. "Murder you, Commissario?"

"At Borgo Genovese—nobody saw you, because nobody imagined that the little old lady in the Fiat 600 was carrying a gun. And when they heard the detonation, they just thought it was a car backfiring."

"Why should I want to murder you?"

"Why, indeed?"

"Murderers are hopeful—they think that, by killing people, they are going to make things better." She turned away to gesture towards the photographs on the piano. "My life is behind me. I have lived long enough."

"Then you had nothing to be afraid of."

She nodded.

"You killed a girl . . . a woman who had all her life before her."

The Baronessa von Neumann had a bright smile. "Really?"

"Why did you want me out of the way? What harm could I do to you?"

"Not you, Piero Trotti—nor anybody else."

"It would never have occurred to me it was you who'd murdered all those old partisans."

She laughed.

"And even if I had found out that you were the mother to my brother's child, what would I have done?"

She raised her glass. "To your health."

"If anything, I would have tried to help you—because that's what you needed."

"I need nothing," she said and drank.

"You had loved Italo Trotti."

"I will always love Italo." The smile vanished. She looked down at her glass and for a few moments there was silence. Then the Baronessa raised her eyes. "I always tried to do what was best."

"Like killing people?"

"For Italo's sake, I always tried to do what was best."

"You wanted to kill me."

"You cannot understand. You didn't know Italo as I knew him." Her voice had lost its brittle edge. It was almost dreamy and she sat staring into her half-empty glass. "The people in the village could be so spiteful. They always accused me of being pro-German—of being anti-Italian. But I was a better patriot than your partisans ever were." She raised her chin towards Fra Gianni.

The priest remained by the door, silent like a stubborn child refusing to sit down.

"When I married Pauli, I thought I was doing my patriotic duty. Duty towards our two countries, duty towards the Duce, towards the Axis. Towards the marriage of Italy and Germany."

"You loved the Baron von Neumann?"

"He never did anything to harm me." The smile softened her face. "Pauli was a good man."

Outside the house, the sound of the river joined that of the wind. The cold smell of the hills.

"I spent the first year of marriage in Germany, and it wasn't until 1943 and the bombing of Hamburg that I returned to Santa Maria."

"You told me that you were in Germany at the end of the war. You now admit you were in Santa Maria?"

A bland smile. "I was happy with Pauli—very happy. A good man—and after so many years of poverty, with Pauli there was no longer the nagging problem of where the next meal was coming from." She nodded. "We are a good people, we, the Italians. We are good and we have generous hearts. But, in our memory, there is always the fear of hunger. And here in the hills, we have never been rich. You know that, Piero Trotti. You're of humble, hard-working stock."

Trotti did not reply.

"When war broke out and there was the possibility of selling food on the black market, people were willing to do anything to make a bit of money." She gestured towards the priest. "About these things, Gianni is so naive. He likes to see everything in black and white. For him the Fascists were all bad and the partisans were all good. He doesn't understand that our politics were determined by self-interest—and hunger. But then he doesn't know about the hunger and the poverty of living in these hills. He is from Piemonte."

"I have lived here for more than forty years, Baronessa."

"And still you don't understand, Gianni."

"Understand what?"

She took a quick gulp of schnapps and smiled as the liquid descended her throat.

"What don't I understand?" The priest's voice was aggrieved, like that of a little boy's.

She turned to Trotti. "Gianni is a good man. Not very intelligent, but good, with a kind heart. Unfortunately, like so many Italians, he doesn't like to face up to the truth." She spoke as if the priest were still in his presbytery. "Or rather, Gianni prefers to create his own truth. He has got it into his head that all the partisans were good and everybody else was wicked." She turned to look at him, her head to one side and talking like a schoolmistress. "Goodness isn't something that you're born with. Goodness comes with the freedom from drudgery, with the freedom from back-breaking toil. Goodness comes from knowing that you can spare the time to help your friends."

The priest said, "We are all born with goodness in our hearts. And evil."

"The hills are a hard taskmaster. You know that, Piero Trotti. The hills have made us a tough and determined lot. The incessant labor. A land that would yield nothing without a struggle."

Trotti held up his hand. "You loved my brother?"

"Of course I loved him. I was a pretty girl in those days, and I could pick and choose. But Italo wasn't like the other men." She stopped and looked at Trotti carefully. "You have eyes a bit like his, Piero. So sad—and yet so warm. Intelligent, brown eyes. And when I saw those eyes again—when Italo returned from Russia, it was as if he had never been away . . . as if I had never been married." She smiled to herself.

"You had an affair with him?"

"How else, Piero Trotti, do you think I got pregnant?"

"You were a married woman in 1944."

"You are all the same."

"You had been married to the baron for three years."

"You men can't understand—because you can't love. You don't know what love is—true, disinterested love." She shook her head. "I loved Pauli—very much indeed. Perhaps, at first, I was impressed by the uniform—Pauli was so splendid in his uniform. And perhaps the idea that a simple peasant girl from the hills could become a German Baronessa." A snort of humorless laughter. "A Baronessa with bare feet. I was flattered—flattered by all the attention, and by the possibilities."

There were the photographs of Pauli again, looking down from the piano. Pauli in the uniform of the Wehrmacht, Pauli smoking a pipe and swinging a golf club. Pauli—his hair now thinner—and a little boy on a windswept beach of the North Sea.

"I loved Pauli very much."

"And my brother? You loved him, too?"

"With Italo it was different, quite different. I loved Pauli, of course. I loved him and I gave him two daughters of his own. He was a good man and I respected him. But Italo was different."

"In what way was my brother different?"

"You ask such stupid questions."

A flash of anger. "I loved my older brother."

"Of course you did, Piero Trotti. Everyone loved him." Again she glanced at the photographs and there was disappointment on her face. "I had always loved him—before the war, before he ever left to go into the army." She closed her eyes. "It must have been 1937—no, 1936—when they sent him to Africa. That's right, he was just eighteen." A smile of nostalgia. "We all loved Italo—so young, so good. He was ten years younger than me and for six marvelous months . . ."

"In 1936?"

"You were still at school, Piero Trotti. You think I don't remember you? An ugly little child you were even then—Italo and I used to joke about you. Thin as a rake—and your long, sharp nose. With your darned trousers and wooden shoes that were two sizes too big for you, you were not a very attractive child."

"You flatter me."

"You could never have been like Italo. You have always been a stubborn and opinionated person, Piero. The complete opposite of Italo. Even as a child, you behaved like a self-righteous priest." She laughed. "No wonder you became a policeman."

"You loved my brother—and yet you wanted to murder me. Because you were afraid that I would find out about the past."

"The past?" She laughed. "You cannot change the past, Piero, not you or anyone else."

"But you wanted me dead."

She nodded. "Of course."

"Why?"

"Because I hate you." She smiled the same coquettish smile.

"What harm have I done you?" Trotti could not hide his surprise.

"Like your mother, Piero Trotti. Stubborn and self-righteous."

"Stubborn enough to want to know why you felt you had to kill me."

"A horrid, snooping policeman. A horrid little man."

Trotti had started to tremble. "Instead of me, you killed a young woman—an innocent young woman."

The Baronessa was no longer listening. She had turned and was now addressing Fra Gianni. "And then Italo came back. We all thought he had died. After so many years away, fighting all those wars, Italo came back. He didn't know. I was married and I'm sure that it was his determination to see me again that helped him stay alive. In Russia he suffered frostbite—but he returned. Italo returned for me—for the only woman he had ever loved."

"Italo was sick."

"You are so like your mother, Piero Trotti." She faced him. "Your mother was a calculating woman. A cold and calculating woman who thought I could get food and medicine from the Germans for her son. It was she who told me that Italo was back. Oh, she hated me, she'd never wanted her son to go with me. She said I was too old for him. But that didn't stop her from telling me he was in hiding in the hills—hiding with the partisans." Her eyes went from the priest to Trotti. "Whatever I did, I did for Italo. Not for that old woman."

"Mother died earlier this year."

She poured more schnapps into her glass. Her pale hand reminded Trotti of a bloodless insect. "So the priest tells me."

"Pauli von Neumann knew that the child was not his?"

"Italo's boy?"

Trotti said, "The man I just met in Como. The German with a strange name. And a rifle in the boot of his car."

"Wolfgang is a dreamer. A poet and a dreamer."

"Your husband knew it was not his child?"

"You believe I would lie to Pauli?"

Trotti shrugged.

"You are a peasant, Piero Trotti, and you take everybody for a peasant like yourself."

Fra Gianni spoke. "You lied to me all these years."

"Because you are a fool, Gianni. A priest and a fool." She turned back to face Trotti. "Of course I told my husband. Pauli wasn't happy. But he was good—and he understood. And later we had our two girls." She raised her eyes towards where Fra Gianni was standing. "Ours was a very united family. I spent twenty marvelous years in Germany. And my daughters now write to me regularly."

"When you came back in 1965, it was then that you started murdering the old partisans?"

"After the war Pauli and I lived in Hamburg. We were very happy. Of course sometimes we quarreled. But we were very happy—and soon after he died, I returned to Italy—and to the hills."

"You murdered Italo?"

"Italo?" Her eyes flickered.

"It wasn't the partisans—it was you who murdered Italo—just as you tried to kill me."

55: Heirloom

"I WAS IN Como with your son. He is in jail. I came here directly with the Captain of Carabinieri."

"A dreamer. Wolfgang is a dreamer like his father."

"Why did he change his name?"

"What name?"

"Schuhmaker—when your name is von Neumann?"

She shrugged. "Pauli's idea—he didn't want the children to be laughed at at school. Very egalitarian, Pauli—he was ashamed of being an aristocrat. That's why he married a peasant girl—an Italian peasant girl."

"And you gave the gun to your son?"

"I didn't give him anything, Piero Trotti."

"Why did he have the gun in his car?"

"You must ask Wolfgang."

"He refuses to talk."

"Wolfgang is a good boy—but he can never be like his father. Because Italo was very special." She smiled. "Italo was in love with me. And it was his love that kept him alive during the march through Russia. That terrible march through the snow when he lost two of his toes."

"I recognized him." Trotti turned to look at the priest. "When I first saw the German, I thought it was my brother. He was sitting in the small cell and it was as if Italo had never died. The same face as Italo—older, and beginning to lose his hair. But still the same face."

"Not the same eyes. Nobody ever had those dark brown eyes." The Baronessa shrugged. "Wolfgang wanted to help me—that's why he came down from Germany. And that's why he wanted to keep the gun."

"He could have thrown it away—thrown it in the river."

"A family heirloom?" A laugh. "He was furious I ever took it in the first place." She glanced at the two men. "Strange how Wolfgang was so close to Pauli. He wasn't the boy's father and yet . . ." She faced Trotti, put her fist to her chin. "I was a good mother, you know. I loved my children—we still write. I am very fond of Wolfgang, who is so like his father. But I could never love Wolfgang the way I loved Italo. You understand that, don't you?"

Trotti did not reply.

Gianni had sat down on the arm of the settee where he had poured himself a drink. He now held the empty glass between his large hands.

"What are you going to do with me, Piero?"

"What do you think, Baronessa?"

The muscles at the corner of her mouth tightened. "A spiteful and vindictive person—even as a child." She folded her arms. "With you, Piero, I can expect the worst."

"I must do my job."

"It was my fault—I shouldn't have talked so much. I shouldn't have told you everything. I regretted it immediately. You are more intelligent than the priest, I was suddenly afraid . . ." She hesitated, then smiled the same coquettish smile that she had used before. It softened her face and lit up her eyes. "You are going to throw an old woman into prison?"

"An old woman who killed a young girl in the prime of her life."

"Like a priest, Piero." A gesture of irritation, but the girlish smile remained. "At times, you can be so self-righteous."

"Brigadiere Ciuffi worked for me, Baronessa. It may not mean much to you—but I was responsible for her. She was an intelligent and good person. She was not beautiful—not beautiful as you were. But kind and hard-working."

"What are you going to do with me?"

"I swore that I would find her killer—and I would see the killer punished."

She frowned. "You are a vindictive person, Piero. You always were. That's why Italo always said—"

"What do you know about Italo? You went to bed with him, you spent a few moments with him—and you think you know all about my brother? What do you know? You don't own him. Because he gave you his child doesn't mean that you own him, that you own his memory."

"I brought him back to life. Without me, without my love and my caring, he would have died."

"You murdered him."

A brittle, mocking laugh. "You say such outrageous things."

"You couldn't have him as a husband—because you would never have given up your German baron and his wealth to go and live with a crippled war veteran. That was out of the question. Live with a poor Italian peasant when you had done everything to escape? When you had a house and money in Germany?"

"The house in Hamburg was destroyed by the American bombers."

"You loved Italo perhaps in your cold and twisted way. I don't doubt that you loved him. But you couldn't accept that Italo would be going to live his life without you. You couldn't accept that. You were carrying his child. And you knew there was no future for you. Not together."

"Absurd."

"And so you killed him."

There was a long silence. Just the noise of the river and the wind outside the house.

"Just like your mother, Piero. You cannot understand—because you don't know what love is. Real, disinterested love."

"Italo never loved you—he never even mentioned you."

A bright flame in her eyes. "It was a secret. Just me and Italo. And the Carabiniere."

"Saltieri?"

"Saltieri helped us. Italo was very sick and his mind wasn't what it had once been. Not even your mother knew about us. I didn't want that interfering woman knowing about us. She knew I was getting food to Italo—food from the Germans. But she didn't know that we . . ."

"You visited Italo?"

"It wasn't easy. The partisans didn't trust me, they never did. For them, I was the wife of a hated German officer. Although, God knows, Pauli never did the evil things they did to their own compatriots. They were monsters, Communists and monsters. Murderers. And your Primula Rosa, he was no better. He was . . ."

"You stayed with Italo in the hills?"

"How do you think I got pregnant?"

"And the partisans didn't know?"

"I would go up into the hills with Saltieri. I wanted to be with him all the time—to be with Italo, to look after him. When we were together, it was just as it had been before he had gone off to be a soldier and fight in all those wretched wars. He was in Abyssinia—and Spain. And in the end he had to walk home from Russia. But he had always loved me." Her shoulders dropped. "And I had gotten married." She looked at Trotti. "It was the least I could do, wasn't it? I would dress up as a man, put on a cloak and the Carabiniere would take me. It was my duty—after all the years. My duty to look after Italo after what he had been through." A pause. "They killed him."

"They?"

"The same wretched people who murdered Saltieri."

"The partisans?"

"Piero Trotti, you never listen to a word I say."

"Such a lot is lies."

"They murdered Italo because he was with Saltieri."

"Then there's no connection between my brother and the SS gold?"

"Italo was witness to the murder of the Carabiniere."

"Why did they kill Saltieri?"

"Because of me—indirectly because of me." She shrugged. "He was fond of me."

"Fra Gianni says my brother knew about the gold."

"Italo was murdered long before the partisans ever took the Nazi gold."

"Then why did they murder him?"

"Because they thought Italo was spying for Saltieri. And perhaps Saltieri really did hope to get Italo to tell him about the partisans." She shrugged. "Or perhaps it was just for my sake that he went up into the hills and took the food and the cigarettes. Saltieri was our go-between—and, in the end, the partisans killed him."

Silence.

"They killed Italo because they thought he had collaborated with the Carabiniere." Again she shrugged. "They were his friends—the partisans and Primula Rosa were his friends."

Trotti could hear the whine of the wind.

"They killed Italo." Suddenly the bright smile. "It was only normal, wasn't it?"

"What?"

"Only normal that I should avenge Italo's murder. They deserved to die, all of them. Dandanin, Draghin, la Nini. And the two others—there were five of them and they were responsible for his death. The only man that I ever really loved—and they killed him in cold blood. I was right, wasn't I, Piero? It was only right that I should kill them. They deserved to die, didn't they?"

56: Return

TROTTI SAID, "SHE must have phoned the Questura and somebody put her on to Centrale—or AV7. She was expecting us. Somebody must have told her that Ciuffi had phoned in that we were going down to the river—looking for a man who was fishing." Trotti smiled at Spadano. "The old woman took her rifle and drove down to Borgo Genovese in the 600. It couldn't have been very difficult to find Vardin—he was the only person fishing at that time of day. The Baronessa was waiting for me."

"Why did she want to kill you?"

"She was afraid."

"What of?"

"She was afraid of me in a way that she'd never been afraid of the priest. She had him round her little finger—but with me it was different. She felt that I'd soon guess she was behind the five murders."

"According to your priest, there were six."

"Tomaso died long before the Baronessa returned from Germany. He fell into the river bed and smashed the back of his head." Trotti shrugged. "Probably his death that gave the old woman her idea. Not the idea of revenge—but made her realize that a woman could kill them all and get away with it."

"And now?"

"Now what?"

"What are you going to do?"

Trotti laughed and put a hand on the door handle. "I'm going to go home and sleep."

"What are you going to do about the old woman?"

Trotti climbed out of the car. "Buona sera, Capitano Spadano."

"You didn't want me to arrest her."

"She's the mother of my nephew."

"She murdered Brigadiere Ciuffi—and there's enough evidence to arrest her for the murders in the hills."

"It can wait. A few days."

"Why?"

"Buona sera, Spadano."

Spadano looked at Trotti in silence for a few moments. Then he nodded. "Buona sera, Signor Commissario."

"And thanks for everything."

The car did a sharp U-turn and disappeared along via Milano, heading back towards the city.

Trotti pushed open the garden gate and went up the steps. He glanced absentmindedly at the potted plants that needed watering. He turned the key in the lock and let himself into the house. Trotti immediately recognized the reassuring, familiar smell. A smell of floor polish and emptiness. He shut the door behind him. His rib hurt. Pioppi's bear was gone from the top of the wardrobe.

He went into the kitchen and opened the refrigerator. He was not hungry. He poured himself half a glass of chilled mineral water and turned on the television. Cold bubbles jumped from the glass on to his hand.

When he closed his eyes, he saw again the old woman's face.

"*Only normal that I should avenge Italo's murder. They deserved to die, all of them. Dandanin, Draghin, la Nini. And the two others—there were five of them and they were responsible for his death. The only man that I ever really loved—and they killed him in cold blood. I was right, wasn't I, Piero? It was only right that I should kill them. They deserved to die, didn't they?*"

Half an hour later the telephone rang.

"Where've you been?"

"Who's speaking?" Trotti asked.

"Where've you been, Papa?"

"In Verona."

"I was worried about you."

"There's no need to worry. Where are you phoning from?"

"They said that you'd been hurt."

"Give me your number, Pioppi, and I'll ring back."

"Nando's here with me. We've been worried about you. They said that you were kidnapped."

Trotti laughed. "A slight exaggeration."

"The man said you'd been kidnapped and that you'd been drugged."

"Who told you that?"

"That nice man who works with you."

"Pisanelli?"

"A policeman came round looking for me and I went to the Questura here. And I spoke over the phone to your colleague. He is very sympathetic."

"I don't know who you're talking about, Pioppi."

"A commissario like you—with a strange name. Minestra or Pasticcio or something."

"Merenda?"

"That's right." A nervous laugh. "Commissario Merenda said that you'd been drugged and kidnapped and he wanted me to come and fetch you."

"Stay where you are, Pioppi."

"Who drugged you?"

"Stay with Nando."

"Papa, you must tell me. Commissario Merenda seemed very concerned about you. He said the whole Questura was upset by what had happened to you—and that's why he had me sent for."

"It's all a mistake."

"What's a mistake?"

Trotti did not reply. He looked unthinkingly at the flickering television screen.

"If you don't tell me, Papa, I'll have to phone Mother."

"Leave Agnese alone."

"Why were you kidnapped?"

He repressed a sigh. "I was looking for a man. And in the course of the enquiries, I met up with an old friend of his. They'd been in jail together."

"Well?"

"According to the Carabinieri, the two men—the man I was looking for and the man I spoke to in Verona—they were about to do a series of hold-ups—banks in the Verona/Mantua area. And so when I turned up asking questions, they wanted me out of the way. They thought . . ."

"Well?"

"They thought that I'd got wind of their projects. They wanted me out of the way for a couple of days. That's all."

"They drugged you?"

"Pioppi, I'm all right and they've been arrested. Two men and a woman so far."

"You always take risks."

"An old man like me?"

"You're not old."

"All I want to do is pick up my pension and retire."

"Go back to the hills?"

"That's right. I will keep bees and I will make my own wine. And perhaps have a few chickens and some cattle. You will be married and you'll come with Nando, bringing the grandchildren."

"You're laughing at me, Papa!" She paused. "And anyway, you don't like Nando."

"Nando's a good boy."

"Papa, do you want us to come up?"

"No."

"We can catch the Milan train on Saturday. Commissario Merenda said . . ."

"I'll come to Bologna next week."

"You promise, Papa?"

"I promise."

"Papa?"

"Yes?"

"Have you found the man who murdered the policewoman?"

"Perhaps," Trotti said. "I'll be in touch. Ciao, Pioppi."

He put down the receiver.

57: Changes

Trotti stepped into the elevator. He pressed the button for the third floor. The elevator smelled of chlorine. His fingers ran reassuringly across the hammer and sickle engraved in the metallic paint.

When the elevator stopped, Trotti was looking in the mirror. He felt less tired, and with a good night's sleep the drugs seemed to have worked themselves out of his system. Still the ache in his ribs.

"Buongiorno."

A man in uniform.

"Where's Gino?" Trotti asked, surprised. "Who are you?"

The man pushed aside the copy of *Epoca* that lay open on the desk.

"Where's Gino?"

"Gino?" A slow Neapolitan accent.

"Who are you?"

"You work here?"

Trotti raised his voice. "Do you know who you're talking to?"

"Your name is here?" A typed list of names had been attached to the desk top with adhesive tape.

"I'm Trotti."

A slight gesture of the hand. "Trotti?" The man wore

pink-tinted glasses that made his eyes appear large, like the eyes of a fish.

"Commissario Piero Trotti."

"Commissario Trotti?" The man shook his head—long hair that had been carefully cut and dyed black—as he ran his finger down the printed list of names. "No Trotti here, Commissario or otherwise."

"Of course my name's there."

"Look for yourself."

"Commissario Trotti. My name is Commissario Trotti and I work here."

"I can't help you. Your name isn't on the list."

"Where is Gino, for God's sake?"

"Trotti?" An accent that was both ingratiating and arrogant. "It must have been you the man wanted to speak to."

"What man?"

"Orsi."

"I don't know any Signor Orsi."

"The blind man—the man I have had to replace."

"Gino? Why's he not here?"

A bland smile. "You'll have to ask the Questore."

Trotti clicked his tongue. "Give me a line, will you? I'll take it in my office." Without hiding his irritation, he turned away and walked down the corridor.

Gino had gone—and with him Principessa. The third floor no longer smelled of the cancerous dog. Like a disease, Trotti thought, that you almost miss once you are cured.

He stepped into the office, thinking about Gino and his dog. Fourteen, fifteen years that the blind man had been on the desk. And now he had left without a word.

The office was empty.

Everything—the filing cabinets, the greasy canvas armchairs, the piles of folders and the old desk—everything had gone. Just the photograph of Pertini on the wall and on the floor, the bulbous green telephone. Between the telephone and the wall, there lay the coils of the dusty, green flex.

For an instant, he thought he had entered the wrong room.

Trotti stood still, his mouth open in surprise. His eyes searched for something familiar. There was no mistake, he identified the wooden partition in the wall. And a couple of sweet paper wrappings lay on the dusty floor; rust marks where the cabinets used to stand.

"My God."

A feeling of pain, of loss, of bewilderment in the pit of his belly. "What's going on in this damn place?" He turned on his heel. "Hey," he shouted.

The man at the desk looked up from the pages of *Epoca*.

"What's happening?" It was hard to speak, the words swelled in his throat. "My office—it's been cleared out."

The man shrugged.

It was as if his hand were autonomous—it wanted to strike the round, complacent face, send the tinted glasses flying. With difficulty, Trotti controlled his anger. "What's going on?"

"I can't help you."

"This is where I work—this is where I've always worked. What's going on?"

"I'm new here."

"Who's given permission?" Trotti choked on his words.

The man looked at him.

"Why's my office been cleared out like that?"

"I think it's something to do with the policewoman."

"Ciuffi?"

"Commissario Merenda said he was making this his HQ."

"That's my office. I haven't been consulted."

The Neapolitan raised his shoulders in simulated empathy.

"Merenda doesn't work on this floor—he's got no right here." Trotti placed his hand on the receiver of the telephone exchange. "You'd better give me a line."

A plump white hand went to the telephone. "No."

"Give me a line."

"I have my orders."

"Give me a line, will you?"

He shook his head. "My instructions are clear."

"Who do you think you are?"

"Not allowed. I do not know you. Your name is not on the list. The Questore is adamant."

"The Questore is going to be adamant about throwing you out on your ear. You, your pimp's glasses and your eau de cologne."

There was no reaction behind the thick lenses.

"This is where I work." Trotti gestured in anger. "That's my office—do you understand? It's been my office for the last seven years."

"The Questore and Commissario Merenda say there have been too many personal calls. I have had to log everything down." He pointed to an exercise book beside the magazine. "Without the permission of the Questore—or of Commissario Merenda—I cannot let you use this phone."

Trotti stared at the round, pale face.

"I'm sure you understand."

58: Leper

"THE BASTARD."

The doors of the elevator closed behind him. In the mirror, Trotti's eyes were red. He had forgotten about the pain in his ribs.

"Bastard Merenda."

He rode the elevator to the basement and pressed the button. A few seconds' wait and then Maserati opened the door.

"What's going on in this place, Maserati?" Trotti stepped out into the archives.

"Good to see you, Commissario." Maserati did not smile.

"My office has been gutted, I'm not allowed to use the phones." Trotti had raised his voice. "What's happening? What's that bastard Merenda doing?"

"I thought you were in the hospital."

"I'm here and I want to know what's going on."

Maserati shrugged.

"You must tell me." Trotti placed a hand on his shoulder.

A slight wince on the young man's face. Maserati was wearing a lab coat and his face seemed to pale. "Tell you what?"

"Am I a leper? All of a sudden, I'm persona non grata in this Questura. What's happening on the third floor, Maserati? They've cleared out my room, there's some Neapolitan gigolo at the desk. And where's Gino?"

"It's the Ciuffi thing, Commissario."

There was the sound of movement behind him.

Trotti turned and he recognized the two men.

Cardano nodded briefly towards him. A thin smile on his narrow face, he headed towards the door. There was an unlit cigarette hanging from his lip. Schipisi was a couple of steps behind him. Both were carrying files. They walked fast, with their heads down.

The two men went through the swing door.

"A warm welcome I'm getting." Trotti turned back to Maserati. "What about Ciuffi?"

"Merenda's set up a major enquiry into her murder. He's making the third floor the central command."

"Apart from your two friends"—Trotti gestured towards the swing doors—"there's nobody around."

"Today's Sunday."

"A waste of time and money."

"The Questore is going out of his mind. We've been getting all the pressure from the newspapers. You know how the Questore is sensitive about that sort of thing. Already been two press conferences. Merenda is keen to get the enquiry sorted out as soon as possible."

"A waste of time, Maserati, because I know who killed Ciuffi."

"You know who killed her?"

Trotti nodded.

Maserati placed his hand on the computer. "Who killed Ciuffi, Commissario?"

"Later."

"Has he been arrested yet?"

"It was a woman."

"A woman? Who?"

"I must see the Questore first." Trotti moved towards the telephone. Beside it, there were three half-full cups of coffee. "At least somebody's working on Sundays." He shook his head.

"Schipisi has been helping me."

"Where's Merenda? Is he at Mass?"

Maserati chewed at his upper lip. "Merenda is in Rome."

Trotti picked up the receiver. "I'll have to speak to the Questore."

Maserati reached out his hand. "Please, Commissario."

"What, Maserati?"

Pressure from Maserati's hand and the receiver was pushed back into its cradle. "I'm afraid that is not possible."

"Not possible?"

"My orders are precise. I have been told . . ."

"You, too, Maserati?"

"My orders come from the Questore. I am not to collaborate with you." A slight frown. "You understand? You no longer work here, Signor Commissario."

59: Cigarette

THERE WAS A shop selling antiques and, beside it, another that had a full window display of knives and scissors. Trotti took the small path between the two shops where the smell of urine and dirt assailed his nostrils. He found himself in a dusty courtyard. A Japanese van, used for transporting the antiques, filled most of the restricted space.

There was a bicycle without a seat leaning against the wall; a sign for the local section of Amnesty International.

The sky was overcast and it shed a grey, disconsolate light upon the city. The weather was hot and humid; soon it would rain.

Trotti went up the two flights of the outside stairs. No noise came from behind the shabby closed blinds. On the third floor, two doors faced each other. The name ORSI, written in ballpoint pen, had been slipped under the doorbell.

Trotti rang the bell and waited.

The smell of death seeped from behind the cracks in the door.

He rang again, this time keeping his finger on the bell. The sound of shuffling feet.

"Who is it?"

"Trotti."

Gino opened the door.

"We work for seven years in the same building. You take all my phone calls for me—and then you go off without a word."

Trotti placed a hand on the man's shoulder. "And you don't recognize me when I come to your front door."

"I'm a blind man." Behind the thick glasses, the sightless eyes appeared welcoming. "Come on in, Piero Trotti."

He had aged in the days that Trotti had been away. Gino was wearing a blue cardigan over his narrow shoulders and his movement was slow. He closed the door and Trotti followed him down the dark hallway, past the ancient bakelite telephone attached to the wall.

Gino walked without raising his slippered feet.

The smell was almost overpowering and Trotti put his hand to his nose. "They didn't want me."

"How's Principessa?"

"It's not the Questore I blame—it was Merenda who wanted to be rid of me. The dog was just an excuse, Piero. The Questore is a weak man."

"What's Merenda doing?"

"Merenda knew I wouldn't stay without the dog." Gino shrugged. "So I have to leave in September. So what? Another few months, and I'd've been retiring anyway." They entered the kitchen.

"You'll get your pension, Gino."

He nodded. "This way, I can be with her."

"Got a cigarette, Gino?"

"You gave up smoking years ago."

The kitchen was dark, but it was clean. The white tiles around the sink were spotless.

"Nice place."

"A woman comes in three times a week."

"I'd like a cigarette if you can spare it." Trotti sat down. He held his hand to his nose and his voice was nasal.

"You soon get used to the smell. I know it's not pleasant."

Trotti laughed. "Give me a cigarette." He did not remove his hand.

"A packet on the sideboard."

Trotti turned in his seat. He took the packet of Alfa and removed the filter-tip from a cigarette. "My third cigarette in twelve years." He lit the end with a match and watched the smoke curl towards the ceiling. He did not place the cigarette in his mouth.

"If you're going to smoke, Trotti, smoke properly."

"You see everything, Gino."

"An advantage of being blind."

"They say it was in Shanghai—is that true? You were on a ship and the boilers blew up."

There was a small verandah and the dog lay outside in a wicker basket. It seemed to be asleep. Trotti noticed that in places the fur had grown thin, leaving ugly patches of pink skin. The body rose and fell softly.

Above the rooftops, the sky was growing darker.

"The vet says she's got another month or so."

"She suffers?"

"Sleeps most of the time, poor beast." Gino lowered himself into a wicker chair beside the refrigerator. "Perhaps that's what I ought to do."

The smell of burning cigarette filled Trotti's nostrils. His eyes had started to water. "Feeling sorry for yourself again?"

"Without her, I won't have much to live for."

"You should get married."

"Married."

"With your pension, you'll be out and about. It's the dog that's stopped you from finding yourself a nice wife."

As if realizing that she was being talked about, Principessa raised her head and turned to look at her master. She blinked sleepily then lowered her head again.

"I don't need a woman—never have." Gino had the tired, sick face of his dog.

"You've got your friends."

"First time you've ever come looking for me."

"I have my problems, too. Don't be harsh, Gino."

"What do you want, Piero?"

"I wanted to see you."

"I hear you got beaten up in Verona."

"Like you, I've been kicked out of the Questura—Merenda doesn't want me either."

"And you don't even smell like Principessa." The unshaven jaw broke into a smile. "Piero Trotti, smoke that thing properly."

Trotti put the cigarette to his lips and inhaled.

"Did you find the person you were looking for?"

"Who?"

"Did you find the girl's murderer?"

"It was a woman, Gino."

"A bastard, whoever it was."

"You never had much time for Ciuffi."

"I don't have much time for women, Trotti—I was married once. All my wife ever did was moan. In the end she went off with some southerner. Glad to be rid of her." He paused. "Ciuffi was all right—even though she hated my dog. And even though you were gaga over her."

"Gaga?"

"Good men like Pisanelli and Magagna—you've always been hard on them, Piero. You came up the hard way and you expect perfection from everybody else. Good men and good policemen, Pisanelli and Magagna—and you treat them like dirt. You treat them like dirt if you don't get perfection. Your kind of perfection."

"Because I get angry when Pisanelli goes swanning off with Merenda?"

"With the girl you were different."

"In what way was I different?"

A dry laugh. "Perhaps you were in love with her."

Trotti stood up. "They told me in the Questura you'd left a message for me."

Gino was still smiling. "A May-December marriage? And why not, Piero? You would have made a good couple. And it was plain to see that she was madly in love with you."

"Sometimes you see too much, Gino."

"Gaga over her—and she, poor little slip of a thing, was head over heels in love with you."

"You really think she was in love with an old man like me?"

The smile vanished. "Who killed her, Piero?"

"Somebody who was trying to kill me." Trotti placed his

hand on Gino's chair. "What was it you wanted to contact me about?"

"You saw the Neapolitan pimp?"

"What was it, Gino?"

He shrugged and he seemed to be looking at the dog. "It's not important."

"What?"

"Podestà?"

"What about her?"

"The ugly woman . . ."

"How do you know she's ugly?"

Gino tapped the side of his nose. "A man came in. It must have been when you were down by the river with Ciuffi. He said he wanted to see you."

"And?"

"After the shooting, he came back again, and I suppose I was the only person who'd listen to him. So he told me."

"What?"

"A married man—he said he'd had an affair with Podestà."

"He's a teacher?"

Gino's head turned. "That's right. He said that . . . he was embarrassed, but he said he felt he had his duty to do."

"Which was?"

"He said Podestà was a liar. That she spent a lot of her time making up stories—fantasies. He said that she'd wanted to marry him—and that he'd even thought about divorcing in order to go through with it. But in the end it wasn't sensible." Gino got to his feet and shuffled over to a chest-of-drawers. "Look, I wrote his name and address down. He would like to see you personally. He said that you weren't to believe anything she said. Not her fault, he said, but she lived in a world of sexual fantasy."

Trotti took the piece of paper that Gino handed him. He glanced at the name. Then he looked into the sightless eyes. "Thanks."

"Shanghai?" Gino asked.

"What about Shanghai?"

"People believe that's how I lost my sight? On a ship in Shanghai?"

"They say the boilers went up."

"Never been on a ship in my life."

"That's not the story I heard . . ."

Gino tapped the frames of his glasses. "In the hills, Trotti. During the war."

"You were a partisan?"

"Partisan? Me?"

"What were you doing in the hills?"

Gino had turned his head towards Principessa. "Doing what everyone was doing—I was doing my duty. Only I chose the wrong side."

"You were with the Fascists?"

"And not ashamed of it. I never changed sides. Mussolini never did me any wrong."

Trotti's voice was incredulous. "You were a Fascist, Gino?"

"When we were caught—me and seven other Repubblichini— I was the only one they didn't kill. Somebody knew my mother." He raised his shoulders. "The partisans spared my life—and instead they blinded me. They thought they were doing me a favor."

60: Friends

IT HAD STARTED to rain: heavy, fat drops that fell noisily on the pavement.

Trotti stood in the doorway of a closed shop until the blue bus pulled around the corner and came to a standstill at the bus stop. As he climbed aboard, he recognized the driver—he had once been arrested for larceny—but the man kept his eyes beneath the peak of his cap and took Trotti's fare with little more than a curt nod.

Trotti sat at the back of the bus.

There was a five-minute wait while bulky peasant women climbed aboard. They shouted to each other in dialect. They had been to Mass in the cathedral. Some glanced suspiciously at Trotti.

He turned and looked out of the window until the bus set off.

They crossed the river and the buildings grew more scattered as they reached the open countryside. It was hot in the bus and the women had brought in puddles of dirty water that ran across the floor in meandering rivulets.

A thin mist hung over the fields.

The bus gathered speed.

At Gravellino they turned left. Most of the passengers got off at a concrete shelter near the war memorial. The driver climbed down from his seat to help some of the older and larger women alight. He joked and he ran his hand beneath the chin of a pretty young mother holding a baby in her arms.

Then the bus drove through the village and soon it was in the new residential area that had grown up in the last few years.

Trotti got off outside a small café. It was one of the few original buildings; most houses were low buildings that imitated the style of the farmhouses they had usurped.

Gardens hidden by high privet hedges and cypresses that demarcated well-kept barriers between neighbors.

It had stopped raining. The air was cool. For a moment, Trotti stood by the roadside, breathing in the air of the countryside—a bittersweet mixture of grass, dung and rain.

The house was at the end of an unsurfaced road. The white Audi was in the garage. Beside it, a motorcycle. Trotti rang at the front door.

It was a while before Signora Bianchini answered.

She was wearing a pair of jeans that accentuated the flatness of her belly and, on her feet, small yellow slippers. It was not the first time Trotti had seen her without make-up but he was surprised by the freshness, the youthfulness of her face. And by her smile.

"Commissario—how nice to see you." She stepped back and Trotti could not tell whether the pleasure was real or feigned.

"Is your son at home, signora?"

"You must come in."

"It is time I spoke to Riccardo."

"I don't think my son has anything to hide."

Trotti looked at her. "Then why have you been hiding him?"

"This way, please." She turned and led him into the house.

The living room was dark and smelt of varnish. An antique grandfather clock in one corner and a vase of freshly-cut flowers on the polished table. Expensive furniture.

Two men sat at either side of the table. They had been talking but they looked up as Trotti entered the room.

Signora Bianchini asked, "Would you gentlemen care for a drink?"

Trotti sat down at the table and his glance went from Riccardo Bianchini to Capitano Spadano of the Carabinieri.

"Some local wine, perhaps, Commissario?"

"And some truffles?"

61: Revelation

"I KNOW SHE is not beautiful—but she has had a hard life. And things haven't always been easy for her. Yet she is very intelligent and when she says she could have gotten married, it's the truth."

"She calls herself a woman of the twentieth century."

Riccardo's face darkened. "You have no right to mock."

Trotti smiled. "I am too old to mock."

"Don't laugh at her. She is a good woman. She has spent her life looking after her mother—and her sister."

"A sister?"

"A couple of years younger than her." He tapped his head. "The sister's not quite normal. Sometimes you can hear her shouting."

"What for?"

"She lives in the apartment above Loredana's. Lately the doctors've put her on drugs—but there's a married brother in Poggibonsi who's always wanted the mad sister put away. Loredana . . ."

"Loredana?"

"Signorina Podestà's real name." Riccardo frowned. "She'd never hear of having her sister committed. So, for the last ten years, she's looked after her. That's why Loredana's never got married. She could have—an intelligent woman like her. But instead, she chose . . ."

"She should have married her teacher friend."

"She believed him." Riccardo shook his head. Pearls of moisture had formed along his forehead. "A man who promised Loredana that he would get a divorce, and for years she really thought he would give up his wife and children to live with her. Loredana believed him until the day she found him upstairs in bed with her sister."

"Intelligent and stupid at the same time, Riccardo?"

Spadano raised his glass of barbera to hide a smile.

"She is very intelligent—very intelligent indeed."

"You should have told me the truth."

Riccardo Bianchini looked unhappy. He was sweating. Three fingers rubbed at his right eyebrow.

"There was nothing for you to be afraid of."

"That's not what you said before. You seemed to think that I had attacked Laura."

"I didn't think anything—I was simply trying to find out the truth." Trotti turned to Spadano. "I was worried about the Vardin child—and the thought that there was some maniac loose in the city." He turned back to Riccardo. "You should have told me what you knew. You must've suspected that Podestà—"

"I didn't know anything. When I came into the Questura, I swear I didn't know anything." The forehead glistened.

Spadano looked at the boy. "At least suspected, Riccardo?"

"That's not what I was thinking about. I was much more concerned about my mother—and about her finding out. You see, I'd been telling her that I was at a friend's when in fact I was with Loredana."

Trotti said, "Signora Bianchini would have had to learn sooner or later about your Signorina Podestà."

The boy shook his head.

"You weren't worried about Laura?"

"Of course I was concerned about Laura. She's nice. Only it never occurred to me that it was Loredana who attacked her. Never occurred to me until Loredana invented her story of rape at Ciel d'Oro."

"What did Signorina Podestà do that for?"

"It was then I realized she was trying to protect me."

"Why protect you?"

"Because of old man Vardin. He never saw Loredana—but that didn't stop him from giving you an identikit of me. He never got out of bed in time to see Loredana running down the stairs. But Vardin hates me—and he wanted to get me into trouble. I was scared when you showed me the identikit and, later, I told Loredana. That's why she felt she had to help me."

"And the soldier?"

"What soldier?" Riccardo looked puzzled.

"Arrested—and they found a knife under his mattress."

"A mistake—a coincidence." He raised his shoulders. "Loredana did it—she told me herself, said that she was jealous. She didn't want to hurt Netta—but she couldn't bear . . . oh, I don't know, she really thought that I was sleeping with Netta." A drop of sweat ran from his temple down the side of his face.

"In the end, it wasn't Netta but Laura that she hurt." Spadano looked at the boy from over his glass.

"Loredana didn't know they'd changed beds."

Trotti said, "But you'd told her how to get into the house?"

Riccardo was silent. "You suspected Podestà, didn't you?"

Trotti shrugged. "You should have told me about your affair with Signorina Podestà."

"Not in front of my mother."

"Why not?"

"I'm all that Mother has."

"With the truth, I could have saved a lot of time. Perhaps even saved a human life."

"I can't hurt my mother."

Spadano's voice was gentle. "A human life was lost, Riccardo—lost because you didn't tell the truth to Commissario Trotti."

"Mother has never minded my having girlfriends—in fact, the more I have, the happier she seems to be." He ran his hand across his forehead. "But a long, long time ago, Mother told me that she was going to hate the woman I married."

"Why?"

"Terrified of losing me."

"You're her son—how can she lose you?"

"In her affections I have replaced Papa. I am the man that she should have married."

Trotti said, "What's that got to do with Podestà?"

"With both Podestà and Netta." He hesitated. "Loredana and Netta are different."

"What do you mean?"

An unexpected, almost wolfish smile broke through the sweating, tense face. "At times, I have been . . . well, very fond of them. And Mama doesn't like that. She is always afraid of my falling in love."

"You're still only seventeen."

"Eighteen." A shrug. "For Mama, I am the same age as her. I am her real husband."

"You're in love with Antonetta Vardin?"

"I used to be—until I realized what she was like."

"And you told Podestà?"

"Of course not." A brief smile. "I should have, I suppose. But I liked teasing her. That way, I could—well, I could get her to do things."

"Things?"

There was a carafe of water beside the half-empty bottle of barbera. Riccardo poured himself a glass. "Loredana is not very beautiful. She hasn't got a nice face, I know—a turned-up nose, as if the skin has been pulled too tight. And eyes that stick out a bit. But she's a woman—and she's taught me a lot of things. A lot of things."

"In bed?"

"Loredana is afraid of losing me."

"So you blackmailed her?" Spadano said.

Riccardo turned his head. "Of course not."

"You blackmailed her, Riccardo."

"She was jealous. Not because Antonetta is pretty or anything, but because she is young. Loredana likes to think of herself as a woman of her century. But she's terrified of growing old." Riccardo hesitated. "I think . . ."

"Yes?"

"I think she would like to have a child."

"By you?"

The boy raised his shoulders. "Why not? She likes me."

"And you'd marry Signorina Podestà?"

Riccardo turned to look at Spadano. "A man doesn't have to be married to give a woman a child."

A tap on the door.

Spadano stood up and quickly opened the door.

The almond eyes seemed anxious. "Do you gentlemen need anything?"

"Most kind of you, Signora Bianchini, but I think for the time being we have drunk enough barbera."

She glanced at her son.

Riccardo ignored her.

The almond eyes went from Riccardo to Trotti.

"Signora, you have nothing to worry about."

Spadano gave Signora Bianchini a reassuring squeeze to her wrist.

She looked down at the thick, strong hand. She smiled shyly at Spadano. "Let me know if you need anything."

Another glance at her son and she withdrew.

"You were telling us about Loredana," Trotti said, when the door had closed. "What things did you get her to do?"

"Loredana really is a woman of her century. She does a lot of things. An open mind and she is always interested, always active."

"You mean she is a good screw?"

Spadano made a snorting noise.

"And you told her that if she didn't give it to you when you wanted, as you wanted and how you wanted—you told her that you would go back to the Vardin girl?"

Riccardo had started to blush.

"You're a little bastard, Bianchini."

"You don't understand."

"A manipulating little bastard."

Riccardo shook his head.

"Sexual blackmail. The Vardin girl wouldn't go to bed with you, and that's why you started to hate her—that's what your friend Raf said."

"Raffaele is not my friend. He knows nothing about me."

"But as for Podestà—a woman who knows that she's not pretty . . ."

"She could pick up soldiers. Before me, there were enough of them."

"With you she fell in love, Riccardo—that's the difference. And so you blackmailed her, threatened her by telling her you'd go back to a girl of your own age. It was only normal she'd fall in love with you—after all, you are young and attractive. As you yourself admit, she'd had a bad time with men."

"You have got a nasty mind, Commissario. You don't want to understand . . ."

"From her you could get what you wanted—even when she didn't want to give it to you. Whenever she refused to open her legs or whatever, all you had to do was tell her you were going back to your Vardin girlfriend." Trotti paused. "No wonder she was jealous. No wonder she took a knife to her."

"But it was Laura she attacked."

"Laura or Netta—it was you who told her everything. To get her jealous, you told her about your girlfriend nestling in bed and how the door was left on the latch and how you would go and see her at nights, go and screw her . . ."

"But I didn't."

"Of course you didn't, Riccardo. Netta wasn't to be had like that. The stuck-up little Vardin girl wasn't as desperate as Podestà—and she wasn't going to give in to your demands. But Podestà wasn't to know that. You exacerbated things and in the end—you knew she wasn't stable—in the end the woman took a knife to the young girl she saw as her rival. Only it wasn't Netta that she hurt—it was Laura."

Riccardo Bianchini had lowered his head.

"Really it could have been you who carried the knife."

"Me?"

"You, Riccardo, who put the knife into Laura's flesh."

"No." Lines of moisture had formed at the side of his chin.

"All along, you were playing—exercising your power over these women—just as your father had over your mother. But whereas with Netta it didn't work, with Podestà it did."

Silence.

"You must be very proud of yourself, Riccardo."

"What do you understand?" The boy looked up. His eyes were wet, and the bright teeth bit at the corner of his lip. "Perhaps I shouldn't have made up the stories about me and Netta."

"Well?"

Riccardo shrugged and he lowered his eyes.

Trotti unbuttoned his collar. "Well?"

"Of course I don't love Loredana like that—and I'd never marry her. But I do like her—that's what you can't understand. I do like her. Like a sister. Or a mother."

Riccardo Bianchini put his closed fists to his eyes.

62: Scratch

THE SHORT HAIR was turning white at the temples.

"You sent her to the hospital, Spadano. I thought it was Magagna—but it was you who sent her with the clothes. You wanted her to keep an eye on me."

The police radio had been switched on and Spadano was driving.

"You came here by bus, Trotti?" He turned his head slightly, but his eyes remained on the road.

"Yes."

"No car?"

"Pisanelli's disappeared."

Spadano had put an unlit cigar in the corner of his mouth. "Today is Sunday—I imagine that even Pisanelli is entitled to his day off."

It was late afternoon and the air had cleared. The rain clouds had gone south, following the line of the Apennines. The valley of the Po stretched out before them; to the north, a discernible profile of the Alps.

Trotti was depressed. Tired, depressed and feeling old. "Even if it wasn't his day off, there's no need for him to work for me. Pisanelli or anyone else."

"You ought to buy a car."

"It would seem I'm persona non grata in the Questura."

"Time you got the insurance for your old Opel." Spadano pulled out the knob of the dashboard lighter. "I'll drive you home."

"If you don't mind, Spadano."

He lit his cigar. Then catching Trotti's glance, he took the packet of Toscani from his shirt pocket. "You want one?"

Trotti lowered the car window. "I think you ought to tell me about Signora Bianchini, Spadano."

"Bianchini?"

"About you and Signora Bianchini?"

The Carabiniere nodded and fell silent.

The tinny sound of a woman's voice, meaningless and insistent, came from the radio, speaking in muted, staccato rhythms, rhythms that formed a continuing leitmotiv that neither Trotti nor Spadano paid attention to.

Spadano did not say another word until they were on the highway leading back into the city.

"Didn't you, Spadano?"

The city was up ahead, the dome of the Cathedral catching the clear light of the late afternoon; to the east there was a thickening band of darkness. To the west, the sky was turning red.

Trotti recalled the drive back with Ciuffi. His eyes felt gritty.

"What?"

"You sent her to the Policlinico, didn't you?"

"Who?"

Trotti raised his voice. "The Bianchini woman—don't deny it, Spadano. How else did she know where to find me? And later, in Verona, how did you know where we were?"

"You're a strange man, Trotti."

"Just now"—a gesture of his thumb over his shoulder—"you think I didn't notice the way you were soft on Riccardo? How you wanted to let him down gently? And you think I didn't see the looks passing between you and the woman."

"You're jealous."

"Jealous." Trotti banged his hand against the edge of the car window. "Of course I'm not jealous. Jealous because her almond eyes are just for you? What the hell was it you once said? Something about finding yourself looking at the kids in the street and wishing that one was yours?"

Spadano's face hardened. "Be careful, Trotti."

They were crossing the Ponte Imperiale.

In the clear afternoon light, the tiered city rose from the banks of the Po like a well-defined photograph.

"A little boy just a little bit like you—perhaps a bit cleverer—who was going to grow up and become like you. Like you, but wiser."

"What are you trying to say?"

"I'm trying to say that you lied to me, Spadano. I thought you were my friend."

"Friend?"

"We have collaborated often enough, haven't we? We were friends—I've always liked you, always respected you. And I believed that the feeling was reciprocated."

"Precisely."

"What do you mean?"

"You're jealous, Trotti."

"Of course I'm not jealous."

"Signora Bianchini and I are friends."

"You used her."

"She is a charming person. You are quite right—both charming and attractive . . ."

"You used her to spy on me."

Spadano laughed.

The woman continued her monologue over the police radio. The car ran along the LungoPò and turned left into Strada Nuova.

"A spy—so that you could know what I was doing."

"Not at all."

"You forget what you said to me, Spadano? About your needing a woman of child-bearing age? You remember?"

Spadano shrugged.

Strada Nuova was empty. They drove past the Questura.

"But you liked what you saw. Nice tits. Those were your words—nice tits and broad hips."

"So what, Trotti?"

"You remember saying that?"

"What are you trying to tell me?"

"You knew her—of course you knew Bianchini. And that's why it didn't take you too long to find me outside Monza at the bogus clinic. You were following me."

"You've got a good memory, Trotti."

"We were friends, Spadano."

"Perhaps you can remember what I also told you—that you put people's backs up."

Traffic lights and over the canal. Then the railway bridge. "Take me to the hospital, Spadano, could you? Somebody I want to see."

"You put people's backs up and you make it hard for them to work for you. People who like you, who respect you because they know you are honest, because they know you are a good policeman—even they find it impossible to work with you."

"Did you send her to Voghera?"

"Impossible to work with, Trotti—because you are proud and you can't admit that you're wrong."

"Did you send her to Voghera?"

"I don't know what you're talking about."

"Bianchini drove me up into Santa Maria, and then afterwards—late at night—I saw her with a man . . ."

"A man?"

"I saw her with somebody in the station bar."

"Signora Bianchini hasn't got the right to do as she pleases, go where she pleases?"

"She was with you?"

"You are incredible."

"Incredible or not, Spadano, you have betrayed me."

They had reached the Policlinico. Spadano waited for the man at the gate to recognize the Carabinieri plates and raise the barrier.

"I respect you, Trotti."

"You betrayed me."

"Betrayed you because I was worried about you? Because I didn't want you to get hurt."

The two men looked at each other.

"You'd almost been killed, Trotti."

"When?"

"Of course I like you, damn it. I wasn't sticking any spy on your tail. Can't you understand? I just didn't want you hurt. And then, when you were kidnapped, I wasn't even there—I was still in Verona."

"You used the woman, Spadano."

The barrier went up and the car jolted forward.

"Signora Bianchini's beautiful—I don't deny it. And if she were to like me, if she just looked at me, I'd be happy, Trotti. The sort of woman I could live with."

"And the child-bearing hips?"

"At thirty-seven, she's not too old to have children." A dry laugh. "With a woman like that, Sardinia could be bearable."

"Over there," Trotti said, pointing to a building. "You can drop me off outside Ostetrica."

"The Sopramonte could be bearable. And I think I could even put up with the kidnappers and the shepherds smelling of the sheep they screwed. But that's not the point."

"What is?"

"The point is that she has eyes for you—for you alone."

"Me?"

"Bianchini doesn't even look at me, Trotti. I don't even exist. It's you she wants—and you can't even see that. At Monza she spent two days looking for you. She wouldn't give up—and she wanted the entire Arma to help her."

"You got her to do what you wanted."

"Never my idea she should sleep in the same bedroom in Verona."

"Spadano, you put her on to me."

"It was her husband I used to know. I didn't know Signora Bianchini. When she found me in the barracks, I didn't know her from Eve. It was because I was a friend of her husband's that she came. She was worried about her son."

"You admit you used her?"

"I told her where you were, Trotti—and that's something she

would have found out from reading the Provincia. No secret you'd been hit by a bullet and were here in the hospital."

"You told her to watch me."

"I gave her my phone number. That's all. It was her decision to phone me. I never asked her to. All I ever told her was to contact me if . . ."

"Yes?"

"To contact me if things got out of hand."

The car stopped.

"Where did you say, Trotti?"

"Where what?"

"At the station in Voghera, you said." Spadano took the cigar from his mouth and threw it out of the window. "You saw her with a man—at the station?"

"With you, Spadano. She was with you."

"With Bianchini." Spadano snorted. "With her husband, Trotti. Bianchini's trying to set up a small shoe factory in Voghera. Making shoes for children."

"Why her husband?"

"Probably wanted some money from him." Spadano turned away. "She's a very beautiful woman, Trotti."

For a moment, the two men sat in their seats staring through the windscreen at the hospital gardens.

Spadano placed his hand on Trotti's sleeve. "Trouble with you, Piero, is you don't know when you're lucky."

63: Incubator

UNDER THE PLASTIC dome, Ivan now lay asleep, naked on the sheet. The tubes had been removed and the baby's body seemed to be larger and more robust than before.

"Such a little thing."

Ivan slept with his minute fists clenched.

"You have come to visit us again?"

Trotti turned.

"Come to see the child?"

Trotti nodded and smiled, "Ivan is doing well for himself."

They shook hands; her grasp was firm. She wore her name on the lapel badge, DOTT.SSA STEFANELLA SILVAN. The doctor said, "We're very proud of him."

An acrylic glass door in the wall of the incubator. Dottoressa Silvan raised it and carefully changed Ivan's position.

The baby frowned in his sleep.

"You're coming along like a house on fire, aren't you, precious? Show the nice policeman your big, fat legs." The doctor made gentle sounds and then closed the door. She ran her finger down the scale on the thermostat.

"Seems to be clinging to life."

The doctor glanced at Trotti. "It's all we've got, Commissario." She was still wearing her gold crucifix, and, like a larger crucifix, a stethoscope hung from her neck. The end had been tucked into her breast pocket.

"Ivan's going to live?"

She had applied a pale lipstick to her mouth. "Of course."

"And somebody's going to adopt him?"

"Not at once."

"When?"

The smile made her look like a young girl. "Ivan will have to remain with us for a bit. But the risk of pneumonia has been dealt with."

"A tough kid."

"A tough mother—she gave birth by herself, all alone in the fields. By leaving the baby with a lot of umbilical cord, she unwittingly saved his life—by preventing serious hemorrhaging."

"When will he leave the hospital?"

"Before the end of the year Ivan will be sent to the Institute— and then it'll be another five or six months before he's adopted."

"Adopted," Trotti repeated.

"And how is your friend?" A hand to the side of her head. "The policeman with hair over his ears—and none on top."

"Who will adopt him?"

"A kind man—he was very good with the mother."

"Who will adopt Ivan, Dottoressa?"

She gave Trotti a shrewd glance. "Good on female psychology, your policeman friend."

"Tell me about the adoption, Dottoressa."

The woman placed her hand on his sleeve. Thin, attractive fingers and a pale skin that was flecked with freckles. "I think I understand." She looked into his eyes and smiled.

"The fact that he's—well, that he's run health risks—how will that affect the adoption?"

"Ivan's health is no problem. But adopting a child is something—"

"Trotti!"

They turned.

The swing door closed softly behind Spadano. He walked fast, his eyes on Trotti. He did not spare a glance for the double row of incubators.

Trotti said, "Dottoressa Silvan—Capitano Spadano of the Carabinieri."

To Trotti Spadano said, "Good job you're still here." A brief nod to the doctor.

"Keeping an eye on me, Spadano?"

A click of the tongue. "Something you ought to know."

Spadano looked out of place in the ward.

"Commissario Trotti was making enquiries about adoption." The doctor bit her lip to stop herself from smiling.

Spadano took Trotti by the arm and he led him to a corner of the small ward.

A poster on the wall showed an African mother breastfeeding her child.

Spadano spoke in a low whisper. "On the radio—I've just heard . . ."

"Radio?"

"The intercom in the car . . . A report from Santa Maria—another body has been found on the edge of the town. Head smashed in."

"Who?"

"Still waiting for a definitive identification. A woman—not a peasant woman. Soft hands and feet . . ."

"Who, Spadano?"

"In the fall—they found her beside the river—the face was disfigured." A taut grimace. "But there are already people who have identified her."

"Who?"

Spadano did not say anything.

"The Baronessa?"

"Listen. She's not at her home."

"Dead."

"A couple of men went to her villa with a warrant. She wasn't there. But . . ."

"Yes."

"In the basement they found several trunks. Containing paintings . . . rolled-up canvasses. Renaissance paintings. And also . . ."

"Gold?"

"You knew?"

Trotti turned away. Tired and depressed, and beneath the lids, his eyes felt as if they were burning.

He moved back towards the doctor.

"Trotti . . ." Spadano said.

The woman stood by the incubator and was looking down on the sprawled, innocent form of the child.

Ivan had opened his eyes.

The young doctor was making gentle sounds in her throat and, with her fingers, she was tapping the acrylic glass dome, trying to win the baby's attention.

It seemed to Trotti that the smile on her young face had grown broader.

A smile that lit up the hospital, that lit up the entire city.

Other Titles in the Soho Crime Series

Stephanie Barron
(Jane Austen's England)
*Jane and the Twelve Days
of Christmas*

Quentin Bates
(Iceland)
*Frozen Assets
Cold Comfort
Chilled to the Bone*

James R. Benn
(World War II Europe)
*Billy Boyle
The First Wave
Blood Alone
Evil for Evil
Rag & Bone
A Mortal Terror
Death's Door
A Blind Goddess
The Rest Is Silence*

Cara Black
(Paris, France)
*Murder in the Marais
Murder in Belleville
Murder in the Sentier
Murder in the Bastille
Murder in Clichy
Murder in Montmartre
Murder on the Ile Saint-Louis
Murder in the Rue de Paradis
Murder in the Latin Quarter
Murder in the Palais Royal
Murder in Passy
Murder at the Lanterne Rouge
Murder Below Montparnasse
Murder in Pigalle
Murder on the Champ de Mars*

Grace Brophy
(Italy)
*The Last Enemy
A Deadly Paradise*

Henry Chang
(Chinatown)
*Chinatown Beat
Year of the Dog
Red Jade
Death Money*

Barbara Cleverly
(England)
*The Last Kashmiri Rose
Strange Images of Death
The Blood Royal
Not My Blood*

Barbara Cleverly cont.
*A Spider in the Cup
Enter Pale Death*

Gary Corby
(Ancient Greece)
*The Pericles Commission
The Ionia Sanction
Sacred Games
The Marathon Conspiracy
Death Ex Machina*

Colin Cotterill
(Laos)
*The Coroner's Lunch
Thirty-Three Teeth
Disco for the Departed
Anarchy and Old Dogs
Curse of the Pogo Stick
The Merry Misogynist
Love Songs from a Shallow Grave
Slash and Burn
The Woman Who Wouldn't Die
The Six and a Half Deadly Sins*

Garry Disher
(Australia)
*The Dragon Man
Kittyhawk Down
Snapshot
Chain of Evidence
Blood Moon
Wyatt
Whispering Death
Port Vila Blues
Fallout
Hell to Pay*

David Downing
(World War II Germany)
*Zoo Station
Silesian Station
Stettin Station
Potsdam Station
Lehrter Station
Masaryk Station*

(World War I)
Jack of Spies

Leighton Gage
(Brazil)
*Blood of the Wicked
Buried Strangers
Dying Gasp
Every Bitter Thing
A Vine in the Blood
Perfect Hatred
The Ways of Evil Men*

Michael Genelin
(Slovakia)
*Siren of the Waters
Dark Dreams
The Magician's Accomplice
Requiem for a Gypsy*

Timothy Hallinan
(Thailand)
*The Fear Artist
For the Dead*

(Los Angeles)
*Crashed
Little Elvises
The Fame Thief
Herbie's Game*

Mette Ivie Harrison
(Mormon Utah)
The Bishop's Wife

Mick Herron
(England)
*Down Cemetery Road
The Last Voice You Hear
Reconstruction
Smoke and Whispers
Why We Die
Slow Horses
Dead Lions
Nobody Walks*

Lene Kaaberbøl & Agnete Friis
(Denmark)
*The Boy in the Suitcase
Invisible Murder
Death of a Nightingale*

Graeme Kent
(Solomon Islands)
*Devil-Devil
One Blood*

Heda Margolius Kovály
(1950s Prague)
Innocence

James Lilliefors
(Global Thrillers)
*Viral
The Leviathan Effect*

Martin Limón
(South Korea)
*Jade Lady Burning
Slicky Boys
Buddha's Money
The Door to Bitterness*

Martin Limón cont.
The Wandering Ghost
G.I. Bones
Mr. Kill
The Joy Brigade
Nightmare Range
The Iron Sickle

Ed Lin
(Taiwan)
Ghost Month

Peter Lovesey
(England)
The Circle
The Headhunters
False Inspector Dew
Rough Cider
On the Edge
The Reaper

(Bath, England)
The Last Detective
Diamond Solitaire
The Summons
Bloodhounds
Upon a Dark Night
The Vault
Diamond Dust
The House Sitter
The Secret Hangman
Skeleton Hill
Stagestruck
Cop to Corpse
The Tooth Tattoo
The Stone Wife

Jassy Mackenzie
(South Africa)
Random Violence
Stolen Lives
The Fallen
Pale Horses

Seichō Matsumoto
(Japan)
Inspector Imanishi Investigates

James McClure
(South Africa)
The Steam Pig
The Caterpillar Cop
The Gooseberry Fool
Snake
The Sunday Hangman
The Blood of an Englishman
The Artful Egg
The Song Dog

Magdalen Nabb
(Italy)
Death of an Englishman
Death of a Dutchman
Death in Springtime
Death in Autumn
The Marshal and the Madwoman
The Marshal and the Murderer
The Marshal's Own Case
The Marshal Makes His Report
The Marshal at the Villa Torrini
Property of Blood
Some Bitter Taste
The Innocent
Vita Nuova
The Monster of Florence

Fuminori Nakamura
(Japan)
The Thief
Evil and the Mask
Last Winter, We Parted

Stuart Neville
(Northern Ireland)
The Ghosts of Belfast
Collusion
Stolen Souls
The Final Silence
Ratlines

Eliot Pattison
(Tibet)
Prayer of the Dragon
The Lord of Death

Rebecca Pawel
(1930s Spain)
Death of a Nationalist
Law of Return
The Watcher in the Pine
The Summer Snow

Kwei Quartey
(Ghana)
Murder at Cape Three Points

Qiu Xiaolong
(China)
Death of a Red Heroine
A Loyal Character Dancer
When Red Is Black

John Straley
(Alaska)
The Woman Who Married a Bear
The Curious Eat Themselves
The Big Both Ways
Cold Storage, Alaska

Akimitsu Takagi
(Japan)
The Tattoo Murder Case
Honeymoon to Nowhere
The Informer

Helene Tursten
(Sweden)
Detective Inspector Huss
The Torso
The Glass Devil
Night Rounds
The Golden Calf
The Fire Dance
The Beige Man

Jan Merete Weiss
(Italy)
These Dark Things
A Few Drops of Blood

Janwillem van de Wetering
(Holland)
Outsider in Amsterdam
Tumbleweed
The Corpse on the Dike
Death of a Hawker
The Japanese Corpse
The Blond Baboon
The Maine Massacre
The Mind-Murders
The Streetbird
The Rattle-Rat
Hard Rain
Just a Corpse at Twilight
Hollow-Eyed Angel
The Perfidious Parrot
Amsterdam Cops: Collected Stories

Timothy Williams
(Guadeloupe)
Another Sun
The Honest Folk of Guadeloupe

(Italy)
Converging Parallels
The Puppeteer
Persona Non Grata
Black August
Big Italy

Jacqueline Winspear
(1920s England)
Maisie Dobbs
Birds of a Feather